The Art
of
Ghost Writing

by
ALISTAIR REY

From

Dark Owl Publishing, LLC

Arizona

Visit us on our website at:
www.darkowlpublishing.com

Also from
Dark Owl Publishing

Collections

The Dark Walk Forward
John S. McFarland

The Last Star Warden
Volumes I and II
Jason J. McCuiston

The Last Star Warden:
The Phantom World
Jason J. McCuiston
Available on Kindle Vella

No Lesser Angels, No Greater
Devils
Laura J. Campbell

The Tension of a Coming Storm
Adrian Ludens

The Nightmare Cycle
Lawrence Dagstine

The Brotherhood of Secret Dark-
ness and Other Cults, Cabals, and
Conspiracies
Jason J. McCuiston

Bad Dreams and Reflections:
A Collection of Weird Horror
Stories
Trevor Kennedy
Coming August 2023

Welcome to Scar Ridge
Jonathon Mast
Coming October 2023

Anthologies
A Celebration of Storytelling
Something Wicked This Way
Rides

Novels
The Black Garden
John S. McFarland

The Mother of Centuries
The sequel to *The Black Garden*
John S. McFarland

The Keeper of Tales
Jonathon Mast

Just About Anyone
Carl R. Jennings

The Malakiad
Gustavo Bondoni

Carnivore Keepers
Kevin M. Folliard

The Wicked Twisted Road
D.S. Hamilton

For Young Readers

Annette: A Big, Hairy Mom
John S. McFarland

Grayson North,
Frost-Keeper of the Windy City
Kevin M. Folliard

Shivers, Scares, and Goosebumps
Vonnie Winslow Crist
The sequels are coming soon!

Buy the books for Kindle and in paperback
www.darkowlpublishing.com

Table *of* Contents

An Autumn Settling

She was a fastidious woman; Veronique could tell from the minute they met. It was the way she pronounced "fifth-floor walk-up," as though the phrase left a bad taste in her mouth. An air of habitual defeat loomed over her husband, whose quiet deference spoke volumes. Veronique vividly imagined the years of disapproving glances and verbal lashings that had emasculated a once proud and maybe even ambitious man. And now, as the woman held out her child's arm to her, Veronique realized over-protective mother could be added to her qualities.

"*What* is this?" the woman asked, tugging sternly at her daughter's wrist in an effort to extend the slack limb. From palm to bicep, the girl's arm was riddled with small red inflammations. Dried blotches of calamine lotion dotted her face, although the girl had clearly been picking at the bites on her cheeks. "For the price we pay, you would think the apartment would be free of vermin."

Veronique looked at the girl, puzzled. "They look like mosquito bites," she said.

"That's exactly what they are," the mother replied.

Veronique was fairly certain that mosquitos were nonexistent in Paris during the winter months. Moreover, the number of bites suggested that the girl was attacked by a veritable swarm.

"Did you see any in the apartment?" she asked, turning to the deferential husband whose name she had since forgotten.

He looked to his wife and emitted a meek, "Not exactly, no."

"Did you sleep with the windows open?"

"It's January!" the woman said. "Who would leave the windows open at night?"

"I don't understand, then. Is it some type of allergy?"

This remark clearly did not sit well with the mother. "My daughter doesn't have allergies," she replied tersely, turning the conversation back to the price they paid for the rental and the complications that *her* mosquitos posed for their vacation.

Having dealt with short-term renters on a more or less consistent basis over the past four years, Veronique knew when to defend herself and when to concede. Here, the choice was obvious. As the woman ran through her litany of grievances, Veronique mentally formulated the terms of her apology. It would be courteous, anodyne, and most importantly, insincere.

***

Veronique liked to think of herself as an understanding person. Her venture into the real estate business, however, had severely tested this assumption.

When her father died, Veronique inherited a modest sum of money. Rather than squander it, she opted to invest. The market for tourist rentals in Paris was secure and seemed a safe bet. She became a *rentier*, living in Poissy and augmenting her income with prime urban real estate. Her father—a dyed-in-the-wool communist like most French intellectuals of his generation—would have probably been disappointed, but then again, he may have been happy to know that his daughter was financially secure. At least this is what Veronique told herself.

She purchased the apartment with the tourist market in mind. It was in a nineteenth-century building in the center of the city. The old spiral staircase winding itself around five floors to reach the apartment might have been slightly inconvenient, but a two-bedroom flat was practically unheard of in Paris these days. The large windows in the master bedroom looked out onto an enclosed courtyard with a cobblestoned patio and well-kept garden. She found it slightly amusing that the top floor offered a panoramic view of the other apartments in the building and hence momentary glimpses into the daily lives of the occupants.

Finding the place should have been the difficult part, but serving as a landlord proved exceedingly more burdensome. Property taxes and insurance—neither of which Veronique had accurately accounted for—were exacting. She also quickly learned that short-term renters were a demanding and inconsiderate breed. They complained about amenities, called at all hours of the night, and frequently left the property in a state of disarray. Veronique began questioning her decision the first time she had to clean semen-stained linens and unclog large balls of hair from the bathroom drains. A year into her venture, she let the place to an American who was staying in Paris for six months on business. The man insisted he was "the bookish sort," and for the next six months, the only contact Veronique had with him was the rent check wired directly to her account each month. The peace of mind was welcomed, and she congratulated herself on having finally let the place to a responsible tenant. That is, until the lease expired.

On the day she showed up to collect the keys and inspect the premises, the American was nowhere to be found. Nothing seemed out of place; the man's coat and clothes still hung in the hall closet. Yet a putrid odor wafted through every room. Stepping into the kitchen, she discovered a mound of rotting fruit piled on the counter. It was more fruit than any one person could possibly eat. The assortment of plums, apples, pears, and melons had liquefied to a pulpy black color. Moving closer, she heard a disturbing buzzing sound and watched in horror as a blanket of flies erupted into the air and dispersed across the walls and ceiling.

Veronique filed a police report, but nothing ever came of the matter. The American had left Paris earlier that month, a fact confirmed by the other residents of the building. They described him as being a reserved and polite individual, unremarkable in almost every respect. He never contacted Veronique to claim his belongings or demand the return of his hefty deposit, a significant portion of which went to pay for an exterminator. Tossing the abandoned shoes and suits into the trash bin, Veronique helplessly anticipated the next renter who would no doubt find some way of violating her trust in humanity. She balled her fists and bit her lip. It was the only thing preventing her from screaming.

Now, three years down the line, she was once again fighting back the urge to scream. The woman had stormed out of the apartment with her browbeaten husband in tow. Even before the door slammed, Veronique had made the decision: she was going to cut her losses and sell the apartment.

***

The property was in a good part of town, the real estate agent assured her. It would not be difficult to find an interested buyer within a month. He was confounded as to why she would want to sell such a place given its potential market value over the next ten years. Veronique did not have the patience to explain that ten years of peevish tenants, clogged drains, and meticulously itemized insurance claims seemed like an eternity. The entire situation had the feel of a bad marriage in which divorce now seemed the only sensible option.

Despite the agent's optimism, though, the apartment didn't sell. Viewing appointments came and went. The agent phoned on a weekly basis providing updates. They were close, he said. The latest prospective buyers that viewed the property always showed "serious interest" in the property, yet none of these promising signs ever translated into an offer. By the summer, the viewing schedules became irregular and the phone calls more sporadic. Veronique lowered the asking price, and when that did nothing, she registered the apartment with a second real estate agent for good measure. The process repeated itself: initial confidence in a quick sale, followed by puzzlement, and finally, resignation. As September rolled around, Veronique began to worry about the financial impact of her decision. Five months without rent had thinned her assets considerably.

"Should I just give up and start renting again?" she asked the agent one afternoon. She tried to mask the defeat in her voice, but it came off badly.

"That is an option," he replied pragmatically.

"I don't understand. Why isn't it selling?"

The agent didn't have a good explanation. He just shrugged and chalked it up to fluctuations in the housing market.

Veronique knew a bullshit excuse when she heard one.

***

What was it about the elevation, the way it induced a sense of falling? Not a terrifying feeling of plunging to the earth, but a pleasant and dream-like one akin to floating. Was it the way the windows appeared to cascade into the courtyard? Or how they seemed to enfold the walls of the building in a honeycomb pattern of mortar and glass? She diverted her eyes away from the walls to the rooftops and autumn sky outside the window. The ground felt solid once more, her bearing restored.

Veronique returned to unpacking her duffle bag, wondering why she had not packed more practical clothing. Realistically, Poissy was not far away. Should she desire a change of clothes she could easily hop on a train and be there within an hour. And yet, this was not the impression she had upon entering the building. Pushing back the heavy carriage doors, home suddenly felt very distant.

Stepping into the shaded corridor, she saw a man standing in the courtyard. He was elderly-looking, and the tweed jacket he wore seemed purposely old-fashioned. It reminded her of the attire prominent in her parents' photo albums, where time was frozen and two-tone plaid and pillbox hats never went out of style. The man did not stir or even move as the door closed behind her. He remained still, his head bent toward one of the flowers in the garden. Veronique could not say that he was smelling the flower so much as had his nose pressed directly against it so that the petals covered his lips and cheeks.

"Hello?" she called.

The man jerked. Specks of pollen dotted his nose.

"Hello," he said after a moment. It sounded more like a question the way he said it, as though he were trying to decipher the meaning of a strange word.

"Are you a vacationer?" he asked, eyeing the duffle bag in her hand. "It's up the flight of stairs just there."

Veronique smiled awkwardly. "How do you know that?"

The old man pulled a handkerchief from his pocket and began dabbing at his nose. There was something unsettling about his gaze. He was looking at her and not looking at her at the same time. "That's where they all go, and you don't live here," he said absently.

She was about to correct him but reconsidered. It was true. She owned the property. It was hers. But she did not live here. She was just as much a stranger to this man as any of the tourists she rented to.

The man swatted the air toward a gnat. "It's warm for this time of year," he offered. "They always come when it's warm."

Veronique just nodded and continued on her way across the courtyard to the stairwell. She couldn't help thinking that half-senile neighbors were hardly a selling point.

Now, sitting on the bed, she could admit to herself why she was here. It wasn't because a break from Poissy felt needed or the fact that she had a vacant apartment in Paris at her disposal that had motivated the stay. It was to understand what precisely was so disagreeable about *this* apartment in one of the world's most frequently visited tourist destinations. Had her instincts been so completely wrong? What had she seen that others did not? These were the types of nagging questions that haunted Veronique as she unpacked her clothes, pulled clean sheets from the armoire, and set to work preparing a modest dinner.

Before bed, she performed a quick inspection of the apartment, checking that all the faucets and electrical outlets worked correctly. She even got down on her hands and knees to inspect the baseboards for signs of decay or dry rot. Nothing seemed out of the ordinary. If anything, the place had a hygienic quality that one wouldn't expect in an old building.

Lying in bed, she listened to the water moving through the

pipes and the silent hum of the electricity behind the walls. The sounds of the building were soothing, Veronique thought as she began to doze. She concentrated on them, allowing herself to be lulled to the edge of sleep. The more she concentrated, the clearer they became. The soft electric hum filled her ears and progressively seemed to fill the room. She turned her mind to other things expecting the sound to dissipate, but the warm buzz lingered, a slight hum just above the silence.

It had transformed so slowly she barely noticed it, but the sound was now different. Alien, even. Rising and approaching the windows, she felt the latches vibrating ever so slightly beneath her fingertips. When she opened them, the sound enveloped the room. Outside, the courtyard was welled in impenetrable shadow, creating the illusion of a vacuous pit. The hum resonated from all sides and in the garden below Veronique perceived a series of incandescent flickers similar to the light of fireflies. They burned in the darkness, each nimbus emitting a hypnotic glow. Had she detected her body listing slightly forward or felt the metal guardrail press against her stomach? She could not recall. By the time she realized the dangerous angle of her body, her mind had seized upon a more menacing detail: buried within the drone was a low chorus of sibilant voices.

***

The unseasonable warmth persisted, even as Paris turned wet and rainy. On most days she sat for long periods of time listening to the rain against the windowpanes with no desire to do anything in particular. The only person she knew in the city was a former boyfriend with whom she had no wish to reestablish contact. The Orsay had an exhibit on Cezanne, but she had always found his work boring. Under the circumstances, Veronique was perfectly content to remain indoors and even entertained the possibility of exploring the building in greater depth. Four years prior, she had accompanied an inspector through the premises prior to buying the place. He had pointed out the old drainage system as they walked through the utility corridor, informing her that it pre-dated Haussmann's urbanization projects of the mid-nineteenth century. The labyrinthine passages lined with piping and modern fiber optic cables were oddly fascinating. They coiled and fed back on one another like the streets of an old oriental medina. In some places, the walls were clammy and rough as though hewn from raw stone.

On the third day, she met the tenant in the apartment opposite hers. Veronique was in the process of examining some scratches on the wood paneling in the hall when she heard him coming up the stairs, two bulging grocery bags in each hand.

"Hello," he said cordially.

As he lowered the bags to extend a hand, a stream of avocados and kiwis rolled across the floor. Veronique picked up the pieces of fruit that accumulated around her feet and politely handed them back. One of those people who followed fad diets, she spec-ulated. It seemed typically Parisian.

"I suppose you're on holiday?" he asked, returning the articles to the bag.

When Veronique corrected him, a smile spread across his face. "Then I suppose that makes us neighbors. I'm 5B."

The man was well-dressed, possibly a mid-level executive at a firm from the look of his suit and shoes. He spoke French with an accent that Veronique could not immediately place.

"Something like that," Veronique replied.

The man asked if she had been looking for something, and Ve-ronique laughed.

"No, I noticed some marks on the wood," she explained, adding, "Have you noticed anything out of sorts with the building? I have heard some stories about the property management here."

If the man realized she was trying to coax an answer out of him, he didn't show it.

"No," was all he said. As far as he knew, the property manage-ment was adequate.

Over the next week, her encounters with the man from 5B ac-quired what she came to think of as an "asymmetrical routine."

They bumped into each other in the hall, engaged in light conversation, or simply nodded in passing. It felt neighborly enough in that informal urban way. Contrary to Veronique's initial hypothesis, it did not appear the man worked in the financial sector. His hours were too irregular. She would hear his footsteps in the hall during the late mornings or catch him whistling some tune in the evenings. Once or twice, she spotted him in the courtyard on his way to the communal trash bins, where he always deposited exactly two black bags in the compost bin. She never learned his name and referred to him only as 5B. Something about the label felt appropriate. It smacked of the anonymity and ordinariness that characterized modern city life.

One afternoon (Veronique thought it was a Thursday), there was a commotion in the courtyard. A vagrant had somehow found his way into the building and had been camping out in the utility corridor. Nobody was certain how long he had been living on the premises, but a child had found his body that morning in one of the passageways. Tenants gathered in the courtyard despite the drizzling rain, their necks craned in the direction of the police and paramedics walking in and out of the corridor entrance. Veronique kept her distance, observing the scene from her window. The throng below traded glances and whispered amongst themselves in small circles.

Even before the paramedics emerged from the corridor bearing the body on a gurney, Veronique knew it was bad. A fetid smell filled the air. The man's skin was black and mottled with flies. When the paramedics hoisted the body into the standard-issue coroner's bag, it landed with a soft thud that sent a frenetic black cloud of insects whizzing into the air. A few of the spectators in the front rows scampered for cover, but most refused to give up their privileged viewing positions. Amid the commotion, Veronique saw the old man who had greeted her upon arrival. Although she was not positive, it appeared that he was looking over his shoulder directly at her window. If their eyes met, neither of them acknowledged the silent exchange.

Watching the paramedics haul away the body brought to mind

a childhood memory. In an effort to teach her daughter English, Veronique's mother had sung an old English nursery rhyme to her each night before bed. While she could no longer recall the entire rhyme, the final refrain had stuck with her.

The king counts days
The queen's in delight
The princess is waiting
For her prince to alight.

With her rudimentary understanding of English at the time, Veronique always heard "prince of flies" rather than the alien Anglo-Saxon word "alight." The phrase conjured up visions of a man dressed in splendid court attire with a mass of ravenous flies feeding on the spoilt flesh concealed within the garments. This creature wove its way into her childhood nightmares. When Veronique, on the verge of tears, told her mother that she didn't want to marry the prince of flies, she laughed. "Whatever gave you such an idea?" she asked, never making the connection between the rhyme and her daughter's active imagination.

The wheels of the gurney made a rickety sound as they rolled across the convex stones of the courtyard. She knew it was inappropriate to think such things, but she imagined the vagrant wandering through the maze-like passages that stretched out beneath the building. Had he first experienced amazement at their vastness? Had this wonder soon converted to terror when he realized that he had completely lost himself in the winding passageways? This was, of course, pure fantasy, because the child had discovered the body near the entrance to the corridor. Nonetheless, she could not let go of the idea.

Throughout the afternoon, Veronique caught herself humming the childish melody of the rhyme. It had been ages since she had last thought of it. The dulcet sound of her mother's voice had been stowed away somewhere in the back of her mind for years, buried but not forgotten. It brought back memories of her childhood in Crécy-la-Chapelle, where her father had taught at the local college. By the time they moved closer to Paris, Veronique had all but forgotten about the prince of flies and the nightmares.

She was still humming the melody when she extinguished the lights and crawled into bed. Closing her eyes, she imagined the prince of flies hovering above her. His face was different now as he smiled and exposed his white teeth through a beard of frenzied insects. Veronique reached out to take his hand and felt a formicating sensation envelop her entire arm. He was drawing her closer, wrapping her in his churning embrace. When he pressed his lips to hers, she could feel him inside her mouth, filling her entire body with moiling, writhing life.

At this thought, she began gasping for air. The room was silent, and she was alone. Pale light trickled in through the blinds, casting a striated pattern across the expanse of floor. Inserting her thumb and index fingers between the venetian blinds, she noted the source of the light. A single window was illuminated two floors down on the opposite side of the courtyard. The kitchen of the opposing apartment was visible from her vantage point. It belonged to the old man, who was sitting alone at a table drizzling honey over a bowl of pears. Veronique was about to check the time when she noticed the man begin to convulse soundlessly. His eyes rolled back, and his mouth stretched and distended in an unnatural movement. Veronique could not believe her eyes as the lower portion of the man's jaw appeared to dislocate, forcing the top portion of his head back at an impossible angle. A long conical tongue sprouted from the gaping mouth and flailed wildly in the air before slithering toward the pears. All the while the man sat perfectly still, his body catatonic.

Naturally, she was still dreaming as she watched the pulsating tongue borrow into the fruit. She was still dreaming when the pears liquefied and the proboscis-like tongue retracted back into the man's throat. She was still dreaming when she slunk back into bed and buried her face deep in the pillow. Perhaps she was even still dreaming when she noticed the first traces of dawn light bleed across the sky.

***

5B found her crouching in the hall with her nose pressed to the ground.

"Something interesting?" he asked, clearly uninterested in whatever it was she was doing.

She pointed at a desiccated fly carcass lying on the parquet in the hall. It had been sitting there on its back motionless when she opened the door.

"Dead fly," she said.

"There are more of those in the courtyard if you fancy them."

"Yes, terrible what happened the other day," she said, rising to her feet. It seemed the only appropriate thing to say.

A troubled look passed over his face. "You know they believe you're responsible," he finally said.

Veronique furrowed her brow. "They don't think that I..."

He shook his head. Talk among the tenants had led some to speculate that Veronique had left the front doors open allowing the vagrant access to the building. Looking at it from their perspective, it was not an implausible scenario: a new person in the building followed by an episode involving a death and the police. Most of the tenants appeared to be older and had probably lived in the building for years without incident.

"Should I speak with them?" she asked after he had finished. "I certainly don't think I'm responsible for this."

5B shook his head again. "No. They'll summon you once they hold a meeting," he said. "It normally works that way."

Veronique doubted she would be sticking around for some building council meeting to decide her fate. She was uncomfortable with how the place was affecting her behavior, and she was pretty certain that the problem with the apartment had little to do with the actual state of the property. Her plan was to spend the day out and return to Poissy in the morning on the first train.

She found a quiet café to pass the afternoon reading the newspaper. Out of habit, she scanned the property values listed in the real estate section. A left bank cinema house was showing *The*

Third Man, finalizing her plans for the night. She spent the evening watching Joseph Cotton and Orson Welles meander around post-war Vienna. It occurred to her that she had only attended a movie alone once before in her life. Some weeks after her father's death, she had sat through a Claude Chabrol retrospective in Archère. Her days then had been filled with sad looks and tepid condolences, and the thought of being surrounded by complete strangers in a dark room felt comforting. There would be no sad looks, no obligatory expressions of sorrow. When the credits opened, Veronique had begun crying. It was the first time she had cried since the funeral. At that moment, with everyone's attention fixed on the screen, it felt permissible.

These thoughts slowly rolled over in her mind as she sat watching *The Third Man*. She found it difficult to concentrate on the film. Her attention continually trailed off and the story seemed hard to follow. More than once she got the impression that something was lurking there in the expansive darkness of the theater, waiting for her. If she listened closely, the faint drone emitted by the old projector sounded eerily like insect noises. Halfway through the movie, she got up and left. Her thoughts were now on packing and catching the first train from Saint Lazare at six.

She pushed back the large front carriage doors with the certainty that tomorrow would be the last time she would ever set foot in this building. The corridor was dark, although she could just barely make out the garden in the ethereal moonlight as she stepped into the courtyard. Her fingers trailed along the wall for the switch to trip the courtyard lights. She located it, pressed the button, and screamed.

As the lights illuminated the courtyard, she saw a collection of bodies making their way through the garden. They were hunched on all fours and moved with a predatory silence. Disjointed limbs thrashed in the air and bent at abnormal angles like the legs of spiders. When they laid eyes on Veronique, a ferocious buzz filled the courtyard. Their faces contorted to expose long tubular tongues that dragged on the ground. A familiar iridescent glow began to pulse in their abdomens. She turned to run but realized that there was nowhere to go. On all sides, tenants were now spilling out of the windows and crawling down the sides of the building on their bellies like beetles. There must have been fifty of them swarming towards the courtyard, converging from every direction. The insectile drone echoed in the air, eclipsing her screams.

The horde fell upon her, and everything went dark. She felt her body being forced to the ground and then raised up into the night. When she opened her eyes she was staring directly at the moon. The contours of the surrounding courtyard walls now framed the night sky and from this position she could clearly see how the enclosure resembled a giant combed hive teeming with gangly bodies scrambling from every window. She felt the creatures roiling beneath her and experienced the sudden sensation of movement. Despite her resistance, she was transferred from hand to hand and inched closer to the gaping black opening of the utility corridor at the far end of the courtyard. She understood now where she was going and attempted to cry out one last time over the shrill drone. Her voice, hoarse from screaming, came out in a disconsolate whimper.

"I don't want to marry the prince of flies," she puled. "I don't want to marry him."

Call *to* Me, Sweet Alecto

Evie caught the scent of the ocean as she pulled into the parking lot, although upon first sight all she saw was a flat terrain of parked cars, their metallic skins glinting in the cold afternoon sunlight. Sedans belonged to the well-off suburban families, the VWs and two-doors to the day-trippers and students. What did she drive? A sleek red Alfa Romeo Spider that she had managed to pry from her ex-husband in the divorce. Evie had always disliked the sports car. A predictable testament to male ego and virility, she had once described it to a therapist. Yet *acquiring* the vehicle, possessing the object which her husband had taken such pride in, invested the car with new significance. Her therapist called it spite. Evie preferred to think of it as catharsis.

The lot was crammed with men in bucket hats and women restraining children eager to explore the waterfront. More than once, Evie slammed on the brakes to avoid hitting a pedestrian. She stared at the threads of bodies massing in the distance like a human ant colony and then let her eyes drift to the boats parked in the harbor and the vacant sea beyond. How many people had come? Certainly not everyone could fit on those ships, she mused.

As she eased the car between an oversized SUV and a Fiat that had seen better days, Evie caught a glimpse of two young men standing about idly, resisting the forward momentum of the crowd. One leaned against the hood of an automobile, flabby arms protruding from a faded muscle shirt, a cigarette pinched between thumb and index finger. As she slid out of the driver's seat, he let out a long whistle. "Nice set... of wheels," he called, eliciting a chortle from his friend.

Evie ignored them, lifting her travel bag from the passenger seat and following the others.

"Don't mind them," a man at her side advised as their paths converged and they merged into the human ant colony.

"Oh, I didn't," Evie assured him.

People bumped and jostled against her. The sheer force of the crowd propelled her forward. Somewhere overhead a gull screeched.

This is a vacation, Evie repeated to herself. *I* need *this vacation.*

"So many people," she muttered, trying to avoid errant elbows and inconsiderate shoes attached to inconsiderate people.

The man at her side gave a wistful smile. "Once every eight years," he said. "It packs them in."

A teenager sporting a tie-dyed shirt featuring leaping whales cut in front of her and then disappeared into the sea of bodies.

"I just wouldn't have thought..." Evie began, eyeing the crowd and wondering why she had decided on a wildlife cruise rather than the beaches of southern France. Wildlife tourism is the new thing, everyone had said. It was *different.*

"The chisel-toothed whales pass through here like clockwork," the man was saying. "It brings out everyone. The tourists. The nature freaks. Biologists. Even religious nuts. Some people think that these whales have mystical significance, did you know that?"

"And which one are you?" Evie asked, half in jest, as they were shunted along towards the greeting stations on the harbor quay.

Once settled into her cabin on *The Odyssey* and after taking half a Klonopin for good measure, Evie began to feel at ease. She wandered along the decks of the ship, passing through empty ballrooms and bars that had yet to be stocked. A crew member dressed in an immaculate white uniform discerned that she was, indeed, lost, and politely instructed her toward the greeting deck where complimentary drinks and hors d'oeuvres were being served.

"Wouldn't want to miss the meet and greet," he said with a smile.

"No, of course not," she mumbled, although Evie was already dreading it. She had yet to spot a lone traveler like herself.

Couples, especially those in the early years of marriage, were associated with an acute type of social discomfort she had come to think of as her own personal form of *Weltschmerz*. In their presence, she would brood, cast pouty looks, and secretly relish in malevolent fantasies. Hardly the type of person you wanted at a party, and eventually, one by one, her friends told her so. They had suggested the trip after all, perhaps with the expectation that she might meet someone or simply to have three weeks free of Evie's incessant self-pity and resentment. Even her therapist was beginning to find her a bore, Evie suspected.

She eyed the couples and families from her position by the deck rail, a flute of chilled prosecco in one hand. The lapping waves below proved more entertaining.

"And then there was one," a voice behind her chimed.

She already knew it belonged to the man she had met earlier on the quay.

He introduced himself as Steve, noting that he was also traveling solo.

All Evie could think was he didn't look like a Steve. A Mark, or maybe a John. But not a Steve.

"Funny, but you don't strike me as the nature type," he said, trying to draw her into conversation. "Why *this* cruise? *This* special event?" He smiled to show he was only being friendly, perhaps a bit curious.

"I wanted to see something that other people hadn't," she admitted. "I wanted something I didn't have to share."

A pained, comical smile meandered across his lips. "Well, you might have picked the wrong shindig," as he gestured to the hundreds of bodies filling the deck. "This occasion packs them in."

Evie laughed, recognizing how absurd she sounded given the circumstances. Of course there would be thousands of people here. Of course everyone would want to experience one of the rarest animal migrations known to man. In an age of mass tourism, a unique experience was something purchased and commodified. It was pre-packaged and converted into irksome selfies and social media updates calculated to incite envy. Kitsch for the digital age.

"You never mentioned what type *you* are," she said, changing the subject. "Religious nut, right?"

Again, that winsome grin.

Standing on the deck in the afternoon sun, pleasantly sedated by the mix of Italian wine and Klonopin, Evie realized that she felt okay for the first time in a long time.

***

"No marriage is perfect," Evie's mother had told her during one of their hour-long phone conservations that passed for therapy in the days before Evie sought professional help. True, perfection was unattainable, but Evie's marriage had been a train wreck. How she had ever fallen for the pseudo-intellectual with a car fetish was beyond her, but it had happened. Falling in love elicited far fewer questions than falling out of it, she appreciated.

In the weeks before she finally decided to break the news to Matt, her soon-to-be *ex*-husband, Evie had painstakingly compiled a list of all the reasons why she knew her choice was correct. Each day she reflected on their four-year relationship, adding memories of hurt, disappointment, and fear. The list was not necessarily to remind her of everything she had put up with and the emotional strife it had caused. It was there as a statement of fact—a raft to cling to as Matt inevitably attempted to make excuses in that persuasive way he had and convince her that the distress and violence they shared together was the natural order of things. Each day, the litany of demoralizing abuse grew longer. At one point, she paused to consider whether she was being *unfair*, just as Matt always accused. Was she failing to "see the other side of things?" Was she retreating into a "feminine worldview of self-obsessive gender idealization," as Matt once claimed, paraphrasing one of the hack social philosophers he was fond of reading? These doubts were followed by shame, frantic discussions with girlfriends, and restless nights that seamlessly blended into sleep-deprived mornings.

On the designated day, Evie left work early and prepared herself for the discussion and subsequent argument that would follow.

She took the precaution of removing any noticeable objects that could be transformed into projectiles. The kitchen knives were stowed away to preclude the usual dramatic declarations of self-harm that made up the *pièce de résistance* in Matt's emotional arsenal. This was not about feminine worldview, she would tell him. It was not about his reluctance to discuss children and family. It was not about menstrual cycles or female hormonal imbalances commonly referred to by Matt as "bitch syndrome." It was about pain and self-worth. In particular, *her* pain and *her* self-worth.

As five o'clock rolled around, she sat with arms folded, list clutched in her hand, waiting for the smooth purr of the Alfa Romeo in the drive. But it never came. By six, she managed to work up the nerve to call. His cell rang and went to voicemail. Evie clenched her fists. He had somehow even managed to ruin her attempt to walk out on her own terms, to have her reckoning. Frustration transformed into a simmering rage. Picking up the phone, she dialed the number a second time. It rang as before, and then the line clicked.

"Yeah?" Matt said.

Evie froze.

"Evie?"

"Matt?"

"Yeah, *you* called me."

"Matt, why aren't you home?"

Don't tell him you were worried. Don't ask what he wants for dinner. Don't apologize. Don't. Don't. Don't!

"Sorry hon, just finishing up some things at the office. Kind of hectic today."

"Matt, when will you be home?"

"Soon. Just need to finish up..."

"Matt, I think you..."

And then she heard it. A soft feminine giggle in the background, faint but playful and suggestive.

"Matt, are you at—"

"I'll be home shortly. Don't worry. See you soon."

"Matt, I—"

But the line was dead.

Evie returned to that moment again and again in the months after the divorce. Whenever she felt lonely or doubted her actions, she would conjure up that soft, feminine laughter and give herself over completely to a rage that knew no expression—a rage that only churned and simmered and expanded like a crescendo that never broke. Hatred, pure and uncontaminated, for everything he was, everything he continued to be. And then she would walk across the living room of her modest single-bedroom apartment and look out the front window toward the driveway where the red Alfa Romeo Spider was parked. For all that Matt might have taken from her—dignity, self-esteem, trust—the car was a poor substitute. But it was, in the end, something.

***

A whine of feedback pierced through the afternoon, sharp and brisk.

"Is this thing on?" came a full-bodied voice.

A long "yesssss" droned from the crowd.

"And you in the back?"

A middle-aged man in a cabana shirt and dark glasses gave a thumbs-up. "Loud and clear."

Evie now saw the man speaking into the hand-held microphone. He was tall and well-tanned, with a warm face. *Affable* was the word to describe it, she thought.

"Okkkaayyyy," he said into the mic. "Welcome aboard, I'm Captain Tom Bering, and I'll be with you for the next three weeks on this adventure. Everyone's getting settled in I hope...? Good!"

Evie braced herself against the deck rail as the ship's motors began to whir and the vessel started its slow departure into the open water.

Captain Tom carefully lay the mic down and cleared his throat. From his pocket he produced a white handkerchief and held it up for the audience to see. Next, he made a fist and placed the white handkerchief over his hand, raising it to eye level. The crowd watched in silence as he waved his hand over the covered fist, making elaborate gestures in the air with his fingers. Then, grabbing the handkerchief, he tore it from his hand in one quick gesture. Three white birds shot into the air, the sound of their flapping wings dissipating as they ascended into the azure sky. A moment of silence ensued, followed by a roar of applause and whistles from the crowd.

"I like to start things off with a bit of magic," Captain Tom explained, pressing the mic once again to his lips. "It makes for a friendlier atmosphere, ya know?"

The crowd concurred with a murmurous "Yesssss."

"Now, we're gonna have a good time here," he continued. "There are a few ground rules I have to go over, and I'll be getting to them in just a sec. But first, I wanted to tell you about what you'll be experiencing. You are in for a treat, folks. The chisel-toothed whale comes through the South Pacific once every eight years to complete its feeding cycle. Now, I know some people might have their own opinions on what this signifies, but to me, it's a celebration. The Great Feeding is a joyous act that we are here to experience together."

He paused for a moment to let the audience digest the meaning of his words.

"Now, I don't know how much you know about these creatures, so I just want to give you some basic facts."

The man in the cabana shirt emitted an audible grunt.

"These creatures are truly a miracle of nature. They only surface to feed every eight years. The rest of the time they remain dormant. Some people find that impossible."

Captain Tom turned to a chalky-faced boy standing in the front row.

"Think *you* could go eight years without dinner?" he asked.

"I'm only seven," the boy replied innocently, drawing a peal of laughter from the crowd.

"Exactly. It's a looonnnng time. But these whales are different. Truly special. And that's why we're all here. We need to remember that *we* are guests in *their* environment. We are the intruders in their habitat. We'll all be good guests, I'm sure, but it means we need to be considerate. Pictures are fine—and we'll get you real close to the action, folks, I swear," as he gave an exaggerated wink, "but under no circumstances should we try to interfere in this miraculous occurrence."

Again, the man in the cabana shirt grunted.

Steve snickered. "I hear you," he said as Captain Tom continued his spiel. "This guy seems a little too keen on the positive vibes."

"You could put it that way," the man replied.

Evie watched the shoreline receding from view as the ship maneuvered a turn and set out into the Pacific. The land looked brown and craggy from this distance; the towering hotels reduced to white blotches on the horizon.

"Eight years," Steve was saying. "I imagine you can work up quite an appetite in that time."

"Technically that isn't true," said the grunting man, removing his glasses and polishing the lenses with the trim of his shirt. "Their bodies are designed to store excess blubber that nourishes them during the dormancy period. They aren't exactly missing any meals, just portioning them out."

"Hey, you must be one of the scientists. Marine biologist? Ichthyologist?"

"Actually, I'm not. I've just done my homework," as he returned his sunglasses and looked past Steve to the women in hot pants and bikini tops on the opposite side of the deck. Every so often, the man licked his lower lip. Evie found the gesture repulsive.

Captain Tom finished his pitch to a loud round of applause.

"Now that guy's a showman," Steve said, joining in the clapping.

The man in the cabana shirt nodded, his eyes fixed on the women.

"Edward?" a shrill voice called out. "Edwaarrrddd!"

The man in the cabana shirt furrowed his brow and looked at his feet. "Right here, dear," he sighed, waving to a woman in baggy shorts and a Moroccan-print shawl.

"Ed, did you hear that? We'll see them right up close. Isn't it wonderful?"

"Hmmm?" Ed's attention seemed elsewhere.

Without an introduction, the woman turned to Evie. "I just knew this trip would be worth it," she said. "My friends wanted to come, you know. But in the end, it was just me and Ed."

Evie smiled, finding the woman's tone and gestures comical. She was patently middle-aged, right down to the heavy makeup applied to her face.

"I like your shawl," Evie said.

"Do you?" the woman beamed. "It's a para-*shawl*. Get it? Like parasol, for the sun?"

"Very clever," Evie played along.

"Okay, let's go see what's on the agenda," Ed cut in, pulling at his wife's arm and towing her across the deck.

"Well, they seemed pleasant," Evie said once the couple was out of earshot.

Steve rolled his eyes. Then, in a complete *non sequitur*, he asked: "Think that kid in the front was a plant?"

"Which one?"

"The boy who said he was only seven."

"I don't..."

"I think he was. Like, absolutely."

"How do you know that?" Evie asked, looking at the child who, she suddenly realized, did not seem to belong to any of the other adults congregating around the drinks table or heading to the poolside lido.

"Show biz instinct. It's a fairly routine setup. Gets the laughs. Disarms the crowd. Basic stuff. Rule *numero uno*: never trust the cute kid in the front row."

"And what show biz instinct are you referring to?" Evie asked, intrigued.

"Oh, I've been around, done my time. I'll tell you about it sometime."

"Careful, I might hold you to that."

"By all means," he replied, smiling.

***

The daily mix-and-mingle activities were just as exhausting as they were boring. There was water aerobics in the morning followed by a round of water polo. Iberian tapas usually preceded the afternoon yoga session hosted by female instructors with muscular arms and tanned bodies. At five, guests congregated in the Retro Lounge for the cocktail meetup where uniformed bartenders doled out endless mojitos. The days acquired their own self-indulgent routine, punctuated by pithy reminders to enjoy the R-and-R and forget your troubles, whatever they may be.

Steve took to cruise life with alacrity, joining in the activities and making friends whenever the opportunity presented itself. Evie, by contrast, found it more difficult to give herself over to the easygoing atmosphere. She spent most days on the sidelines listening to inspirational podcasts with titles like *Find Your Zen* and *Renewal for the Modern Soul*. She looked out across the water from time to time and monitored the movement of *The Odyssey*'s sister ship, *The Aegean*, a mile to the west. She found it slightly amusing to think that everything taking place on *The Odyssey* was being replicated just a short distance across the water on its counterpart: women lounging about the pool in two-piece bathing suits; paunchy men hunched over exercise bikes in the gym; couples wrapped in white bathrobes on their way to the sauna, the only difference being the insignia on the breast reading *The Aegean* in swirling blue script.

"*You are in a special place,*" the soothing voice on the podcast whispered in her ear. "*It is empowering. It is liberating.*"

When she did explore *The Odyssey*'s many amenities, it was always at Steve's behest. Mud baths in the Revitalization Center or wine tastings at the bistro. She felt guilty pampering herself in such a flagrant manner and told Steve so.

"You paid for it," he assuaged. Steve was stretched out in a tub of Red Sea silt, arms dangling over the sides. Evie had selected the more alluring Infused Amazonian Mud for her own bath. It was only day three of the cruise, but it already felt much longer. "All-inclusive means just that."

"I don't know how to react," Evie confessed. "It's all new to me."

"These are just the perks, the add-ons if you will. We're all here for a reason. The Great Feeding is the context, but everyone attends seeking something different. A personal revelation or self-discovery, ya know?"

Evie mulled this over as she felt the cool mud cake on her naked skin. "What's your reason?" she eventually asked, trying not to sound intrusive.

He was quiet for a long time. Then, "I think I'll know when I see it. When the Great Feeding begins, I'll just know."

Evie had to admit it was nice sharing a level of intimacy with someone again. The conversation, the activities, the slow revealing of the self; she had forgotten that life need not be a sentence of solitary confinement, that pain did not preclude enjoyment. Most of all, Matt and the past four years were far from her mind when she was with Steve. His laidback nature had a certain power of its own.

Every evening as twilight streaked the sky, Evie sat on the deck and watched the lights on *The Aegean* slowly illuminate. The ship floated like a diadem in the night. The effect was oddly mesmerizing, and she wondered whether her counterpart was sitting on the deck of *The Aegean* at that very moment, contemplating the lights of *The Odyssey*, a sad and inaccessible not-Evie grappling with her own anxieties and self-doubts.

You require nothing but yourself for inspiration. Each day is a creative moment of infinite possibilities.

Evenings were hit-and-miss. She had taken to dining with Steve, who seemed to have a knack for making friends. Each night, a new person or couple joined their table, expanding the dinner circle. Evie was less than thrilled at what she quickly came to interpret as an intrusion. For the most part, they were retirees, accountants who managed corporate assets, and women whose opinions were lifted from the pages of *Cosmo* and *Elle*. Brigette, an attractive blonde from California who Steve had met at a volleyball session, was the exception. Fresh off her big break as a model in an online clothing catalogue, Brigette talked about traveling to Milan or Paris, of meeting celebrities, of *making it*. She was full of hope and idealism, and Evie hated her for it. Steve, however, listened attentively to every word. He would lean back in his chair, arms folded across his chest, nodding approvingly as she prattled on about the fashion world and the power of influencers.

"Say, didn't you mention you were in show biz?" a smooth faced tech-support specialist sitting across from Steve butted in.

Steve flashed a boyish grin. Evie couldn't help but notice Brigette return the smile. "That was a long time ago," he said.

"And?"

"Child acting. Teen stuff. Ever hear of *Afterschool Freak Out* or shows like *Beat Kids*?"

Brigette's face lit up as she placed a hand on Steve's outstretched arm.

"Yeah! Those nineties teen dramas!" she squealed. "I used to watch all of them in reruns when I was a kid! You were in *those*?"

"A few of them. Here and there."

He was being intentionally modest. Brigette beamed, her mouth contorting into a rictus of semi-awe. Her hand closed tighter on Steve's arm. Evie wanted to believe the gesture was involuntary, but still...

"Like I said, a long time ago."

"I think I need some air," Evie said, excusing herself and exiting the dining room. Nobody stopped her.

Retreating through the corridors, she passed empty recreational areas and barrooms packed with young people enjoying the evening. In the gym, rows of exercise machines lay silent and inert. It was hard to believe she was somewhere in the middle of the ocean. Everything had the cold, sterile feel of a shopping mall, office building, and apartment complex rolled into one.

She fumbled through her purse and jammed her earbuds in.

You require nothing but yourself for inspiration. The power to regenerate comes from within.

She recalled a line scribbled on a sheet of folded note paper she had kept in a dresser drawer. *Somewhere on the other side of this wide night and the distance between us, I am thinking of you.* Matt had placed the note in her mailbox two days after their first date. She remembered thinking the sentiment did not match the blocky, masculine script printed on the paper, as though poetry demanded a fluid and elegant script. Only later did she discover that Matt had taken the line from another poem—that plagiarism and deception, rather than poetry, were where his actual talents lay.

She was letting him back in again, invoking his presence.

Stupid! Stupid! Stupid!

Only once you have let go of what you are, can you become what you will be.

***

Breakfast buffets always divulged character. Pancakes were simplicity. Eggs benedict *au saumon* suggested extravagance. Fresh fruit was emblematic of sincerity. Listening to her daily dose of morning inspiration, Evie watched as each guest unknowingly revealed an intimate part of themselves to her. Ed, donning a fresh cabana shirt, selected pancakes; his wife, the eggs benedict. Others indulged in heaping plates of bacon, Belgian-style waffles, continental fare.

"You missed the disco last night," Steve said as he took a seat *sans* invitation. "Fun night."

He had chosen the breakfast burrito, symbolizing indecisiveness and ease.

Evie pictured Steve and Brigette dancing amidst strobing lights and pulsing dance music, their bodies touching and entangling.

"Not my scene," was all she said.

One table over, Ed and his wife were engaged in an argument about the air conditioner in their room.

"For once, Lydia, can you take my side?" he grumbled. "Just *once* would be nice."

"What do you expect from *me*?"

"Luxury, my ass. I'm dying in this heat!"

"You're making a scene," she reprimanded, casting a furtive look around the room. "Please, don't humiliate us," she moaned. "*Please.*"

"Us? *Us*? Couldn't have that, right?" with an arrogant laugh.

Steve, who had been listening to the entire exchange, gave Evie a wide-eyed look across the table. Couples like Ed and Lydia were walking advertisements for divorce. Others concealed their misery and frustration behind a staid conjugal exterior. As to which was preferable, Evie didn't know.

After breakfast, everyone migrated onto the south deck where Captain Tom was preparing for the morning briefing.

"The hour grows near, friends," he intoned. "The Great Feeding will soon be upon us."

Evie looked over the faces in the crowd. Brigette stood on the opposite side of the circle, her face shaded by a stylish Ipanema sun hat. She smiled and waved. Steve reciprocated.

"I have felt the expectation, the anticipation," Captain Tom continued, his voice thunderous, sermonic even. "We stand upon the threshold of a new day. Yes, a *new* day! In our own personal way, we too feel the hunger. It is a hunger that stirs us, that leads us to seek, to question, to re-evaluate who we are. *What* we are."

"Are you kiddin' me?" Ed mumbled, earning an abrasive shush from his wife.

Captain Tom paused, and Evie had the sudden impression that he was speaking directly to her.

"We may think that the hunger is insatiable, that we are destined to wander unfulfilled. But I tell you: *it* is out there! We all must travel through our own vast oceans, struggling against powerful currents. But our instincts are strong! We may fear. We may question. We may supplicate in moments of weakness. But we also prevail. We seek transformation and, through it, transcendence."

The crowd stared up at him, enraptured.

"The hour comes when each in their own way will know the ecstasy of satiation. We will bear witness! And in one miraculous moment, we will experience this fulfillment together, for it is *our* fulfillment, each and every one of us."

He paused and cast a long look out toward the rolling waves. A poignant expression bled across his face, as though he were looking past the depths of the horizon into the promised future.

Slowly, the crowd stirred as a few clapping hands swelled into a climax of applause. The spell broke and the audience came to life in a buzz of chatter.

"I told you, a real showman," Steve said with a nudge.

Evie, momentarily entranced, followed Captain Tom's stare. *The Aegean*, half a mile away, was the only object in the expanse of sea and sky unrolling before them.

"Amazing," Brigette trilled, gliding through the thinning crowd. "I could almost feel it. Like something was *calling* to me."

"Powerful stuff," Steve concurred. Then, turning to Evie, "Coming to the sports meet-up later?"

"Think I'll pass."

"Suit yourself," he said with a shrug.

Evie remained on the south deck for most of the morning, avoiding the pool and recreational areas. The quiet suited her, and she could think of doing nothing save stretching out in a sun chair and admiring the vastness of the ocean.

"You are in a special place," she muttered to herself. "It is empowering. It is liberating."

The words sounded hollow and devoid of meaning.

As the sun climbed toward its zenith, Evie withdrew inside. In the recreational area, children and elderly couples were busy painting little ceramic figurines. Further afield, bare-chested men and girls in bikinis socialized on the lido over tall piña coladas. Evie considered ordering a margarita at the pool bar but decided against it, noting the older single men in loose-fitting floral shirts congregating there. Passing the sports center, however, she immediately regretted her decision. Through the massive window, she spotted Steve standing astride Brigette. Hand on her wrist, he was gently guiding her arm forward to demonstrate the proper motion for retuning a volley. As he pulled her arm back, Brigette's body pressed against his. Although their voices were silenced behind the thick wall of plexiglass, their body language said enough.

Evie bit down on the inside of her cheek and tasted blood.

Steve was placing his hand on Brigette's hips to adjust her stance when Brigette turned her head. For a split second, their eyes locked through the glass and Brigette flashed a razor-thin smile. It felt malicious and cruel. Although lasting only an instant, there had been something communicative in that look; a cold recognition of one another.

The taste of blood lingered in Evie's mouth as she rushed down the corridor, pushing past oncoming men in towels and boys carrying waterboards. She could feel it again. That emotional churning, a certain sense of spinning out of control. It had been there all this time, she now realized: latent, ravenous, waiting to resurface.

Her hands were steady as she pried the lid off the prescription bottle and queued up a power session of *Find Your Zen*. By the time the calm yet assertive female voice informed her that failure was merely a stop on the path to success, Evie was fast asleep. And she slept for a long time.

***

Somewhere in the middle of a dream, she heard quick, heavy footsteps coming from the hall. Crepuscular light filled the windows, bathing the room in a warm glow. Evie rubbed her eyes and pulled herself from bed, groggy and slow to comprehend. There were more footsteps in the hall, excited voices trailing through the corridors.

Outside the windows, the sea was crimson. *The Aegean* floated listlessly a quarter mile out. It was the closest Evie could remember seeing the ship to *The Odyssey*. At this distance, it looked dense and less ethereal. Different, she thought, before placing her finger on it. The ship was dark. Despite the twilight, the lights were extinguished. It rocked there in the ocean, black and silent.

More footsteps came from the hall and Evie poked her head out the door. People hustled past, some half-dressed, cameras in hand.

"What is it?" Evie asked a scurrying woman.

She halted, her face eager and expectant. "They're here. It's begun," she said as she continued along the corridor toward the main deck.

Evie didn't bother to change. She exited the room and joined the stream of people.

Even before they arrived on the deck, she heard the noise: a deep, resonant wailing coming across the water. It saturated the air, sounding omnipresent.

The silhouette of *The Aegean* loomed off the starboard side, ominous in its darkness. Captain Tom was speaking from the bridge.

"The hour is upon us," his voice thundered through the PA. "Behold the Great Feeding. Bear witness! Bear witness and succumb to the hunger! Embrace it! Transcend *through* it!"

As Evie listened, she wondered how she understood. Captain Tom's voice was melding together with the plangent wailing filling the air, becoming one with it. They were not words. The noise itself resounded deep in her being. A calling coming from across the water. Isn't that how Brigette described it? A *calling*?

"There!" somebody shouted, pointing into the distance.

Heads swiveled. There was movement in the water. Shadowy forms broke through the surface, leaping and splashing before plunging back into the depths. People sprinted to the rail, pushing, cameras at the ready for the next surfacing. When it came, there was the click of cameras followed by a collective exhalation of amazement.

The movement of the distant animals was strange, Evie thought. Their bodies were long and slender. Not as she had imagined a whale's body to be. Each leap and splash brought them closer. Evie couldn't tell whether the ship was moving or whether the animals were cutting through the water with such stealth. The wailing grew louder. At closer range, the splashing and jumping didn't appear playful. Rather, it felt precise and predatory.

"Oh, God! Help!" a voice screamed.

Taking her eyes from the water, Evie saw Ed hunched over Lydia. She was sprawled out on the floor, violently convulsing.

"Somebody!" he called, his hands cradling his wife's head.

Steve and Brigette were first on the scene, and as they knelt to assess the situation, Evie heard further calls for help echoing across the deck. A young Asian woman had collapsed, followed by a little girl. There was a confusion of voices and then the ship lurched to an abrupt halt as though running aground. The water surrounding the vessel roiled. Dark shapes circled just beneath the surface.

Evie heard a commotion and then an ear-piercing scream. Lydia was sitting up now, blood running down her chin. A large chunk of mangled flesh was gripped between her teeth. Steve was attempting to bind Ed's wound with his shirt when Lydia shoved him aside. Without a word, she pounced and began frantically clawing at her husband's face.

Screams were coming from all parts of the deck as people lunged and tackled one another to the ground. Steve and Brigette huddled against the rail, inches from where Lydia assailed her flailing husband. A scene of complete carnage unfolded around them. Women convulsed, flailed, slashed, and tore, streaking the deck in rivulets of blood. They cried out in anguish, joining in the deep wailing sound growing louder by the second. Husbands, sons, lovers—all were being surrendered to the Great Hunger. Horrified, Evie looked back to Brigette, the same dawning realization evident in both their eyes.

A sound like grinding metal cut through the air and the ship listed. Brigette screamed as a spider-like claw snaked over the rail and landed on the deck. Below, a slurping sound came from the water, and Evie saw the dark shapes moiling beneath the waves start climbing up the sides of the ship. The deck was littered with butchered flesh, bodies torn limb from limb. Off the bow, a form was rising from the water, something black and mammoth emerging from the depths. It rose up tall into the twilit sky, its massive form alien yet strangely beautiful. Evie attempted to scream, but all she heard was the wailing sound coming from her throat. She stood, awe-stricken, gazing up at what she knew could not be towering above them. Its smooth contours were magnificent in the oncoming moonlight. Paralyzed with wonder, Evie understood. She must yield to it, must allow it to suffuse and possess her. She could feel it mounting inside her like a crescendo, a torrent of intense and rapturous joy begging for release.

Tearing her gaze away, Evie's eyes settled on Steve. He stood back against the rail, a spectator to the unabating carnage surrounding them. When he noticed Evie's stare, an expression of dread stole across his face. Brigette was nowhere in sight as she started out across the deck, her shoes slick in the blood pooling on the deck floor.

"You are in a special place," she reminded herself, her heart quickening with each step. "It is empowering. It is liberating."

The Past is a Foreign Country

He must have been dreaming. He can still vaguely see the frozen river and the boy with the sled who kept speaking to them in Russian even when it was obvious they did not understand a word he was saying. It had been their trip to Moscow three years ago. Abby was ten and fascinated by the pocket atlas at the hotel, relishing in her dawning realization of the world's immensity. "Who goes to Russia in the winter?" his brother-in-law had asked. Liz, rolling her eyes, declined to explain the appeal of airline discounts or the logic of off-season travel. It didn't prevent her from complaining of the cold and snow the whole time, he thinks now, rousing from his reminiscence of vacations past as he hears the soft knocking at the door.

"Sol, you going to answer that?" Liz calls from upstairs.

Awake, leaping over the couch, he opens the door to find a man in a bland brown UPS uniform. He requests a signature before turning over a small package wrapped in decorative paper. There is no card, he realizes as he closes the door and places the package alongside the others that have been arriving all week. Abby is going to be spoiled, he thinks, looking at the array of presents.

"Another one?" Liz asks, eyeing the boxes neatly stacked on the table. "When I turned thirteen, I got a few dolls. You?"

"My parents had the decency to spare me the dolls," he says, smiling and eliciting a playful swat from his wife.

"Don't forget you need to pick up the cake," she reminds him, sliding into her high-heeled shoes as she makes for the living room.

"I'll have to take Abby, you know. Who else will watch her?"

"Just distract her when you go to the bakery. Try and keep it a surprise." She frowns, plants a kiss on his cheek and finishes the last of her coffee.

Setting the mug down and clearing some magazines from the dining room table, she begins to hum. The melody is familiar and for a second Solomon has the impression he is still asleep on the couch dreaming. He listens carefully and verifies as Liz absent-mindedly attends to her last-minute chores.

"What are you humming?"

She stops, thinks, and shrugs. "I don't know. Something I heard?"

"Where?" He is noticeably distressed.

"I don't know... On the radio maybe? Why, what's wrong?"

He shakes his head. He must have been mistaken, he thinks. The Moscow dream is still fresh in his mind, roiling other parts of his waking brain, blending dream and reality. Yet still, he thinks he hears her humming it again as she picks up her bag, checks her appearance in the mirror and heads out the door. It lingers in the room after she is gone, running through his thoughts. He couldn't have heard it correctly, or had imposed his own melody on the notes she was humming under her breath, transmogrifying some generic pop song into a somber hymn.

As he mulls this over, he hears Abby padding along the upstairs hallway, her socked feet whisper-soft on the carpet. His parental responsibilities call, blotting out all other considerations.

***

He swore he would never return. It had been a promise made to himself on his final day at Stanhope standing in his soon-to-be former room and looking at the vacant space that for three years had served in turn as domicile, study, and sanctuary. Now, having passed through the campus gates, Solomon acknowledged the betrayal to his former self. The intervening years had softened his resolve or perhaps simply given him a more accurate perspective on the naïve obstinacy so characteristic of youth. Yet the fact remained. He had made that promise once, whether seriously or not.

And now he had violated it.

Nothing had changed in twenty-two years. The ivy still clung to the redbrick buildings. The heavy boughs of the trees still drooped over the footpaths. The Georgian portico with its handsome columns remained intact. The only detail amiss was the truck parked in the drive and the team of workmen hauling a large packing crate from the bed of the vehicle. Establishments like the Stanhope Academy prided themselves on tradition and heritage; change was an alien concept. Even Collingwood, who accepted the position as headmaster, had come from within the academy and first walked through those gates as a student of music, just as Solomon had. It was a peculiar type of inbreeding, he thought. Venerable institutions clung to old ways and nourished themselves on unhealthy fears of the outside world.

Entering the atrium occasioned a flood of dormant memories. Here they had sat on warm afternoons, gathering as the Stanhope Trio and planning for yet unrealized futures. During the winter months they migrated inside, colonizing the antechamber with the small upright Baldwin and shelves lined with music folios. Preston would lounge idly in one of the embroidered armchairs beside the bust of Liszt while Collingwood hunched over the cold hearth, repeatedly swearing he knew how to build a fire. Conversation was punctuated by turns on the piano as each played bars and the others guessed the composer. Preston had taken to smoking a pipe during their second year and the sweet smell of the tobacco always hung heavy in the room. An old-fashioned habit, Collingwood liked to remind him with a dry expression. Preston never failed to grin, curls of smoke coiling around his face. At least he knew how to get a fire going, he taunted. Of course it was an old-fashioned habit, but the pipe never seemed unnatural or affected in any way. That was Preston's charm: the ability to pull off those mannerisms and idiosyncrasies as though they were completely authentic.

He had spent some happy days here, Solomon reminded himself, running his fingertips over the ivory keys of the Baldwin and eliciting a series of faint, ghost-like notes that lingered in the empty room. It was easy to forget. Everything had become clouded by the more unpleasant details as if it were perfectly natural for the shadow of the future to cast itself backward over the past. Retrospectively, it was impossible not to try to discern the telltale signs that must have been there all along, indecipherable yet latent, waiting to be placed in their proper context. Reading time in reverse was like watching a movie for a second time and piecing together the plotline in advance. Solomon had first entertained such thoughts the day following the memorial when he stood in Preston's bedroom surveying the unclaimed objects and keepsakes. A daybook open on the desk with a half-page of writing scribbled in it; the tangled sheets of an unmade bed; the pipe resting atop the nightstand, listing to one side. The scene appeared absolutely commonplace, giving the impression the room was still inhabited and that the occupant might return at any moment. Picking up the pipe, Solomon pressed the bowl to his nose and inhaled the traces of cherry resin and burnt tobacco. The briar was cold to the touch.

He hammered out an A-minor chord on the piano and listened to the sound resonate deep inside the instrument's cavity. In the hall, workers maneuvered the large crate through the corridor, flexing their hypertrophied arms and barking in broken syllables. An instrument for an upcoming performance, no doubt. A grand piano or harpsichord judging from its size. Solomon channeled his thoughts elsewhere, drowning out the background noise with the aid of the Baldwin.

How had Collingwood managed to remain, he wondered? Over the years he had rarely thought of him, although when he did it was always through the wan light of their past lives. To imagine him now as a serious middle-aged man with a career and adult responsibilities was inconceivable. He was forever a nostalgic remnant of his years at Stanhope, a mental image sketched from the dust of memory that never quite dissipated.

The chord rang out and a faint applause followed from the hall. Collingwood, dressed in a blue blazer and tie, emerged from the adjoining chamber, his feet mute on the thick Oriental rug. The thin face and receding hairline were those of a stranger, although Solomon could not ignore the haunting familiarity that nagged at him all the same.

"Hello, Sol." After all these years, it was the most basic of greetings he offered. "Still sounds the same, doesn't it?" He gestured toward the Baldwin and placed a slender finger on the C-sharp key in the upper register. A tinny note trilled, slightly off-key. That particular key had always been out of tune. During those winter evenings when they sat testing each other's compositional knowledge, it had frustrated them to no end, eventually becoming a running joke within their little coterie.

"It's never been fixed."

"Some things never change," Solomon replied with a wry smile, adding, "especially here."

"Especially here," he agreed.

The rectory office still smelled of floor wax and brass polish. He wondered if the janitorial staff had stayed consistent over the years or whether the new one simply used the same cleaning products. Afternoon light crept in through the window, latticing the room in streaks of gold and dusty shadow. Collingwood eased into the leather-backed chair behind the desk and habitually cracked his knuckles as though about to perform. Solomon recalled Spencer Erskine, the former headmaster, filling this same chair two decades previous. He had an incorrigible habit of fidgeting with his fountain pen or letter opener when he spoke. "How was that man ever a cellist?" Preston had mused, imitating the movement of Erskine's nervous fingers. But he had been a world-class cellist in his lifetime. The alumnus newsletter had made a point of noting it in the obituary it printed.

"This room looks the same," Solomon offered, taking his customary seat across from the large oak desk. "Although, if memory serves me right, Erskine always had a bowl of confectionaries on his desk."

"Those dreadful lemon drops," Collingwood said, making a face, "the ones with a medicinal taste." Then, clearing his throat, "Sol, I have to ask if you were surprised by my letter asking you to come."

"Well..."

"I didn't invite you here to trot down memory lane." Collingwood paused. He was carefully weighing his words, perhaps knowing that a misphrased utterance could stir raw emotions resistant to the mellowing influences of time. "I located it," he finally stated.

It took Solomon a moment to comprehend, and in the split-second between presumption and understanding he could not help thinking that Collingwood looked misplaced in Erskine's former seat, like a mannequin temporarily holding the place of its rightful owner.

***

"Earth to Dad? Come in, Dad?"

"Huh?"

"You spaced."

She's right.

He squints and focuses on the road, disregarding the sprawl of strip malls and gas stations that line the stretch of highway. Cars dart in and out of lanes, spitting up rainwater as they maneuver through the hazy drizzle at a moderate speed. All morning his head has been in a fog, his thoughts scattered and elsewhere.

"Not a great day for a birthday," he says looking at the streaks of water running down the windshield. "Sorry, pumpkin."

Abby is preoccupied with her phone, oblivious.

He angles the car into the mall parking lot and nestles in beside a family-sized sedan. The sticker in the rear window advertises "My Son Is A Music Scholar At Marshall Elementary." Solomon gives a dismal laugh, feeling the sticker somehow suits the day and his drifting recollections.

"What?" Abby asks, checking to see if the laugh is on her account.

"Nothing," he says.

How could he begin to explain? There are no musical instruments in their house, no artifacts from his student days. When he and Liz began dating, she discovered some old books of piano arrangements stored in a box. "You play?" she asked, intrigued. They belonged to his father, he lied. She didn't ask any questions when she saw them lying on the rubbish heap the following day. Every trace was meticulously scoured away as if it were possible to quarantine the past. The letter he received and the trip he took last month have gone quietly unmentioned. He only lies to her on this one particular subject, and for reasons he cannot properly understand or articulate. There is a sacred and ritualistic quality to his secrecy that he cannot bring himself to relinquish.

People mill idly along the mall promenade, gazing into windows, meandering in and out of stores. He tells Abby she can go to the toy store and hands her a crisp bill.

"How old do you think I am?" she scoffs, heading for a clothing retailer that caters to young adults.

He takes a place in the line twisting through The Baker's Dozen. The cozy artisanal-sounding name does not match the size and layout of the store. People browse through catalogs of cakes and pastry assortments; they push shopping carts along stark aisles containing industrial baking supplies, frozen delicacies, and made-to-order baked goods. The quaint Baker's Dozen logo is reflected backward in the storefront window, its folksy script evoking nostalgia for a time when large supermarkets and made-to-order goods did not exist.

He concentrates on the music purring through the loudspeaker. It takes a moment to detect it over the drone of voices and buzzing checkout lines, but it is definitely there, too sad and elegiac for a large retail store like this. Again, he experiences the sensation of dreaming and believes he is mistaken. The notes float over the din of modern commerce, barely noticeable, yet perceptible all the same. He could whistle the melody on cue if he wanted, Solomon realizes with a sudden pang of distress. It is tattooed on his memory like a scar, and he suddenly wants to know—*needs* to know—how this song is being played in this place at this exact moment. His thoughts are in such a frenzy that he doesn't hear the woman at the counter call out, "Next!" or detect her contemptuous look when he fails to respond to her brusque command.

"Name and order number," she says, as he approaches the counter.

"Where is this music coming from?"

"What?"

"The music. Why is this playing? Who put it on?"

She fixes him with an aggravated expression. "The managers play it, sir. I think the playlists are determined by the main office."

"That's impossible," he protests, placing his hands on the counter.

"Sir, name and order number, please," she repeats, visibly alarmed by his behavior.

"You're saying they play this music here *all* the time?"

"Name and order number."

Her voice is deliberate, the syllables even and stressed. She is not going to ask again.

Without a word, he hands over the receipt with the order number. As he waits for the cake, he listens to the low drone of the music mixing with the background noise. The song has now changed, though. A woman is singing a cover of a popular eighties song. The last haunting traces of the melody evaporate into thin air, folding back into the recesses of his memory.

***

They had been four at first: Solomon, Collingwood, Preston, and a spindly young violinist named Harper. Peers dubbed them the Stanhope Quartet, although Harper distanced himself once students began referring to the Stanhope *Queer*-tet. Hence, the Stanhope Trio. It had a certain ring to it, sounding more like an old-style gang of bank robbers than an informal student fellowship.

The clique was not without its rivalries and petty jealousies, of course. Solomon was always aware of that special type of competitive ambition that existed among young students aspiring to Carnegie Hall and the national symphony. He learned to detest it, although it was part and parcel of academic life. Stories abounded of students sabotaging recitals and spreading rumors to undermine potential scholarship and prize winners. Collingwood resented the fact that the academy had awarded Preston the annual bursary rather than him, although he never admitted as much. To acknowledge the achievements of others was to admit to one's own shortcomings and deficiencies. Better to mock quietly, to criticize in whispered breaths rather than aloud, to nurse resentments that bloomed into antipathy. Spite and malice drove greatness: this was what they were taught; this is what they lived and breathed while gracing the hallowed halls of Stanhope.

Solomon could never recall whether Preston or Collingwood first mentioned the name of Johannes Aehrenthal. Their interest in the composer seemed to develop collectively, emerging out of the unnatural hive-like consciousness shared among them. Aehrenthal, with his esoteric appeal and bizarre compositions; Aehrenthal, who had reputedly been invited to perform at the Schönbrunn Palace and debuted his *Freiheithymne* to the horror of Empress Maria Theresa and the Austrian nobility; Aehrenthal, whose name never graced the lectures they attended at the academy. In this obscure composer, the trio found their patron saint, and it was through their shared fascination that they first learned of the black legend and the infamous Fugue in B minor, allegedly written to summon the devil.

"This chap gets better and better!" Preston trilled, leaning over the old leather-bound volume as curls of fragrant smoke filled the airless room.

"A legend used to justify his ban from court," Collingwood pointed out dismissively. "Are you really that gullible?"

True, the notorious fugue had never been performed. A few collectors demanding exorbitant prices claimed to possess rare copies of the composition manuscript. A black market for these types of curios was not unheard of, and the Aehrenthal legend certainly attracted its fair share of enthusiasts willing to dole out large sums for such a coveted item. Who could not be at least tempted to speculate on what such a piece of music might sound like? A melody with the power to summon unspeakable darkness and evil, the sheer macabre nature of these stories elevated Aehrenthal to near-mythic status.

It was, therefore, with a mix of anticipation and wonder that Preston disclosed his discovery on that cold December evening as they congregated in the antechamber. Collingwood had been leaning against the fireplace, looking down dejectedly at his latest disaster. It snowed that night. Solomon could distinctly remember sitting in a meditative silence watching the white crystals accumulate on the latticed windows as he listened to Preston's quiet voice. When Preston stated he had obtained a copy of Fugue in B minor, his words seemed to mix with the cold air and hang there, heavy and solid, demanding recognition. Collingwood soured, mumbling that his upcoming recitation was more important than an arcane piece of folklore. Still, Solomon could detect the underlying envy, the recognition that Preston had once again bested him in some vital way.

In the privacy of his room, Preston carefully removed each leaf of the sheet music from a brown paper envelope and assembled them on the bed. The trio huddled 'round, indulging in the secretive and almost conspiratorial nature of their investigation. A small Reich swastika was stamped in red ink on the first page of the manuscript, under which in neat typeface was printed the words *Fuge der Verdammten*. Solomon felt his mouth go dry as he stared spellbound at the symbol. He had never seen an actual Nazi swastika before and its sight made all the horrific details repeated in his history lectures feel real and concrete. The manuscript had been held in a German music conservatory during the war, Preston explained. A British collector had smuggled it out of occupied Berlin unknown to Allied authorities.

"Unbelievable," Collingwood whispered, rubbing the corners of the paper between his fingers. "How can this possibly be real?"

Preston had paid a significant sum for the manuscript by borrowing against a trust overseen jointly by his parents.

"And they were perfectly fine with this?"

Preston never answered the question, and the subject was dropped until the official inquiry months later when the illegal procurement of funds became a topic of contention.

They agreed to play the fugue over winter break when the students and faculty departed for the holiday season, leaving only a skeleton crew of custodians to mind the premises. Collingwood and Preston spent the long afternoons confined to the recital chambers practicing their own compositions. Solomon was content to pass the days reading paperbacks in his room, already aware that he was losing what the instructors called his "competitive spirit." Unlike his peers, the future was far from his thoughts.

Confined to grounds during the recess period, it felt as though the rest of the world ceased to exist. From the large front windows, Solomon stared out over the empty campus and expanse of well-manicured lawn. The footpaths tread by students lay abandoned and covered with snow. At night the buildings slumbered in darkness, enduring their own winter hibernation. Even the electric lanterns lining the walkways remained dark and unlit.

On the day, they gathered in the main salon. Preston tested the concert piano by running through a Bach prelude and then carefully arranged the illicit sheet music on the stand. His collaborators sat in the wingchairs, eagerly waiting for him to begin. "Don't botch it like you did the Tchaikovsky concerto last fall," Collingwood called out, forever masking his viciousness behind an air of playful comradery.

The music had a somber quality and exhibited none of the frenetic energy that Solomon had expected from such a piece. He watched as Preston's agile hands played note after note, descending the keyboard into the lower register and producing a drowning chorus of deep resonant tones. His hands inched lower as they crept toward the last set of keys and then unexpectedly tumbled off the board in a clatter of discordant notes. The silence that followed was piercing. Collingwood and Solomon exchanged perplexed expressions as Preston squinted feverishly at the sheet music in front of him.

"What the hell?"

"Did your fingers cramp?" Collingwood asked, mildly ecstatic.

"No. I can't reach the notes," Preston said.

"What do you mean can't reach them?"

He pressed his finger to the sheet music, trying to decipher the bars. His fingers mimicked the bass notes in the air, moving like an agitated spider. He shook his head and started again. "It's too low," he finally said. He played the bars again, this time slowly, and as he reached the end of the keys his fingers once again slid off the keyboard.

The notation was either incorrect or the manuscript was a joke. Either way, Fugue in B minor was unplayable. The notes simply defied the normal register of string and wind instruments. For the next month, they worked on the composition, attempting to find the error. By the end of January, Collingwood had concluded the manuscript must be a hoax. "You've wasted those hard-earned pennies," he teased, knowing full well Preston had purchased it with his parents' money.

Preston continued to toy with the fugue, spending night after night running through the score. Each time he reached the impossible section he would pause, swear, and bang on the keys in frustration. Eventually, he took to practicing in private, rehearsing the workable sections and perfecting them like a diligent student attempting to emulate the work of a master. "Still playing that damned fugue?" Collingwood would ask, offering the by-then standard chuckle at his own *bon mot*. He was, and he was getting nowhere.

Solomon liked to think it had been the intense pressure—a monomaniacal genius even—that drove Preston to do what he did. He pictured him sitting at the piano, sleep-deprived and wild, anxiously attempting to find the correct arrangement of notes that would make sense. However, in the end, he knew that this was his own romanticized version of events and that the truth was far more banal. The missing funds had been noticed. The piece had been a forgery. There were questions that had to be answered, but the answers provided were hardly satisfactory.

The school organized a slapdash memorial service. The headmaster was keen to accent the issue of missing funds and guilt to divert attention from any discussion of Stanhope's rigorous curriculum or the strains it might impose on overly ambitious students. "Student experience" at the academy was a centerpiece of his brief speech. Collingwood took the podium next and sermonized on the value of friendship, emphasizing the positive role he believed he played in Preston's short life. Solomon declined to speak. The entire memorial felt wrong. During the service, he continually glanced over at Preston's mother and father, who remained composed throughout the speeches and remembrances. Only once the gathering dispersed did his mother break down in tears. Solomon made a gesture to comfort her but stopped himself. He had nothing to offer, nothing to say that would ease the pain.

That evening, he stood in Preston's room holding the pipe, trying to wrap his mind around the immensity of what had occurred. At some point, Collingwood popped his head in the door, a grave expression on his face. He looked as if he were about to say something but then hesitated before proceeding across the room and shuffling through the papers on the desk.

"I feel sorry for his parents," he said, his voice cold and without inflection.

Solomon remained silent and watched Collingwood draw the brown paper folder from the debris on the desk and tuck it under his arm. They stared at one another across the room for an instant, each trying to decipher the other. Then Collingwood patted him on the shoulder in a friendly sort of way.

"Why would you want to summon the devil anyway? What would you ask for? Did we ever think about that?"

Without another word he exited, vanishing into the thick evening shadows accumulating in the hall.

Collingwood took the envelope, and he took the pipe. A week later, he stood in his own bedroom, the walls stripped bare, his personal effects neatly sorted into boxes. He was finished with Stanhope, he told himself. He was finished with the academy, with professional music, with everyone and everything associated with this place. He would never come back, and he meant it.

***

Jared grins at his niece, watching her unwrap a set of dolls that she is clearly too old to enjoy. "Happy birthday!" he bellows as the final shreds of paper are torn from the box. Abby is well-mannered enough to feign excitement and pose for the obligatory photograph. They raised her well is all Solomon can think, his head buzzing from the click of the camera and the two glasses of wine he had with dinner.

The table is strewn with plates and half-emptied glasses. The cake sits in the center, three-fourths devoured and the remaining quarter looking oddly sad and abandoned.

"Those all of them?" Solomon asks, checking the wall clock and surrendering to his parental instincts as he observes it is twenty minutes past Abby's usual bedtime.

"One more," she warbles, picking up the last present.

It is the package delivered this morning, Solomon notes with interest as Abby eagerly tears at the colored paper and ribbon to unveil a small wooden box.

"Who's that one from?" Liz asks, admiring the object.

"Doesn't say," Abby replies, turning the box over in her hands.

There is a slight mechanical noise as she opens the lid. Two small figures begin to orbit the box. They are cast in silver, one a boy playing a pan flute, the other a goat dancing on its hind legs. The two miniatures circle round as the box emits a jangly melody that Solomon instantly recognizes. He stares horror-stricken at the scene of his daughter watching the boy and goat frolic to the doleful music.

"Neat," Liz says, reaching out for the music box.

"No!" Solomon shrieks, slapping her hand away.

"Hey! What was that for?"

"Is this some kind of joke?" he shouts, looking from Liz to her brother.

"What's wrong?"

He snatches the box from Abby, unaware of the small white card that falls lazily to the floor like a dead leaf. He squeezes the two figurines, halting them in mid-rotation to stop the music and then proceeds to scrutinize the box feverishly as his wife and brother-in-law look on in shock.

Liz is afraid to reach out and touch his shoulder or place a hand on his arm. "Sol?" she whispers, realizing for the first time in her life that her husband can inspire a feeling of complete fear in her. The man standing here with the ashen face mumbling to himself is a stranger she does not recognize.

"Dad?" Abby calls.

Her voice draws Solomon from his trance. He stares at her, a mix of terror and confusion on his face.

She holds out the cream-colored card in her hand with a puzzled look. "It says it's for you."

***

Taking a seat at the Baldwin, he ceremoniously cracked his fingers and began playing the familiar notes. Through the fog of memory, they sounded even more elegiac and mournful. The beauty of music is its ability to instantly transport the listener, to conjure and evoke like a witch doctor summoning old spirits. Solomon hung onto every note, remembering the way Preston's hands moved across the keys and fumbled to touch what could not be touched. The anticipated discordant notes followed as Collingwood's hand slid off the keyboard. He had heard it so many times that it seemed part of the composition, an intentional Schoenberg-like dissonance.

"Familiar, no?" A thin smile crept across Collingwood's lips. Even now, he received pleasure remembering this particular miscarriage, repeating it perfectly for effect.

"Did your fingers cramp?" Solomon asked dryly.

"He wasn't wrong, you know?" as he drew the cover over the keys. "It wasn't a mistake."

Solomon began to feel irritated. After two decades, Collingwood had contacted him out of the blue only to revisit this moment. No, not revisit it. Relish in it. There was a sense of triumphalism to this charade, that old competitive spirit bordering on malevolence and cruelty. Outliving a rival was not enough. Spite required continual affirmation. It had a long memory that hid behind sophisticated concepts like tradition and heritage.

"Do you want me to applaud?" Solomon asked. "Bravo then."

"You misunderstand," Collingwood said, drumming his fingers on the keyboard cover. "The manuscript was authentic. Aehrenthal had an organ specially designed for him with a keyboard possessing an additional two octaves. Fugue in B minor could only be played on a single instrument, Aehrenthal's organ, which was kept in the Göttingen Konservatorium."

Solomon realized he had bitten his inner lip. The taste of blood entered his mouth as he thought about the workmen hauling the large crate through the hall. It had been intended for an upcoming concert, a private one. "You can't be serious?"

"Quite."

"Hasn't this gone far enough? Why drag all this out now?"

"You can't say you're not curious. All these years, wondering what exactly he died for?"

"This isn't about that or him and you know it," Solomon retorted, rising.

He recalled those last words in Preston's room ages ago. *Why would you want to summon the devil anyway? What would you ask for?* An older and more embittered man might have an answer to this question. It wasn't simply that Collingwood had settled for headmaster at Stanhope because he knew nothing else. He lacked the very attributes he despised in others: creativity, grueling dedication, virtuosity—the qualities essential to a life beyond the safety of tradition and honorable names. He genuinely hated those who could do what he could not.

"I'm going to leave," Solomon said, slowly.

Collingwood nodded. "It will haunt you, you know? It will," as he continued to drum his fingertips against the wood. "You will always wonder what we were trying to achieve back then, what it was all about, why exactly he did what he did."

"That's where we differ. I'm not like you. These things don't eat me up inside. I don't lose sleep over them like you. I'm not stuck here."

"Aren't you?" he asked with a mirthless grin. "You're here now."

"And I'm leaving."

"You're here, just like me. Our thoughts, our memories: we're emotionally invested in this place. We can't escape it. It won't let us."

Solomon rolled his eyes. He felt sorry for Collingwood despite his aversion. He paused at the door and, turning, rested his hand gently on the doorframe.

"Why would you want to summon the devil?" he asked, reminding him. "What would you ask for?"

"Why don't you stick around and we'll find out."

Solomon just shook his head and exited the room.

Unlike Collingwood, he was not bound to this place. He never had been. And as long as he could help it, he never would be.

***

Morning finds him sitting on the sofa, the translucent dawn light slowly creeping through the drapes and accumulating in the room like an unwanted presence. It makes the pestering agitation and broken sleep of the past hours all the more intolerable, conjugating them into something real and definitive. He turns the card over in his hands, studying the neat calligraphy etched into the grain of the paper: *For Solomon, toujours et à jamais.* How Liz recoiled when she read it, gathering her face in her hands and admitting that she had known about the trip, had let the possibility cross her mind only to dismiss it. She never paused to consider that the script looked conspicuously masculine in its tightly wrapped loops and pronounced curls. *Always and forever.* He cannot correct her misperception nor explain the weight and gravity of its precise meaning. Nor can he bear to lie in bed beside her, aware that the silence is the smoldering silence of resentment and festering doubt rather than the mute repose of slumber.

At a quarter-past, the alarm clock in the bedroom comes to life and familiar music fills the room. On the television, the well-known theme song to The Breakfast Hour has been inexplicably replaced with a more lachrymal melody. The talk show hosts discuss the daily headlines and partake in their usual banter, never once commenting on the change. During the interludes, commercials advertise products to the accompaniment of sad organ music. Solomon picks up the music box from the table, cringes, and watches the boy and goat chase one another in endless pursuit. When Liz finally descends the stairs, this is how she finds him: bathed in the pale glow of the television, staring intently at the two figurines, wondering whether the boy is chasing the goat or, on the contrary, whether it is the animal that is chasing the boy.

People *of the* Land

On my last day at Breckenridge, I sat in the antechamber watching my father pace about in his usual fashion as he flipped through a magazine. My mother sat across from me in silence, her face difficult to read. Nobody said much, although I was conscious of the looks that passed between my parents from time to time. Eventually, the phone rang, and the assistant informed us the chancellor was ready to see them. My father put a hand on my shoulder, indicating for me to remain seated.

I shuffled absentmindedly through the stack of magazines for a bit and threw glances in the assistant's direction, trying to see what her expressions or gestures might convey. Was it serious? If so, *how* serious? If she knew, her face betrayed nothing. I could hear the chancellor's murmurous voice echo through the corridor. It sounded affable enough.

After a while, I grew bored and excused myself. At the end of the hall was a small passage that led to a rear loading dock. Despite the placard on the wall informing that the passage was for staff access only, I was quite familiar with the route and could, if necessary, navigate it blindfolded.

I propped open the heavy steel door at the end of the passage and stepped out into an arc of sunlight. Taking a seat on the cement floor, I fished through my pocket, dug out a pack of cigarettes, and sat with my legs dangling over the deck edge. It was here that what I had come to think of as "my deed" had taken place.

Most afternoons, our little clique congregated on the deck during recess hour when the truancy officers were busy patrolling the outer perimeter. We would sit about smoking with our shirt sleeves rolled up, ties loosened at the neck, and jackets slung over our shoulders in that casual way clothing models exhibit in advertisements. The chatter was predictable. Which members of the rowing team were being disciplined for drinking after a match? Had Dirkman really catnipped Mike Trefflin? Who was snogging one of the girls from Fairfield this week? These and other subjects passed for sociability among our group.

As I sat alone smoking and taking in the afternoon sun, my eyes drifted over the stones scattered about the loading dock floor. I then looked to the iron guard rail that encircled the deck and squinted. Flecks of dried blood, unwashed and barely perceptible. It suddenly started to feel like I had been gone a long time, so I extinguished my cigarette and eased the heavy door closed behind me.

My parents were still in the office when I returned to the antechamber. I could hear the chancellor more clearly now.

"...Appreciate the very generous donations you have made in the past, but that is not the issue."

"Oh, isn't it...?"

"No, naturally. The board has ruled on the matter."

"A preliminary decision."

"Yet one that will be finalized shortly. We simply cannot tolerate that kind of behavior here."

***

Our kind anticipates these sorts of incidents. There are contingency plans for just such occasions and unspoken agreements with relatives possessing manor homes in the north country. A secluded residence; a few months of rehabilitation under stern yet compassionate, avuncular supervision while your parents ring up every headmaster in the book inquiring about openings; and then it's all right as rain. When Alfie White was expelled from Codderdale, he spent six months at his guardian's home in Somerset practicing archery and playing stoolball at the local sports club. Not ideal, but not necessarily bad either.

I, on the other hand, didn't have a flush relative moldering away on some country estate. It is one of the indignities that come with being *nouveau riche*. The closest we had was Chambliss Morgan, a "friend of the family" as my father liked to say. That was one way of putting it anyway. My father had made the acquaintance of the tough old Welshman during his days as an RAF serviceman. Meeting him as a boy, I remember my eight-year-old wonder at how his massive hands seemed to envelop mine in a handshake. Morgan, now retired, spent his days in the Welsh countryside occupied with animal husbandry. His wife had passed away the year prior, and it was suggested that given these circumstances he might enjoy some company. I began to form an inkling of what I was in for. I was being shipped to Blackenwell. In other words: unofficial boot camp under the tutelage of a seasoned military veteran.

The car ride passed in virtual silence. For most of the trip, I was content to gaze sullenly out the window. With every mile we crossed the landscape appeared more hostile: looming hills and thick bracken lost in grey mist; fields dotted with all varieties of animals; towns that became increasingly smaller and forlorn. Morgan's home was situated on a large estate surrounded by nothing but fields, hills, and woods. A dense thicket of trees encircled the property, boxing off Blackenwell from the rest of the world.

The person who met us in the drive was a shrunken and aged version of the man with the large hands I remembered from childhood. Slightly stooped and hair greyed, he still possessed broad shoulders and a solid build. Nothing I couldn't handle, I thought to myself.

"Cham!" my father trilled as he exited the car. "Good to see you, tough old bird."

"And I hope that the city hasn't softened you up any," he replied, patting my father on the shoulder. The first thing that struck me was his accent. He had a robust and warm voice like you might imagine of an opera singer.

After planting a polite kiss on my mother's cheek, he then turned to me. "And this must be Benjamin. All grown up, I see?"

"Mr. Morgan," I nodded.

He let out a hearty laugh. "Cham," he replied. "All my friends call me that," adding, "and we will become good friends while you're here."

I smiled politely, concealing any annoyance I might have felt.

***

Under different circumstances, Blackenwell may have been considered charming. The large estate was mostly grazing fields and rolling hills extending as far as the eye could see. In the pen near the house, sheep wandered back and forth in a chorus of bleats and grunts. A ram strutted about the yard, confidently bobbing his head and bleating to the ewes in his midst. I suppose I would have been confident too, were I the only male among a herd of vulnerable females.

"Of course, his cocksureness is a fantasy," Morgan told me as we watched the animals circle the pen. He angled his head toward the small abattoir located beside the barn and smiled.

Aside from the sheep, Morgan shared the land with a few local families who assisted with the herding and husbandry work. Their homes, which I assume were leased in exchange for labor, sat at the edge of the grounds where the fields gave way to the woodlands. None of the families seemed particularly friendly, and most were content to go about their own business. I noticed small packs of children scuttling around the pens and barn where the adults worked. Like the adults, they were dirty and shabbily dressed. I had often heard stories of rural poverty, but these people exceeded every stereotype I might have imagined.

On my initial tour of the grounds, I was conscious of the looks we received. Every time we passed a group, they stopped their chores and cast long, furtive gazes in my direction as though trying to decipher who I was and why I was there. They never spoke or plied me with questions and Morgan never introduced me. In fact, during my first week I cannot recall any of them uttering a sound or even acknowledging our presence aside from the apprehensive looks. The laborers never spoke among themselves and none of the children sang songs or played in the normal way children do. They simply stood about mute and attended to their affairs as if we were not there. I got the impression these people did not care much for their landlord and perhaps even hated him.

People claim to enjoy the countryside, but I imagine these types have rarely spent a great deal of time away from cities. For all its scenic beauty, the country is quite dull. The appeal of rustic charm wears off in a day or two, especially once you realize there is nothing beyond fields, sheep, and decrepit houses awaiting you. Morgan never showed much interest in enforcing discipline, as I thought he might. Usually, I was left to my own devices and so I explored the immediate vicinity, wandering the paths that wound their way through the fields and hills. After I had covered these, I ventured off into the woods, avoiding the shanty town where the locals dwelled. Aside from birds and the constant bleating of sheep, the land was desolate.

One afternoon about a week after my arrival, I was walking along the path leading through the pastures when I felt the ground beneath my feet start to quake. A deep rumbling filled the air, and the earth emitted a loud groan. I planted my feet and felt vibrations run through my entire body. Birds nesting in the overhead trees let out a series of furious cries before exploding into the sky and disbanding in every direction. Then, as quickly as it had begun, the violent tremor subsided. A strange hush descended on the landscape, the only noise being the chaotic bleating of the sheep coming from the fields.

Sprinting back to the house, I found Morgan by the pen attending to the startled ewes. He was accompanied by a well-dressed man I had never seen before. In his right hand, he clutched a traditional-looking medical bag made of brown leather. I couldn't help noticing on first observation that the bag matched his shoes perfectly.

"What was that?" I asked, half out of breath.

"A tremor," the man said, as though it had been a stupid question to ask. He had a Scottish accent. The man's eyes remained fixed on the fields in the distance where the sheep were beginning to calm down.

"There's a fair amount of seismic activity around these parts," Morgan added. "Nothing to be alarmed about."

I had never heard of earthquakes occurring in this part of the world and when I mentioned this the two men laughed, raised eyebrows, and exchanged looks. I had a lot to learn about Wales, Morgan told me, and then introduced the man at his side as Dr. Campbell. He was the local veterinarian.

"I'll be heading on up to the cabin, Cham," Campbell said, shuffling his feet in the dust. "I'll take a look at that ewe after lunch."

Morgan just nodded and Campbell set out along the path. We remained standing there for a while, watching him get smaller and smaller until he disappeared over the hill.

The next morning, I found Morgan out in the field dragging an animal carcass through the grass. The ewe had fallen sick and died during the night, he told me as he paused to shift his weight and reposition his hands around the animal's torso. I helped him transport the body to the abattoir, cringing at the bristling sound the animal's coat made against the dry grass and leaves. The body felt unnaturally heavy, like dragging a sack of cold meat across the yard.

The interior of the abattoir resembled a modern surgery more than a slaughterhouse. We lifted the body onto a stainless steel examining table and Morgan turned his attention to a collection of surgical tools arranged on the counter. Uncertain of what role I would be performing in this procedure, I took a seat and watched him sterilize the instruments with rubbing alcohol. His actions gave the impression of a well-rehearsed ritual as he rolled up his sleeves, selected his instruments, and set to work.

Planting the blade in the sheep's abdomen, he made a long incision running from anus to throat. I was surprised at the ease with which the blade cut through skin and the small amount of blood that seeped from the gash. His actions were effortless and methodical. The way his hands sought out the proper organs or the way he delicately worked the blade through the flesh and paired away muscle from bone: every stroke was precise and executed with care.

"The sheep were my wife's idea," Morgan said, making general conversation. "This farm was her way of doing things."

Having nothing to add, I nodded and asked, "And how did she pass away?"

Morgan halted his dissection and I immediately felt ashamed for having made such a gauche inquiry.

"Like everything else," he said after a while, resuming his work. "She died. She's one with the land now—*her* land—just like she wanted it."

I winced at the cracking of the ribs and the slopping noises as Morgan emptied the entrails into a bucket.

"What do you need the intestines for?" I asked quietly. "They're not important."

"On the contrary, they were once quite important," he chuckled. "Druid priests used to divine omens by reading the entrails of animals. Shamans made prophesies after carefully examining extracted livers."

"Hepatoscopy," I said.

"Very good," he replied with an approving nod. "The parts we throw away were the most vital parts of the animal for the ancients. They were the medium for communicating with the gods."

He forcefully pushed down on the sternum, breaking the ribs and collapsing the lungs. The sheep's head listed to one side so that I was staring directly into its gaping mouth. The black tongue lolled lifelessly on the metal table, and I closed my eyes.

"You the squeamish sort?" Morgan asked without taking his eyes off his work.

I shrugged.

"But it's not the blood that turns your stomach, is it?"

This was a statement, not a question, and Morgan shot me a knowing glance.

"No," he said when I didn't respond, "certainly not the blood."

I didn't like his suggestive tone or his insinuation that he somehow knew me better than he did. I fixed him with a cold stare and turned my eyes back toward the sheep's splayed body. A faint smile stretched across his lips as he pushed back the broken ribs to access the organs located deep within the cavity. Extracting the liver, he worked the blade through it, carefully pruning off thin slices which he deposited in the bucket one at a time. When he was finished, he did the same with the heart and kidney. There was no reason to perform these procedures. He was putting on this demonstration for me alone, testing me.

"Your da' ever tell you about his time in the military?" Morgan asked when I did not prove forthcoming. The tone in his voice had noticeably changed.

"No," was all I offered.

He nodded at this. "As it should be. A talkative soldier is an undisciplined soldier."

"What did this sheep die from?" I asked, changing the subject.

He mulled this over. "You're asking the wrong question," he finally replied. "You ought to ask *for whom* did this sheep die?"

"Sheep don't die for people."

Morgan was about to comment when the surgical instruments on the examining table began to rattle against the metal. A low growling noise, like the crunching of rocks and dirt filled the room. I braced my body against the wall, clenched my teeth, and gave myself over to the jolting movements coming from the earth. The overhead lamp rocked back and forth, sending cones of pale light spiraling across the room. A peculiar expression appeared to creep across Morgan's face, one I could not read with any accuracy.

"Aftershocks," he said dismissively once the tremor ceased and he had resumed his dissection. "You'll grow accustomed to it in time."

***

On a warm afternoon in late September, I sat in a hospital room wondering whether it would be the worst day of my life. The window was open, and a light breeze stirred the curtains. Every time the nurse entered the room to remind me of the time she would point to the window and ask if I preferred it closed. It is funny what you remember—the odd details that stick with you for no good reason.

Tommy lay in bed, his face swathed in bandages. He never woke or stirred while I was there, and I never spoke to him or told jokes like they do in the movies. The silence felt appropriate, punctuated only by his labored breathing and the bleeping of the monitor. Had I really come to watch him die, like they said? Maybe the rumor mill at Breckenridge had it right for once. I couldn't say why I was there or what compelled me to sit at his bedside like some angel of death. I simply wasn't thinking about possible consequences or repercussions. In fact, I never really had to begin with.

I had the urge to remove the bandages and see his face. Silvia Hitch had said he'd lost the eye. I felt like I needed to know for certain. I assumed it was gossip, but it didn't stop Arron Matthews from inserting a peeled grape into one of his sockets during lunch and asking everyone "Who am I? Look, who am I?" Nobody laughed. They talked and murmured, but nobody dared laugh. All the levity had been sucked out of them. It was going to be a lean year for a class clown like Matthews.

When the nurse returned, her expression was taut and serious. I knew what that meant and hopped to my feet. The clock on the wall told me I had overstayed my visit by five minutes.

"Take the stairs at the opposite end of the hall," she advised.

I didn't listen.

As I walked down the corridor, I saw Mrs. Sheldrake exiting the elevator. Her face looked tired, but I wondered if this was because she wasn't wearing the heavy layer of makeup she normally did. When our gazes crossed, I swore time stood still. The soft footsteps in the hall and the white noise ceased, and for one distended moment, it was just the two of us standing in the absence of everything.

"What are you doing here?" she asked me. Even her voice sounded hollow and dead.

I can't remember what I said as I passed, although I know what I didn't say. I did not say "I'm sorry," because we both would have known it was a lie.

***

Stepping into the autumn dusk, I heard soft singing trailing on the breeze. The local people were out. They huddled around the barn and sang in a strange language by candlelight. The words sounded alien and primeval in the impending night.

I spotted Campbell some distance from the gathering smoking a cigarette and quietly observing.

"Evening, Ben," as I approached. "Come to view this anthropological spectacle?"

I understood what he meant. The mutilated carcass of the sheep lay in the dirt, eviscerated and skinned, the lean pink muscle stretched tight over the skeleton. Stripped of its coat and fatty tissue, the body looked emaciated. Like a medium-sized dog or the size of a wild cat, I thought. The families huddled close, wreathed in candlelight. Their song was a dirge, a hymn to life and sacrifice.

"Unbelievable, isn't it?" Campbell muttered, keeping his gaze on the ceremony. "It's the tremors. It's got them spooked."

I had nothing to say so I watched in silence.

"Who are these people?" I asked when the group brought their ceremony to a close and began wrapping up the carcass.

"They're the people of the land," Campbell told me.

Over the coming week, I discovered Campbell was the talkative sort. Unknown to me the day we met, he was a regular at Blackenwell. His routine visits to check on the animals often required him to remain on the estate for weeks at a time. There was a small cottage located in the far pasture which Campbell had come to think of as his personal *pied-à-terre*. During the day, he and Morgan disappeared into the hills to survey the livestock. In the evenings, Campbell was free of all responsibilities and content to sit about the parlor in the main house drinking, chatting, and killing time. We quickly got into the habit of meeting after Morgan retired for the night, and Campbell had no reservations about pouring me out a tumbler of malt whiskey, which was one of the reasons I looked forward to our nightly encounters.

Conversation was bland at first. He didn't ask too many questions regarding why I was at Blackenwell, although he seemed to have a general idea of my situation. Over the span of a few nights, we became progressively more comfortable with one another and the drink usually loosened Campbell's lips. I was curious why a Scottish veterinarian would make regular visits to northern Wales. Campbell only shrugged, replying somebody had to do it.

One night, the conversation turned to the people of the land.

"You know that's why he eviscerates them like he does? The sheep, I mean," Campbell said wryly. "Otherwise, they'd be liable to dig up the body and make a mess of it. Better just to remove the innards and be done with it."

"Has it happened before?" I was genuinely intrigued.

Campbell nodded.

"Why does he tolerate it? Why not just hire new workers?"

He furrowed his brow. "Those are Mrs. Morgan's kin, her people. They've been here a long time."

"*That's* her family?"

"*Kin.* I said her kin. That's different. This whole place—all this land— belonged to Aeronwen and her kin. You can't escape something like that, which is why I suppose she came back, bringing Cham with her."

I let this set in as Campbell kept talking.

"This land is old. It's got a history, a violent history. Wars, conquest, and slaughter, from the Anglo-Saxons to the Romans to the Civil Wars. It's etched in the land, as if the soil were fertilized by all that blood and violence."

"Isn't that a line from the Marseillaise?" I asked, half in jest.

"Yeah? Well, maybe the French got that right. You can feel it here sometimes though, that history and all that violence and blood that was spilt. It's like the soil has to be fed, like it *needs* it. Aeronwen knew that, and that's why she came back and that's why those people are here still."

Campbell was evidently drunker than usual, and I thought it best to keep the conversation focused. "And how did she die?" I thought about the way Morgan reacted that day in the abattoir.

"Who? Aeronwen?"

I nodded and Campbell waved a hand. "I'm a veterinarian, not a medical doctor," he said, staring vacantly into the bottom of his glass.

***

That night, the bed shook and the windows rattled. After an hour I grew accustomed to the trembling, as Morgan said I would. I drifted in and out of sleep, waking periodically to the soft clattering and rumbling noises that filled the house.

It was early morning when Campbell nudged me awake. The predawn light trickled in through the windows and I could still feel the vibrations.

"Get dressed and meet me outside," he whispered.

I did as instructed and joined Campbell in the yard where he stood propped against the end of a shovel. A wheelbarrow containing the rotting sheep carcass was parked next to him. He handed me the shovel and said we were going to bury it.

We set out along the path. The surrounding landscape was barely visible through the morning mist creeping across the fields. After what seemed like a long time, Campbell veered off toward the woods. I followed without a word through the thicket, going further than I had ever dared to go on my own. The mist was thick, making it difficult to gauge direction and distance. Campbell, however, showed little hesitation in his navigation. He walked briskly, the cart trundling along in front of him. When we entered a clearing Campbell indicated for us to stop. The outlines of the trees were just barely visible through the haze, suggesting an area of significant size. I could see the silhouette of a ruined building in the distance.

"Dig," Campbell instructed. "No more than six inches. Keep it shallow."

Campbell removed a hatchet from the cart and began hacking the lamb carcass into bits. The blade made a moist sound with each blow.

I could still feel the ground quaking slightly. When I plunged the shovel into the earth it sent painful vibrations coursing through my hands. I had expected the blade to go in easily, but to my surprise, the earth was hard and stony.

"Soil's thin here," Campbell advised.

I nodded and worked the earth slowly.

"What's that?" I asked, angling my head toward the crumbling edifice in the distance.

"Romans built it."

"Didn't know the Romans settled here."

"They didn't. It was a military occupation. That was a garrison," he explained, pointing with the hatchet blade. "The Romans knew better than to settle this place. They could feel it, the *genius loci* or whatever you want to call it. It's poisoned."

The soil below the surface was damp and less compact. Working the shovel blade became easier. As I turned up clumps of moist trembling earth, I noticed pieces of bone packed in the dirt. I couldn't tell whether they were animal or human remains. The bones looked like nothing I had ever seen. Ribs, femurs, and tibias melted together and fused in unrecognizable patterns. I excavated the debris with an unsettling feeling. As I did so, a thick black substance began to pool in the hole. It gurgled like raw petroleum coming to the surface.

Campbell looked panic stricken. "I told you six inches," he yelled. "Quick, get the body into the hole and cover it."

We tossed the carcass into the ground and began shoveling dirt over it. Campbell got down on his knees and moved large piles with his hands to expedite the process. When we were finished, we both lay on our backs, exhausted, feeling the earth churn beneath us.

"There should be an easier way to reform a boy," Campbell said after a while, staring into the gray morning sky.

Somewhere in the distance, a bird cried out.

On our way back, a light rain began to fall, turning the path into mud. Neither of us commented on the way the earth seemed to writhe and shake beneath us. I imagine we made quite a sight walking along that road: Campbell pushing the empty cart and me with the shovel slung over my shoulder, pressing forward through the oncoming drizzle.

By the time we got back to the house, the rain had gotten heavier. Morgan was standing on the front porch, silent. Campbell fixed him with a stony look.

"Just like her," Morgan said, shaking his head. "You know it doesn't do a thing. You know what *needs* to be done."

"Not now," Campbell muttered.

Morgan balked. "You feel that, don't you? You know it's time."

"Not now."

"It's time," he repeated, descending the steps.

Campbell shifted his gaze to the field and then, turning to me, said, "You're going to want to change those clothes. It gets messy."

Twenty minutes later we were back on the path, the earth shaking and the rain coming down. I followed the two men in silence, Morgan in the lead and Campbell in tow carrying his doctor's satchel. We walked the path and then cut across the fields back into the woods, heading toward the shanty town where the people of the land dwelled.

Residents looked out from windows and doorways as we passed the dilapidated shacks in silence. They huddled 'round and trailed behind us at a safe distance. Looking up, I saw the grim faces of children, their eyes cold and expressionless. At the opposite end of the settlement was a large hut with a rotting domed roof. Morgan marched along with determination, never once intimidated by the stares or the violent quaking. His movements had a regularity to them. Everything assumed the air of ritual and ceremony. Even the people trailing at our backs felt a part of this.

The interior was dark and thick with animal stench. As my eyes adjusted to the gloom, I discerned a form wriggling there on the floor. I was still trying to make out what I was looking at when Morgan lit the two electric lanterns. The shadows dissipated to reveal a person chained to the wall. A cloth bag was placed over the head, stifling the low moans. I realized why I had been unable to first identify the shape as human when we entered. Only a single leg was attached to the body. The other limbs ended in short grotesque stumps, giving the body a vermiform quality.

Morgan lifted the hood to reveal a gaunt face. The man winced and then started screaming and thrashing about like an animal. His cries were choked, and staring into his gaping mouth, I saw that the man's tongue had been removed. Despite the thrashing, Morgan patted the man's head and ran his palm over his long stringy hair.

"It's time, Jacob," he said in a soft voice. "It's time."

Campbell was already fishing through his medical bag. His hands trembled, whether because of nerves or the violent quaking. I wanted to turn away when I saw Campbell produce the surgical saw, but I didn't. I stood immobile, observing the struggle and listening to the agonizing screams fill the room. For the second time in my life, I experienced that strange sensation of existing outside of time. All the noise and people there in the room ceased to exist, leaving just me and the horrific scene playing out before me in slow motion. When I eventually looked up at Morgan, I saw that his eyes were neither on Campbell nor the man. He was staring directly at me.

Finishing his work, Campbell placed the amputated leg in a cloth sack. His hands and shirt were smeared with blood and in the soft light of the lantern his face looked drawn and disconsolate. Jacob undulated like a worm, his body tracing circles in the blood pooling on the dirt floor. I thought he might have been sobbing, but listening closer I realized I was mistaken. He was laughing.

As I watched him writhe, I felt something cold and smooth being placed in my hand.

"Do it," I heard Morgan say, "and this time finish what you start."

The people of the land gathered just outside the ring of the lamplight, inert and motionless. Jacob squirmed at my feet, and as I lifted the stone, I felt all those eyes focused directly on me, watching, silently judging.

The first strike is always the most difficult. Everyone stands around numb trying to comprehend what they are seeing, to grasp the logic of it. By the third strike, the spell is broken, and they are trying to restrain you any way they can. However, here, among the woods and fields, the spell never breaks. It is one long moment extending into infinity.

***

Evening fell as we walked through the woods. The cart's wheels made a vile squishing noise in the mud, carving out a long, sluggish trail leading back to the village. Morgan dug the hole this time. Campbell and I watched as he laid the severed leg in the earth. The soil clung to the limb, releasing faint gasps and gurgling noises as it drew the offering deeper into itself, accepting what was given.

I listened to the night as we made our way back to the house. Blackenwell was completely silent save for the low rumbling echoing deep within the ground. The tremors were abating. By morning, Blackenwell would be restored to its normal rustic calm.

The people of the land were assembled on the main lawn, clustering around the barn like a strange flock of nocturnal birds. One by one the congregation drew onyx-hued stones from a cast-iron pot. Just before I closed the door, I heard a babble of voices. A girl had drawn the sole white pebble from the lot. She couldn't have been more than seventeen, I thought, locking the door; the exact same age as me.

***

My parents drove the convertible the day they came to retrieve me. My father was fond of showing off his little luxury car and liked taking it for rides through the country whenever he got the chance. I had always found the purchase in poor taste. It was exactly the type of thing expected of a parvenu. They were all smiles as they exited the vehicle.

"Cham, tough old bird! I hope Ben wasn't a handful," my father said cheerily, patting me on the shoulder.

"I should say not," Morgan replied in his amiable way.

It was all quite jovial as my father chatted with Morgan and my mother planted kisses on my cheek and filled me in on the comings and goings of the neighbors. After a minute or so of polite conversation, my mother beamed her radiant smile and told me that I had been accepted into Codderdale on late matriculation. I was scheduled to begin just after the New Year.

"See, right as rain," my father said, ruffling my hair in that irritating way he always does when trying to encourage me to see his side of things.

"You do think he's ready to attend?" asked my mother, turning to Morgan.

"I should think so."

Then, turning to me, her face noticeably more earnest, she asked, "Ben, do *you* think you're ready?"

The tone in her voice was solemn, and I was conscious of the way the three of them stared at me, anticipating my reply.

Yes, I told them. I was ready.

Jorge *the* Younger

The guests slowly arrived at Jorge Regatta's annual spring gathering, congregating at the picnic tables and making small talk at the amply stocked bar. Mark first spotted her through the sea of gingham, faux Japanese parasols, and sunhats dotting the spacious lawn. Although she wore large, dark glasses, he was certain their gazes locked for a fraction of a second. Not long enough for a formal encounter, but enough to convey interest. He watched as the woman walked across the grass, smiling at the guests, a small child following behind her in tow. Stopping at the buffet table, she filled a paper plate with spoonfuls of potato salad and soft-shell crabs before fixing a child-sized plate for her son.

What was it that was so attractive about young mothers? Something maternal, perhaps? Even Freudian? Mark couldn't say. But as he watched the woman fill up her plate with heaping mounds of food, he knew instinctively that they had a future together. Maybe not tonight, but definitely a future.

For most of the afternoon, Mark wove in and out of small clusters of guests, striking up awkward conversations with people he barely knew. He kept an eye on the woman, who seemed to be well acquainted with many of the attendees. He always seemed to be in her immediate vicinity but never close enough to strike up a private conversation. Later, after consuming a few plastic cups of red wine, it would be different, he told himself.

As the hours passed, he watched the shadows on the lawn grow long and angular. The debris of the afternoon festivities, consisting of discarded Dixie cups and balled-up napkins, accumulated on the trampled grass, emphasizing the thinning ranks of the guests. The woman was among those remaining, Mark saw, although how he might initiate a conversation still remained unclear. It was best to leave it to chance. As the hour of Jorge's arrival approached, an opportunity would surely present itself.

The woman sat stretched out on a checkered blanket watching her son swing a badminton racket. The child darted from one end of the net to the other, wielding the racket like a sword as he batted a shuttlecock across the lawn. Jorge the Elder sat idly in his chair watching the child play. His frame sank into the lawn chair, contorting at awkward angles. Two arthritic hands rested lifelessly in his lap, twisted into claws. The eyes that peered out of the emaciated face were the only things that hinted at life in an otherwise depleted body. As he followed the child's movements, it was evident the old man was admiring the boy's youth and agility. Conscious of the stares, the mother smiled kindly at the man. For all her compassion though, she was unable to hide the hint of sadness implicit in the gesture.

Mark was never certain why they invited the Elder each year. It seemed cruel and unnecessary. Why subject him to public humiliation for the sake of ceremony? Each year he sat in the same worn-out lawn chair under the tree crumpled up like a formless heap of rags. His presence visibly upset some of the guests. Everyone socialized and laughed, but it was a feigned conviviality, a conscientious refusal to acknowledge what was preferable to ignore.

It took Jamie Kessling, a smug obstetrician whom Mark had always disliked, to introduce them. Jamie was discussing the ongoing studies at his clinic to stabilize embryonic tissue samples. It was the typical self-congratulatory bragging that Mark expected from Jamie Kessling, a man who never failed to use kernels of knowledge and anecdotes as a means of conveying his own inflated sense of importance. Mark was on the verge of excusing himself when Jamie waved to the woman sitting on the lawn. "Let me introduce you to the latest member of the team," he said.

Jamie was noticeably intoxicated as they walked across the lawn, a detail Mark found troubling. Two glasses, three at max was the rule of thumb at these gatherings. Anything more and you ran the risk of being impaired when Jorge the Younger arrived.

"Doctor Mark Clempson, meet Deborah Peters," Jamie said, gesturing to the woman. "She's our latest specialist in cellular therapeutics."

"Pleased to meet you," Mark said, extending his hand.

"There are so many doctors present here I imagine there's a joke in there somewhere," she said.

"There is the one about two doctors and an HMO manager who—"

Mark never had a chance to deliver the punchline. His attempt at a lame joke was punctuated by an ear-piercing scream. People began murmuring and craning their necks in the direction of the commotion. A crowd had gathered at the far edge of the lawn. Mark and Deborah joined the circle to find the lawn chair over-turned and the Elder splayed flat on his back in the grass. The child stood above him, a paring knife clutched in his fist. The man screamed as the child thrust the blade repeatedly into the Elder, soaking his loose-fitting clothes in blood. Nobody stirred as the screams subsided and the limbs ceased to twitch, leaving only the sound of the blade hacking through cold dead meat.

When the child finally ceased, he arose and faced the guests. The stillness was almost palpable in the seconds before the audience erupted into loud applause and whistling.

Mark looked over at Deborah and noticed tears beginning to stream down her cheeks. They were both a part of this moment, of something bigger than themselves, he thought as he moved closer to her. It would mark their commencement, their collective beginning as one.

The child began to convulse and dropped to the ground. Nudged by maternal instinct, Deborah rushed to her son's side and proceeded to wipe beads of sweat from his brow. His abdomen and throat engorged, inducing a series of spastic movements. The child's face drained of color as the jaw detached to reveal a gaping mouth filled with broken teeth. A single talon-like hand pro-truded from the throat, eliciting a tearing sound of muscle and flesh.

"Jamie! Jamie! It's time!" somebody shouted.

Not for the first time, Mark stood spellbound watching the limbs claw their way out of the throat and grasp at the balmy night air. The spectators gathered around in awe, relishing the sublime moment.

Then came the familiar cry that echoed each year.

"Jorge's arrived! Jorge's arrived!"

Montauk's Design

He was a peculiar-looking man. Probably middle-aged, although his wire-rimmed glasses and attire made him appear older. He wore a wide-brimmed black hat reminiscent of a Victorian pastor. Over his left shoulder was slung a leather rucksack that had seen better days. A cross between a missionary and college professor, Lacey would later think, although at the moment this juxtaposition was far from her thoughts. She was distracted by what he had said upon her answering the door: "This is *my* house."

"Excuse me?" Lacey asked.

The man gazed up at the eaves of the porch, nodding to himself. "Unmistakable," he said. "This is certainly my house."

Her initial reaction was confusion, followed by a sudden urge to bolt the door and call the police.

Lacey had been a homeowner for the past five years and was certain that this was, indeed, her house. She had lived in small studio apartments for most of her adult life in order to save up for a down payment on a place of her own. Upon first sight, she knew that *this* house was the one: a three-bedroom stand-alone dating from the turn of the century, complete with neo-gothic décor and a wrap-around porch. The asking price had been slightly higher than anticipated, but a few years' extended mortgage was a tolerable trade-off for domestic happiness, she wagered.

"You must be mistaken," was all Lacey could say. "This is *my* house." She was struck by how ridiculous the statement sounded.

"Yes, I don't doubt that, but it's also mine," the man replied. "I'm not mistaken."

Lacey leaned against the door with the intention of shutting it. The man cracked a thin smile.

"I realize how strange this sounds, and I could have done a better job of explaining," he began. "What I mean is that your house resembles my house. But not just resembles... It *is* my house."

She peered at him through the narrowing crack in the door. "I'm not following here," she said honestly.

"Please, if you let me come in, I might be able to elucidate what I am trying to convey."

Sound judgment dictated that inviting a complete stranger into your home was a bad idea. However, Lacey had never been one to think of herself as "sound" in any strict sense of the word. Besides, did psychopaths use words like "elucidate?"

Stepping into the foyer, the man cast a sweeping look around the parlor, taking note of the furnishings, wall hangings, and other belongings that filled the room. He appeared to be sizing up the interior, framing it as a painter might before executing a masterpiece. Honestly, Lacey was dumbfounded, and it was only when the man began speaking again that she realized she was still standing in the doorway, clutching the handle's brass knob.

"My name is Cyrus Case. Most people call me Cy."

He slid the rucksack off his shoulder and began rummaging through it, eventually drawing out a brown paper envelope. "Please?" he said, motioning to the dining room table.

He dumped the contents of the envelope onto the table and sorted through an array of photographs, newspaper clippings, and scraps of paper filled with illegible writing. Lacey thought of offering the stranger a glass of water or a drink, knowing it was the customary thing to do in such a situation. For some reason, she couldn't move.

He arranged a series of photographs on the table.

"This is my house," he said, pointing to one of the photographs.

Lacey looked at the image. The gothic arches of the porch overhang, the latticed window on the front door, the distinctively carved newel posts at the bottom of the front steps: it was obviously a picture of her own house. A pang of fear gripped her, and

Lacey understood now that she had made a terrible mistake in allowing this man to enter her home.

"Looks familiar, doesn't it?" Cy continued, oblivious to her trepidation. "But, this house—*my* house—is located in Richmond Hill, Georgia, where I live."

He pointed to a second photograph showing a wide-angle view of the house. Indeed, the surroundings indicated that it was not Lacey's house. She lived on a scenic, semi-urban New England street lined with single-family homes. The house in the picture stood alone on the banks of a river dotted with drooping trees and flowering plants.

Lacey squinted at the picture. "It looks similar," she agreed.

"*Similar*? It's exact. I bet I can describe the entire layout of your home, from the small hexagonal-shaped room on the eastern side to the stained-glass window above the second-floor landing."

"How...?"

"I know it because it's also my house. Two houses, virtually identical in structure and appearance. Odd, right? But..." He tapped his finger on a third photograph, a faded black and white print of the same house, now situated on a hill surrounded by farmland. The neat writing on the yellowed border read: *Willard, Kansas, 1948.*

***

I became reacquainted with Lacey Andrews at a dinner party hosted by a mutual friend. It was winter, and Boston was still recovering from a nor'easter that had recently terrorized much of the North Atlantic coast. Cars were snowed under and plows made regular sweeps of the streets, depositing their glacial mounds on curbs and along gutters. A stillness enveloped the city in those first few days after the storm, as though everyone was too stunned or too beleaguered to do much other than remain indoors and let municipal services attend to the aftermath.

The gathering I had attended was winding down. Lacey was standing beside the buffet table, staring at the discarded paper plates and empty wine bottles. She seemed lost in thought, but when she noticed me, she smiled and made polite conversation, asking how I was doing and whether I was still working as a copy editor for a local magazine. I filled her in on the details of my life over the past few years and then mentioned that I had just been contracted to write a book on the historic homes of New England for a small press.

"Is that your specialty now?" she asked.

"Not really, but I received an advance."

"Pays the bills, then?"

"I'm not quitting my day job," I admitted, "and I'll have to do some research since my knowledge of historic buildings in the area is minimal."

"*Historic Homes of New England*. What a quaint title."

"It's a work in progress."

"Huh, well, if you need a place to get started, I certainly have one," Lacey told me with an uneasy laugh. "The last house I lived in. It had a history."

"Don't all houses?"

"No, I mean it definitely had a history. A man named Cy Case was working on writing it before he died. He told me a few things, and I also discovered a few bits myself." She paused, and then added: "I had to move eventually, though. I couldn't live there anymore."

I asked if it was because of the house's past, and Lacey gave me a pained expression, as though uncertain of how to answer. "Not exactly," she finally replied. "I learned that the house was not all that... *exceptional*, I guess is the word. That it wasn't really *my own* house because it was somebody else's. Does that make sense?"

I told her quite honestly that I had no clue what she was hinting at, and we both laughed at this. She told me to look into it myself, gave me the address and some details, and left it at that. I wouldn't be disappointed, she promised.

***

Historic Homes of New England
Entry Twenty-Five: The Montauk House

   Among the many gems of Art Deco and Georgian style homes that northern Massachusetts has to offer, the Montauk House of Haverhill remains unique unto itself, in light of its gothic fixtures and customized design. The first known deed of sale for the residence dates from 1901, although the building was most likely constructed during the late-nineteenth century, by architect Clarence James Montauk. It features various stylistic flourishes representative of American gothic revivalism, a style for which Montauk was well known. Among its more distinguished residents have been Simon Greenleaf Whittier, a relative of the renowned Massachusetts poet John Greenleaf Whittier, and the librettist and musician Barret Dorsey.

   The most distinctive features of the building include the front portico and tympanum, the gothic spire attached to the eastern roof, and the four stained glass windows that adorn each side of the house. The tympanum and stained glass share a common motif. One might initially assume that the content of the decorative pieces is Biblical, although further examination would quickly reveal that the images featured within do not correspond to any known Christian iconography or narrative.

   C.J. Montauk, who both designed and built the house, was an architect of some renown in his day, although his notoriety has since diminished. A native of England, he immigrated to the United States in the mid-nineteenth century. Records pertaining to his arrival in the country are scarce, although various municipal reports attest to his living in Boston by the end of the Civil War. His claims to have studied under the inimitable François-Christian Gau remain unsubstantiated, but certain stylistic elements of his work do recall both French and Imperial Gothic traits. In addition to architecture, Montauk was known for his works on theosophy and his naturalist writing. His study of the natural world compelled him later in life to travel extensively throughout North America, and he planned and commissioned a variety of buildings during these years of travel. His architectural work can be found today in cities as far-flung as Savannah, Georgia; New Orleans, Louisiana; and Lincoln, Nebraska.

The Montauk house of Haverhill is Gothic in both design and spirit. Its decorative elements are eclectic, mixing English, German, and French styles to convey a sense of harmony through multiplicity. As with many Gothic Revivalist houses, the arrangement of the interior rooms is uneven and disproportionate. The design appears to have been based entirely upon the exterior attributes of the house, with the interior rooms planned to accommodate it. This technique might best be described as "Form over Function." The result is oddly angled rooms, the most obvious being a hexagonal chamber located in the eastern wing. The only exception is a perfectly symmetrical room on the second floor, the shape of which is made unusual in this structure only by its relative normalcy. At times, the effect of the overall design on the viewer is disorienting. At least one observer described the sensation as "vertigo-like." Barret Dorsey noted similar impressions in the daily journal kept during his years of residency in the Montauk house. "I stared for a good twenty minutes, studying how the angles of the floor and the wall came together," he recorded in 1934. "It appeared all the lines converged in a corner, at a single, fixed geometric point. I wondered whether they might extend an infinite distance, never completely touching at all but only giving the illusion of such from my vantage point. The spell was broken only when Maestro, my cat, jumped onto my lap." Later that night, Dorsey reputedly began work on "I'm Under Your Spell," a jazz number that would become a standard of the big band repertoire during the late 1930s.

***

Lacey mulled over the seven photographs arranged in a fan-shaped pattern on the dining table. She listened diligently as Cy recounted the details of the book he was working on and afterward did not object to his request to examine the interior of the house in detail. She watched detachedly as he unrolled a long tape measure and began recording the width, length, and diagonal distances of all the ground-floor rooms in a dog-eared spiral notebook.

"Amazing," he said after consulting the figures. "The measurements are exactly the same."

"The same as what?" Lacey asked.

"As my house, as the house in New Orleans, as the houses in Willard and Lincoln... And despite the odd shape of the rooms, too. They're not random at all. Each one was precisely measured, down to the nearest centimeter."

Lacey looked at the photographs once more and tried to hold back her disappointment. One of the most attractive qualities of her house had been its assumed uniqueness, she suddenly realized: its oddly shaped rooms, its paneled walls and quaint stained glass windows. A certain pride—or perhaps arrogance—had come with the belief that her house was not like the generic buildings lining most American streets, that it was better than the uniform townhouses and split-levels that popped up everywhere like mushrooms after rain. For better or worse, Cy had shattered this illusion, revealing her to be the self-important dupe she was. And for what? To satisfy his own curiosity? Disappointment quickly melted into resentment.

"So, what you're saying is that my house is just like all the others? I had always thought my house was special and it wasn't, right?" Lacey didn't bother to hide the disdain in her voice.

"That's the problem, though. It was never *your* house to begin with," he explained. "It was always Clarence Montauk's."

She found his pragmatic tone insulting and remained quiet as he finished his inspection.

Once Cy was gone, Lacey poured a glass of wine and began flipping through the photographs he had left. The anger she had felt earlier re-emerged, and rather than considering the matter further, she tore up the photos he had left and deposited them in the wastebasket.

Later that night Lacey was washing out her wine glass in the kitchen sink when it accidentally slipped from her fingers and shattered. She stared at the shards of glass for a moment, appreciating the way they glistened in the light. Then, picking up one of the larger pieces from the basin, she impulsively pressed it to the kitchen wall and carved a narrow gouge into the wood.

Screw you, Montauk, she thought.

***

Dear Brother Roderick,

I have traded in the familiarity of New England for the obscure meridional back-country. The savagery that one encounters here cannot be understated, yet with it comes a certain picturesque and virginal quality. The work is slow, with all lumber and resources necessitating a haul by cart across expanses of forest and swampland. Two horses have already perished. The countrymen complain daily of the arduous work, reminding me that in former days no white man would have been forced to submit to such menial labors. Many of the village elders do not hide their fondness for the recent past and evoke warm memories of days that are no more. Nostalgia infects the land like a blight. I have never encountered a place so populated with phantoms. The ravages of history remain fresh in the mind, especially as one wanders about the wreckage on the outskirts of Savannah.

Before my departure, you had inquired as to the nature of the designs which have so fastidiously occupied my days and nights these past seven years. I confess I remained reticent on the subject at the time. Yet, after much contemplation, I have now considered how best to articulate my vision to you. Yes, I say "vision," because a vision it is.

Do you recall the old brotherhood? I can state with certainty that our efforts were never futile, as some of our fellow brothers have since come to profess. In particular, I reference the night on which Brother Sylvanus first became struck by the odd somnambulism that would afflict him for the rest of his life and, ultimately, drive him to the most immoral of acts. I do not doubt that his passing came about by his own hand. I only doubt that it came about through his own will. Surely, we are not naïve enough to believe that calling upon the gods does not demand a sacrifice?

Upon the night in question, we convoked at Brother Mathew's residence. We intoned the usual prayers and performed the ceremonies as was our custom. As we stood about the circle, a most startling form revealed itself to me in the thick shadows. I saw a shape completely perfect in its configuration, there in the darkness, light made visible. This particular form has since haunted me. It materializes before me in my waking moments and is conjured from the substance of my dreams. So familiar am I with it that I have committed its every detail to memory, studying it like a monk might study a sacred text.

I know now that what I glimpsed was an idea of perfect space, an abstraction capable of being willed into material existence. Imagine a space without a history, a space that collapses time and the singularity of experience within its very structure. I believe you now have an inkling of my plan and can perhaps understand the tireless work that I persist to undertake. We have been given a singular opportunity. Perfection is not to be found in the communal correctness of republics or the arithmetic of political economy but in the production and reproduction of pure form. Although our brotherhood dissolved following the tragedy which befell Brother Sylvanus, I intend to imprint its legacy upon the sinews of this land. And for good reason; while still a young country, it is already acquiring geriatric habits. America is beginning to buckle under the weight of her accumulated memories and the refuse of her past agonies. Need I remind you that such is the condition of a people in its dotage? Those who seek solace in the reminiscence of youth resign all hope for the future.

De profundis vocat te.

***

In the winter, the house assumed an oppressive quality. The rooms felt constricting, the air stale. During this period, Lacey developed two odd habits. The first was an uncontrollable desire to mar the walls and fixtures of her house on a semi-regular basis. For no particular reason, Lacey would be suddenly struck by an overwhelming urge to mark the paneling with a butterknife or make an incision in the doorframe. The nicks and scratches she left were always small and barely noticeable, yet they accumulated over the winter weeks, leaving a trail of her comings and goings throughout the house.

The second habit she developed was a proclivity for spending abnormally long periods in the cellar. It started one evening when the living room lights went out and Lacey descended the creaky wooden steps to examine the fuse box. Once below, Lacey realized that the fuses connecting the cellar lights had also blown. Squinting into blackness, she fumbled along with her hands stretched out in front of her. As she moved through the dark, she swore that she could feel familiar objects occupying the room with her: the downy surface of a blanket, a cold metallic smoothness, the contours of a human face. She knew that the cellar was empty save for a few boxes stowed away at the far end. Somehow, despite this, the darkness had become haptic, and stranger still, there was nothing threatening or remotely disturbing in this discovery. She wriggled her fingers and felt a rough, bristly texture. She moved her hands and touched the softness of well-moisturized skin. Each step further through the void yielded a new sensation.

She thought she might go on like this forever until finally, her fingertips grazed the metal covering of the fuse box. She managed to change out the fuses in the dark. The pale antiseptic light from the overhead exposed a stark and empty room, nothing more. She looked about, bemused and a bit disenchanted. Then she pulled the chain, restoring the room to darkness before making her way back toward the stairs.

***

They stayed in touch. Cy's first letter arrived in the spring. There was an old-world quality to receiving letters via post that she liked. The letters continued for the span of a year, and through them, Lacey learned a great many things. She was slowly fed details on the history of her house as Cy churned out his manuscript. She discovered what Georgia autumns were like, even though she had never been to the southern part of the country. She also learned of the submissive humility that comes when a doctor puts a definitive time limit on your life, the indignity of hospital rooms, and the tedium that solemn bedside visitors invite. Cy had been diagnosed with terminal cancer that winter. Lacey kept her replies light and optimistic. She knew that one day soon the letters would simply cease, an interrupted conversation never to be resumed.

One spring afternoon, after emerging from the cellar, Lacey was dusting the windows in the bedroom. Looking out, she saw a man standing in the street, his face hidden behind a camera. She took him for a bird watcher at first, before realizing that that camera seemed to be pointed directly at her window. Instinctively, she hid behind the drapes. It took a moment to admit that she was probably being foolish. When she returned to the window, the man was still there, too distant to identify with any certainty. He now appeared to be waving at her.

That night, Lacey began a letter to Cy that she would never finish:

"Today, I imagined you on that day last year when you turned up at my door, when you were just the odd man with the pictures..."

***

In the Boston library, a cream-colored envelope lies sandwiched between the mess of documents and notes contained within the Townshend Family papers. Nobody has been able to determine its proper place among the body of correspondences spanning generations. Its crimson wax seal remains unbroken, tempting the inquisitive. A single phrase is scrawled on the overleaf in faded blue pencil: *Received three days after death of Roderick P. Townsend, misc.*

***

By late spring, the Louisiana heat was already thick and oppressive. I sat in a seminar room listening to the drone of an air conditioner. Out the window, shimmering waves of heat hovered above the macadam. I was the only person watching. The other five attendees sat at desks arranged in a semi-circle, concentrating on the seminar leader. They were all like me: mid-thirties, relatively well-educated, and enthusiastic about starting a career in journalism despite having only a modicum of talent. The leader paced about the room, posing open-ended questions to us. The theme of the seminar said it all: "How to write for the New York Times (and why it shouldn't matter)." Desperation hung over the room like a cloud. I reconciled myself to the fact I had wasted nearly a thousand dollars on the seminar fee and accompanying travel. By the third day, my thoughts were on packing and the impending deadlines waiting for me back in Boston.

I had been working on *Historical Homes of New England* for six months, and as the seminar wound down, I remembered from my research that C.J. Montauk had worked in New Orleans during his career. A quick search later, I was able to locate the address of the only remaining Montauk building in the state. Renting a car and driving from Baton Rouge felt like the saving grace of an otherwise fruitless trip.

I booked a cheap motel room in Maître and then proceeded to Algiers Point, where the address was located. The neighborhood was quiet and scenic. Driving along the winding banks of the river, I believed that an authentic New Orleans could still exist just at the periphery of the tourist traps and vulgarized Dixieland heritage that drew visitors to the French Quarter on a regular basis.

My work on *Historic Homes* had sparked an interest in Clarence Montauk. By this point I was already considering writing a biography of the man, imagining it as an epic American story told through buildings. The problem was the lack of reliable sources. His life in Massachusetts was patchy, and his travels throughout the country were only recoverable through a mix of letters to unidentified recipients and extant work contracts in local record offices. The letters did, however, give insight into an interesting mind. By the end of his life, Montauk had become fascinated with Pythagorean mathematics and geometry. On numerous occasions, he provided details on his own work, suggesting that the designs were based on ideas communicated to him by God. If this was to be taken at face value, it painted a picture of the architect as a man driven by an attempt to reproduce an architectural structure based upon divine principles. A man on a mission, I liked to think, not unlike the Puritans who sought to reconstruct God's kingdom here on earth.

Pulling around the bend, the house came into view. It was identical to the Montauk house of Haverhill. Even the weathervane crowning the spire appeared to lilt at the same wind-bent angle.

I got out of the car and snapped a few quick photos as the evening light descended over the Mississippi. Having become familiar with Lacey Andrew's former house through my research, I couldn't help but feel a certain connection with its twin sister. After a while, I began to feel mosquitos dancing across my bare arms and knew it was time to leave.

"So long, Clarence," I said and waved. "You build a hell of a home."

I got in the car and proceeded back along the river. I turned on the radio and listened to the voice of the broadcaster reading the evening news, paying only minimal attention to the empty streets. My mind was elsewhere when I saw the Gothic spire poke out from behind the tops of the trees ten minutes later. The entire house came into view as I rounded the bend with an odd sensation of déjà vu. I had driven in a complete circle. I stopped the car at the place I had taken the pictures earlier and laughed.

"Fancy meeting you in a place like this," I said to the house.

It remained silent. Its features seemed more defined and angular in the evening light, as if I was staring at a detailed sketch rather than the actual structure.

I put the car in reverse and went in the opposite direction this time, imagining that I had missed the turn for the highway at some point. The news broadcast had ended. A southern preacher discussing the benefits of a personal relationship with God now murmured from the radio. I listened for amusement, considering it a little "local color" to complement my Louisiana adventure. The preacher had a thin voice, and I found it difficult to imagine him sermonizing before a congregation. At some point, he transitioned into the subject of how and whether we could know with certainty what God intended for us.

"In the beginning was the original idea," the crackling voice continued, "the idea of form that structures God's universe. And although obscure to us, God's master architecture embraces and includes us in its infinite design and wisdom. The unfathomable will…"

Twisting the dial to lower the broadcast, I cast a gaze toward the treetops in front of me. The point of the spire stood silhouetted against the failing light. The same abandoned street stretched out in front of me. I stopped the car. The low buzz of the broadcast was barely audible.

"…to know the symmetry of its form. For as it is written, He has inscribed a circle on the surface of the waters at the boundary of light and darkness…"

***

She awoke to the sound of a pebble striking glass. She ignored the disturbance at first but felt obliged to crawl out of bed when the noise repeated. Padding into the hall, Lacey saw a zig-zagging crack stretching across one of the stained-glass windows. The snaking fissure had misaligned some of the glasswork. The window usually contained an image of a man standing on the shoreline, pointing out to sea where a whale was rising from the depths of the ocean. The man now seemed to be pointing at a star-studded sky while the whale keeled over in the water.

Lacey pressed her finger to the cracked pane. She noticed a faint glow coming from the hall below and a man walking the corridor. He held a candle, and in the flickering light, she was certain the intruder was Cy Case. He moved through the house quietly, his feet shuffling on the floorboards toward the cellar door. Lacey waited until the glow of the candle subsided and then followed him down. Yet once she was in the cellar stairwell there was no sign of Cy. The candlelight had been extinguished, leaving only a scorched scent in the air. The empty darkness enveloped her body like silk, its consistency denser with each forward step.

After walking for an indeterminate amount of time, she glimpsed a doorway filled with starlight. She exited into a balmy summer night. A field extended before her. In the distance, shadowy trees sat pitched against a star-filled sky. She could hear the chirping of night insects and the faint sound of rushing water. The shadow of the house loomed behind her. It was dreaming, Lacey thought as she walked through the field and felt the wet grass brush against her ankles. The house was dreaming of her, and not the other way around.

Her feet moved along, treading a familiar path. The scorched smell she had first detected in the cellar became stronger as she walked through the woods. Eventually the trees receded, and Lacey entered upon desolate streets lined with ruined buildings. Houses with roofs caved in, walls blackened with char, exposed beams protruding through plaster like bones—an image of absolute destruction. The burnt smell lingered over everything, seared into the landscape.

Among the wreckage, Lacey saw one building untouched by the devastation. Tramping across the rubble, she ascended the front steps, running her fingers over the newel post in a familiar way. She knocked on the front door, admiring the latticed window and the shadows cast by the eaves overhead. A woman answered. Her face was familiar, but Lacey could not say how she knew this person or in what capacity.

The woman cast an inquisitive glance at her. "Are you lost, dear?" she asked.

Lacey shook her head. "No, this is my house," she told her.

"Excuse me?"

"This is certainly my house. I receive letters here," Lacey laughed, as if this detail corroborated her claim.

The woman looked at her placidly, and some instinctive part of

Lacey already knew that no further letters would arrive—that they hadn't arrived here for a very long time. She would never hear about another Georgia autumn, never know the complete story of how Montauk designed and built his perfect house.

"You must be mistaken," was all she said before closing the door.

Sightseeing

As a general rule, speech is a commodity in Morocco. Conversations and friendly greetings quickly transform into veiled sales pitches at a moment's notice. Merchants in the medina hawk their wares. They call out in multiple languages, beckon you to their stalls, and aggressively place unwanted objects in your hand for consideration. In Fes, I purchased a small lamp after enduring a prolonged lecture on artisanal craftsmanship. I had no desire to own the object, but in the end, it proved more expedient to pay the hundred dirhams for the lamp than waste the afternoon explaining myself to an insistent storeowner. Those volunteering restaurant recommendations will typically lead you to the establishment of a business partner. If you are lost, pedestrians offering to show you to your destination will strategically steer you in the direction of their uncle's workshop where you can sip tea and examine Arabian carpets. Not that these types of encounters are without their charm. It was simply something to which I was unaccustomed. After a few days in Fes, however, I acclimated to the street culture of the bazaars and even came to enjoy it in a strange way.

I was traveling to Marrakesh—the second leg of my journey— when I met the man who would tell me about the Wādī. He was unassuming at first glance: slightly past middle age, well-dressed, and clean-cut. He introduced himself as Abbas and inquired about my trip, where I was from, and whether I was enjoying Morocco. It was the type of polite chatter you might expect on a long train ride in which two strangers know they will be spending a significant amount of time together and try to make the best of the situation. When I told him I would be spending a week in Marrakesh, he made a face and asked whether I would be taking any excursions. I hadn't considered it, I told him.

"There are many places to visit in the area," he said. "Most people tend to spend a few days in Marrakesh and take day trips outside the city. Tour companies run regular service to these destinations."

When I said I didn't much care for the company of tourists, Abbas laughed and nodded approvingly.

"You could consider Wādī al-Dimā then. Not many people go there."

Four hours southeast of Marrakesh was a city that had been uninhabited since at least the turn of the twentieth century. It had originally been a Berber settlement prior to the Roman invasion. In the early Christian era, the site had served briefly as an Augustine monastery before being overrun by Arab conquers. Abbas seemed well-informed on the locality. I sat listening to him discuss its history, trying to form an image of the place in my mind. I stared out the window at the passing landscape, imagining what such a city might look like with its mix of Roman, Christian, and Islamic architecture.

"And now, it's completely abandoned?" I asked when he finished.

He nodded sadly. "No money. It's located in the valleys of the Atlas Mountains. They don't get much business that way. People have left. It's a sad thing. Inevitable, but still sad."

Abbas dug into his wallet and pulled out a card. I felt stupid for letting myself be disarmed by his congeniality and expected a well-rehearsed sales pitch recommending a restaurant in town or offering some type of local service. But he didn't launch into a polished sales pitch. Instead, he simply held out the card, indicating for me to take it. He knew a person who could take me to Wādī al-Dimā if I was interested. There was no obligation, he assured. Tour companies didn't usually run buses out to that part of the countryside, and I would need a private guide.

I tucked the card into my rucksack and told him I would

consider it. Abbas nodded and changed the subject. For the rest of the trip, we discussed North African politics, the Arab Spring, and his impression of British tourists—which, to be honest, was quite amusing. Arriving in Marrakesh, he wished me a nice trip, hopped into a cab, and left me to haggle with the cab drivers milling about the station entrance. I never saw him again.

I enjoyed Marrakesh with its mosques, large squares, and winding streets. Each morning, I awoke to the *adzhan*, listening to it drift across the morning like strange and enchanting music that summoned the faithful to prayer. Other tourists in the hotel were not as enamored with its resonant beauty and complained about the noise.

"Can't you do anything about it?" asked one man who had been woken at sunrise by the muezzin's call. The manager at the hotel desk stared at him helplessly.

His expression reminded me why I despised tourists. Aversion for one's own kind is a peculiar type of loathing.

I recalled the card that Abbas gave me. The idea of an isolated village seemed appealing. By my fourth day, I had already managed to visit all the major attractions in Marrakesh. My afternoons increasingly degenerated into wandering from café to café, trying to occupy my time and avoid the sightseers congregating at Jemma el-Fnaa.

Why not head further afield and explore the environs?

I called the number on the card, and a man answered in French. As I worked through some clumsy greetings recalled from my A-level French classes, the man fluidly switched to perfect English.

"I know Abbas," I said. "I want to go to Wādī al-Dimā."

I was instructed to meet at a nearby café in an hour, an austere building made of dirty stucco and flaking plaster. Once inside, however, the courtyard opened onto an impressive restaurant with a rooftop terrace overlooking the city skyline, where I sat drinking a glass of wine, always a rare find in Moroccan cities.

As I waited, I watched the sky slowly fill with soft evening light and listened to the *adzhan* resonate across the city. I became transfixed by its low, rolling utterances and must have momentarily closed my eyes because when I opened them again a young man was seated across from me at the table, smiling. He introduced himself as Ayman.

We chatted for a few minutes as I gave him a brief summary of my trip. Ayman took it all in, listening attentively and interjecting when appropriate.

"And you are traveling *alone?*" he finally asked, a bit taken aback by this revelation.

I nodded, smiling at his disbelief. A young Irish girl was not the stereotypical lone traveler, I agreed, although I was quite capable of handling myself when necessary.

"My father had reservations about me traveling alone," I said. "He advised Spain as an alternative, but everyone goes there."

Ayman scoffed. "No, not Spain. Morocco is better."

Why I wanted to go to Wādī al-Dimā puzzled him. Not many people knew about the place, and it was not listed in the travel books.

"There is nothing there. It's a ghost town." He mulled over this phrase and asked if he had used the proper English expression.

"If you mean it is completely abandoned, then yes."

"*Abandoned.* That's the word I was thinking," he said, more to himself. "Well, it is. Nobody has lived there for a hundred years."

"And why is that?"

Ayman shrugged. "Economy dried up. Lack of water. No infrastructure. Take your pick. There have been some other theories, too. In the 1950s, a French entrepreneur had plans to turn it into a retreat for artists. I'm not so knowledgeable in the details, but something went wrong. Mainly, it's just a sad place that doesn't attract tourists."

"Perfect," I said. "Will you take me?"

We negotiated a price and planned to leave the next morning.

Ayman arrived at my hotel at daybreak in a pristine SUV. The ride into the mountains was pleasant. An hour into the trip, Ayman turned off the main highway and navigated along the local roads. We passed towns and villages, many of them poor and decrepit looking. You could tell the places leased to European contractors by the modern apartment complexes and swimming pools. The unequal distribution of wealth was evident everywhere. At one point, we passed an old man sitting on the side of the road selling vegetables from a cart. At another location, a child directed a herd of goats across the road. The craggy mountains gradually came into view, towering over the shrubs and Argania trees. For most of the trip, I snapped pictures of the people and scenery as Ayman educated me on local points of interest.

"You might be the first person to visit the Wādī in a long time," Ayman said as we cruised along. "Nobody has ever asked me to take them out there."

"That so?"

"Yes. I am curious."

"So, you've *never been*?"

He shook his head. "No, not many people go there. Setti Fatma, Tidssi, yes. But not to the Wādī. Once the people left, it was forgotten."

He cast a look in my direction. His eyes concealed behind dark sunglasses made it difficult to read his expression, but I imagined he was trying to instill confidence in me. "I know where I'm going. It's difficult to get lost out here."

I just nodded and returned to snapping photos of the countryside.

As the afternoon progressed, the terrain became more mountainous and barren. The craggy formations took on strange shapes as though hewn from an alien substance. The peculiar way they reflected the light caught my eye, making them appear to shimmer in the distance. I chalked it up to the rising heat, although this reasoning hardly explained the odd effect of the mountains, which cast long shadows across the earth despite the high declination of the noon sun. It was almost as if they defied nature and obeyed laws known only to them.

The walls of the city came into view as we turned onto a stretch of rutted dirt roads leading into the valley. Unremarkable on first inspection: flat sallow plaster mottled with water stains and scabby paint. Judging from the length of the walls, the city was not large. The gates that had once protected the settlement were in a state of complete disrepair and jutted from the earth like teetering giants. Outside the walls, wild and barren fields extended upward along the sloping mountains. The city had sprouted up in the sterile wilderness like a mushroom clinging to the craggy incline of the valley. I could not help feeling slightly disappointed as the car came to a halt.

A small row of crumbling buildings was visible through the gate's entrance. The worn brick and arches suggested that they were Roman, although this was simply an inference on my part. I snapped a few pictures of the exterior as Ayman laced up his hiking boots. What would my friends back home think when they saw them? They were not the typical photos of tourist attractions or people lounging around the pool.

"Crazy Laura," they would say in that playful way meant to conceal their envy. "Always has to be different."

"Ready?" Ayman asked as I adjusted my camera settings.

We entered through the gates, passing the old, crumbling structures. Behind these, a network of deserted streets fanned out before us, snaking in odd directions with little sense of structure or design. Dust littered each avenue, and debris crunched under our feet as we advanced further into the medina.

The height of the surrounding buildings seized me with a sensation of vertigo. The buildings pitched and weaved at peculiar angles, seeming to take the shape of the winding streets with their curved and convex facades.

The tan-colored stone glistened faintly in the afternoon light, reminding me of the rocks we had seen coming into the valley. Despite the afternoon heat, they were cool to the touch.

Further along, the buildings became noticeably more modern with windows, doorframes, and decorative features. Some of the ornamentation was quite beautiful. The engravings along the walls resembled a fine stone filigree reminiscent of the gothic stucco calligraphy and girih-like panels in Fes. A surreal silence permeated the streets with no tourists elbowing for a view and no chattering voices intruding on the stillness. The isolation was complete.

It was paradise.

"Have you noticed the streets?" Ayman said, as though he whispered this in my ear, but when I turned around, he was crouched in the debris a good five meters behind me, examining an engraving running along the base of a building.

I shook my head, and he made a spiral shape in the air with his finger. "Not straight."

A shadowy outline in the window of the building opposite me looked like a person slumped against the wall, although the shape didn't stir when I called out.

Inside, we found a bare, cavernous room. Bits of broken rock covered the floor. A mannequin made of dusty rags and twigs was propped against the windowsill. The face was blank except for two crudely formed eye sockets and a stitched mouth. The angle of the body, however, gave the dummy an unnatural life-like quality—an idle spectator casually gazing out to the empty street.

"What is it?" I asked Ayman, prodding at the bundle of rags and sticks, half expecting it to leap at me.

Ayman stared at the thing in silence and shook his head.

I took a few photos of the mannequin, and we continued down the empty avenue.

On the next street, we discovered a second mannequin huddled in the corner of a gutted building.

A third and fourth turned up in the following two constructions we explored.

In each room or building we entered, the same grotesque sculptures greeted us. Although each was made of rags and sticks, none were identical. Evident care had been taken in positioning these objects in such a way as to give a semblance of life and movement. Limbs made of branches and husks bent at just the right angles, matted cloth bundled together to create the illusion of contrapedal balance and poise.

Wandering in and out of the demolished buildings, we were surrounded by these mute, inert creatures. We had entered their world. We were the strangers among them.

"This is creepy," I told Ayman candidly after mulling over our latest discovery. "I think we should leave."

Ayman agreed, and we marched back along the street leading toward the gates. I had not taken particular note of the buildings we passed upon entering. Many of them looked similar, and their fluid, curving designs often made it difficult to detect where one building ended and the next began. An impression of warped and towering walls surrounded me on all sides.

As we passed them a second time, I gave greater consideration to the particularities of each building, scrutinizing them for familiar markings or distinctive features that might indicate we were headed in the right direction. However, this proved impossible. None of the buildings jogged my memory. The streets turned and coiled with greater frequency as we walked, and I remembered the way Ayman had made a spiraling gesture in the air with his finger.

Not straight, he had said.

When we came to a plaza with a building I was certain we had never passed, I paused. A soaring Gothic construction had statues running along the expanse of the entire facade. The carvings were a mix of human and animal forms arranged in an intricate arabesque pattern. In the pale afternoon light, the adornments looked like petrified bodies.

Every structure in the city had an unusual organic quality as though having been turned to stone rather than carved from it.

"I think we went the wrong way," I said after studying the plaza and adjacent arcades.

Ayman looked up at the carvings and nodded.

We followed the winding street back the way we came. The quiet, which I had found so pleasant earlier in the afternoon, unnerved me as we trekked along the vacant streets. Everything around us hinted at life, yet nothing stirred—the only noises were our footsteps and the wind. Not even the call of birds or the slithering sounds of lizards through the rocks punctuated the silence.

"I feel like those things are watching us," I said with a light laugh. I offered the comment simply for the sake of conversation. I wanted to concentrate on something other than the crunching of stone and brick under our shoes. Not that it wasn't true. I couldn't help thinking about the mannequins concealed behind each wall and enclosure, how they silently observed us meandering back and forth.

Ayman cast an unsettling look around. "No, not them. Someone else."

"What do you mean?"

He only shook his head.

Ayman seemed to be losing command of his English, his responses terse, often abrupt. Whereas earlier that morning he communicated with the fluidity of a native speaker, he now seemed to search for the proper words and became frustrated when he couldn't find them. Of course, it could have been that he simply preferred not to talk. Our current circumstances hardly encouraged gratuitous conversation.

Despite our change of direction, the streets grew shorter and wended at sharper angles. Every time I thought we were about to come upon a street or building we had passed before, I was mistaken. Street after street, new buildings, squares, and courtyards appeared, like walking in a maze.

At each intersection, I paused to consider which direction looked most promising. After a while, they all looked the same. We wandered aimlessly, hoping to stumble across a recognizable landmark that would direct us back to the gates.

The afternoon shadows elongated. By my calculation, we had been lost for a few hours, although the light in the sky suggested it was considerably later. The flat blue rapidly diminished to a burnt orange. I could not spot the sun or tell in which direction it was setting, but it was clearly advancing toward evening. Daylight didn't appear to drain from the sky like a normal sunset. Rather, it seemed to absorb color, ingesting tints of azure, umber, and vermillion like a canvas stretched tight above us.

"What time is it?" I asked, looking up at the sky.

If he heard me, he paid me no mind. His gaze fixed on the far end of the street where a succession of minarets stood silhouetted against the sky, their tapering outlines stark and imposing in the dusk.

Ayman placed a finger to his lips.

"*Shhhhhhh.*" He gestured to his ear.

I listened. The wind echoed through the empty buildings and passages—a desolate sound, reminiscent of barren desert landscapes and inhospitable terrain. Yet, something else—a low, sonorous reverberation just above the wind—lifted. Difficult to discern at first, I soon recognized the *adzhan*. It bled out into the evening, growing from a murmur into a resonant chant that progressively filled the air.

We stood there for a long time, listening. In the distance, shadows moved along the horizon without definite cause.

The sky turned a deep crimson, bathing everything in blood-red light.

The shadows flickered and moved in spastic gestures.

Squinting into the twilight, I was certain they were people, scuttling along the streets in single file.

Ayman's panic lined his face. Before I could utter a word, he bellowed something in Arabic and ran headlong in the opposite direction.

I followed him but could not see how he managed to dart across the rock and debris with such agility.

I called after him as he vanished into the darkness but only heard his retreating footsteps.

I called out louder, trying to project my voice over the incantatory *adzhan* pealing through the night, but he had fled.

The figures in the distance continued to writhe and gyrate, although they were now receding into the scarlet light. The file moved along, heeding the summons as the people disappeared one by one over the horizon.

Once the *adzhan* trailed off, emptiness surrounded me. Darkness completely veiled the streets and buildings. A faint red afterglow lingered, but it scarcely illuminated the area. I whispered Ayman's name, but silence was my only reply.

Certain that Ayman would not return, I shuffled through the debris and rubble with my hands extended in front of me. With each step, I expected my fingers to graze rough stone or make contact with a wall, but I encountered nothing. I inched along, uncertain of the direction I traveled. The absolute darkness wasn't the most unsettling thing. The *feel* of the darkness was. Something lurked there with me, something silent and just out of reach.

After a while, my imagination conjured up a variety of monstrosities culled from old folk tales I had heard as a child. It was silly, but the more fantastical the beast I imagined, the more at ease I felt. I had just about managed to calm myself and concentrate on finding my way through the dark when I heard the quiet sound of labored breathing.

"Ayman?" I kept my voice low.

The breaths grew hoarse and asthmatic, like somebody gasping for air. I stopped moving and listened.

"What do you want?" I asked the darkness.

I had not expected an answer, but a soft voice came through the blackness.

"Nothing that you can offer," it said.

Irregular footsteps scuffled through the debris ahead as Ayman staggered out of the dark, his movements rigid and jerky. Two flaccid arms dangled at his side, hanging there like bits of wet cloth. Although I knew it was Ayman from his clothing, I barely recognized him. His face deflated and shrank as though someone wore a mask of Ayman's face. Even the skin on his body looked loose-fitting and shapeless, like a garment pinned to an armature. His mouth dropped open in a mechanical gesture and emitted a choked squawking sound as he lurched towards me. He tried to speak, like he was saying "dispossession" over and over in a garbled language.

I closed my eyes, awaiting the feel of his limp hands on me, but it never came. The hand that touched me was firm and warm.

A voice spoke in French, and I opened my eyes.

"*Ça va, madame? Ça va?*"

I lay in the dirt. The officer's hand gently nudged my back as he repeated the question. I blinked into the sunlight and sat up just outside the gates of the medina. The police officer handed me a bottle of water, speaking in French. When it became evident I didn't understand, he simply pointed to the gates and I nodded.

A second officer exited from a nearby car and approached.

The two spoke between themselves for a moment as I looked about for Ayman.

"Ayman?" I asked. "*L'autre homme?*"

The two puzzled men offered to help me to my feet.

The SUV was parked where we had left it, its pristine white now covered in a thin layer of dust. I shielded my eyes from the sun and cast a long look around the valley with its sloping hills and sparse Argania trees.

No Ayman, although one of the officers stood around a single chair near the entrance of the gate. From my vantage point, it looked as though a person sat in it, their face turned toward the city gates.

The chair had not been there when we arrived, and I moved closer. It was not a person at all. It was one of the mannequins made of sticks and rags, its posture oddly human and slumped in the chair like a dozing spectator. The face was plain with crudely molded eyes and a sewn mouth, like the others.

However, the mannequin wore Ayman's clothes.

The officer murmured something in French and prodded the dummy. It made a dry sound like cornhusks rubbing together.

I shook my head slowly.

The officer assumed I was responding to his inquiry and left it at that.

They escorted me to their vehicle and helped me into the back seat. Making a U-turn sent up a trail of dust into the afternoon.

I nodded when I felt the officers were asking me a question, although I had little idea of what was actually said. I still felt numb as the city receded from view behind us and the car glided along the roads winding through the valley.

The officer in the passenger seat unhooked the handset of a two-way radio, and I made out the phrase, "found a tourist" during the communiqué.

I hugged myself closer and passed the remainder of the trip in a rueful silence.

In Marrakesh, I went to a police station where an official recorded my statement. He patiently scribbled down my account with an incredulous expression. After the interview, I was given the contact information for the Irish consulate in Casablanca and told that I could follow up on the report there. I arrived at my hotel late and fell asleep quickly that night.

I thought I might still be dreaming when I woke at dawn to the tolling cry of the muezzin. I sat up in bed, listening to the *adzhan* with a shudder. It seemed to extend indefinitely, summoning God knew what at this hour.

After what felt like a long time, I got dressed and made my way to the hotel lobby, empty save for a lone man at the desk working the night shift. His gaze shifted from me to the pages of the paperback he read.

I shuffled over to the ice machine in the corner and filled a bucket.

The *adzhan* resonated, pervading the lobby and rooms of the hotel.

The deskman remained oblivious, his eyes fixed on his book.

"Is there any way to make it stop?" I asked him in a weak voice. "Can't you do anything about it?"

The helpless look he gave filled me with shame, an all too identifiable and familiar kind of shame.

The Big Idea

It all went south once the fatties got the gliders.

That afternoon, I was sitting with Mr. Popadokalus in the rec room on the twenty-first floor. The old man took his breaks every day at twelve sharp. You could practically set your watch by it, or so the joke ran. As noon rolled around, the other employees would mill about the salesroom floor, dividing their attention between their wristwatches and Popadokalus, looking for telltale signs that the veteran was about to break. As he reached to unfasten his nametag, their eyes would bulge and diligently chart the movement of second hands crawling around watch faces.

"Bingo!" Crowley exclaimed, pointing to his watch as Popadokalus exited the salesroom. "The veteran's right on time!" The veteran: that's what they called him.

Whoever's watch was closest to noon when Mr. Popadokalus took his leave got lunch *gratis*. On some days, the wager came down to a matter of seconds, often eliciting quarrels over whose second hand crested first or whether digital watches had an advantage over mechanized ones. This is what passed for normal among our group: timekeeping, the hope of free lunches, and Popadokalus' predictable habits.

I watched as Mr. Popadokalus sat at the industrial-sized table in the rec room and carefully unpacked the contents of his lunch from a crisp brown bag in silence. My eyes drifted to the far end of the room, where a large window looked out over the Midtown skyline. From this vantage point, the city was reduced to near-microscopic proportions. The streets, bustling pedestrians, and steady traffic flow transformed into a chaos of atoms and neutrons in motion. I was contemplating the tricks that altitude and distance play on perception when I saw the dark shadow appear in the sky, followed by a forceful whoosh of air as a man enveloped in the triangular cut of a hang glider darted past my field of vision.

Next, I heard Mr. Popadokalus's thermos tumble to the floor as he shot up from his seated position.

"Good God, they're airborne!" he squawked, pointing to the window.

I remained silent, watching as the thermos rolled about the floor, dribbling concentric circles of coffee on the linoleum.

**

Winter mornings when the winds come blustering off the lake are the worst. I cringed as I lay in bed, listening to the currents of air whip through the streets. I can recall once hating the cold. I would contract my body and draw the blanket close, idly dreaming of skipping school and spending the day in bed listening to the drone of the radiator. Now I hate the wind and its ferocious wail. It means that the sky will be teeming with them.

Around ten, I get a call from Crowley. He wants to know why I haven't bothered showing up for my shift.

"Waiting for the winds to die down," I tell him.

"Everyone else made it in this morning," he snaps. "I gotta come all the way from the West Side. You know what *that's* like? But I got my ass in on time."

Crowley never misses an opportunity to remind you that the West Side was ground zero or that he had a front-row seat for the Great Waif Rebellion. He's a modern day martyr, a model waif. Each day he punches his timecard marks a new chapter in his personal hagiography. I sometimes wish I could accrete mass just to avoid being lumped together with people like him.

After ten minutes of his pedantic badgering, I'm done.

I hang up the phone, ditch the pajamas, and pull on the parka I found last summer while rummaging through the China Town dumpsters with Darcy and Joanie. Darcy spotted it first atop a heap of garbage bags and discarded boxes. I wear it now because the large hood covers my entire head.

"Nice threads," Darcy said, smiling at me.

"You think?" I asked, modeling it for her and pulling up the hood so that it came down over my eyes.

She laughed and ran her index finger over the parka's fur-lined hood.

I like to think I wear the parka because I recall this memory every time I slip it on. I can't, however, deny the utility of the large hood, which is an excellent protective covering against aerial bombardments of drool, sweat, and other bodily fluids that might randomly fall from the sky. On bad days when the winds are high, waifs rush about the streets carrying umbrellas or darting from store canopies to covered bus stops with a cautious eye turned to the sky, but not me. Bundled in my parka, I have perfected a style of leisurely walking as I move through the streets. It's the type of gait I imagine a European aristocrat might have. In August, the heat was excruciating, and the sweat that poured down my face would elicit peals of laughter from Darcy. "Weirdo," she called me as we walked through the park. "Screwball," she said to me as we cavorted around the abandoned lakefront arcades. Utility aside, I wore the parka for her amusement and the offhanded comments that came my way whenever we were together.

I pause in the doorway and listen to the wind rattle the traffic lights suspended above. The streets are desolate; the sky is clear. I take it as a good sign as I begin my mile-long trek to work.

Alone, I drop the aristocratic stride I have perfected and remain vigilant. At the bakery on Wentworth, old Chinese men sit huddled around tables, smoking cigarettes and playing cards. Their faces are always long and even, as though the world hasn't imploded. They focus on their cards, rattle small spoons against glasses of tea, and murmur amongst themselves. I envy their composure. It's a testament to human fortitude in some strange way.

"Watch out, kid!" I hear, as a large shadow pools around me.

I've been staring at the Chinese card players, distracted. Instinctively, I hit the pavement just as I feel a rush of air pass over my head, followed by a familiar whooshing sound. Looking straight ahead from my position on the ground, I watch as one of them alights on the sidewalk ten feet in front of me. His mass is hidden behind the triangular form of the glider, but from the shadow that flew over, I can tell he is large. He throws a look over his shoulder and our eyes momentarily meet. Despite his capabilities of flight, there is nothing graceful in his movements. I am suddenly reminded of the old expression "...when pigs fly." It's dead on. He resembles a giant hog, and I watch as he starts into a waddling trundle along the sidewalk, picking up a wind current and taking to the air just as suddenly as he descended.

I let out a breath I had been holding in and feel a hand grab the back of my parka.

"Kid, you okay?"

The person helps me to my feet, and I am about to respond that I am fine when I see that it's Mr. Popadokalus. The words don't come out and I'm left staring at the veteran, numb.

"Kiddo, you've got to be more careful," he says as he dusts flecks of dirt from the front of my coat.

I want to tell him about the Chinese card players and human resilience, but I can't find the words. "Yeah," is all I mumble.

Then I ask him why he isn't at work.

"High winds this morning," he says, pointing to the sky as if the currents of air were visibly there rolling about overhead like a van Gogh painting. "Better to play it safe. On days like this, there's only one person who comes in before noon, and I think we both know who that is," Popadokalus says with a grin.

I nod.

Crowley's a bastard, is all I can think.

***

In the beginning, there was Jan... Or at least that's the way most people tell it.

Dutch political spokesman and EU finance minister Jan Huitzja watched his career take a sharp nosedive as the financial crisis of the aughts unfolded. At some point during his transformation from political trailblazer to persona non grata, he developed a taste for pastries. He would inhale three warm croissants for breakfast, making sure to lick the buttery residue from each of his plump fingers. With the paper-thin crumbs of the croissants still clinging to his beard, he commenced nibbling on pain au chocolate accompanied by three espressos. After lunch, a platter of cream puffs, Napoléons drizzled with caramel, and cinnamon beaded Apfeltaschen usually followed. At each interval of the day, Jan's office became a veritable bakery with plates of jelly-filled cakes, fruit-stuffed strudel, and small pies oozing cream. To watch him cram these goodies into his mouth was sickening. The licking of the fingers that followed was almost ceremonial.

Gorging on baked goods took its effect as the muscular physique of youth melted into the flabby contours of middle age. Jan certainly had a paunch, and one might expect it was filled with cream like so many of the pastries he devoured daily. He still possessed his thundering laugh, although lately, to everyone's surprise, it had been subsiding into a soft and muffled snicker. One time, while delivering a speech at the European Monetary Forum in Zurich, he had even lapsed into a series of warm giggles after telling a joke. The following day, the communist paper *L'Humanité* ran a cartoon satirizing the event in which Jan, depicted as the Pillsbury Doughboy, addressed a drowsy audience of wolves in pinstripe suits. While he brushed off the cartoon, it did serve to highlight an evident truth: at the age of forty-nine, Jan, who in college had been described as athletic and well-built, resembled a bloated cartoon character. In his late thirties, he had discovered a sweet tooth that he had not been conscious of before. His stomach suddenly began rumbling, his mouth watering like one of Pavlov's dogs. There was a *need* to be filled, and somehow baked goods satisfied this need.

On the day news of his dismissal from the finance ministry arrived, Jan was sitting at his desk in the office he rented off Rue Wiertz. He had recently had an indentation cut in the desktop to accommodate his protruding gut, giving observers the impression that he was somehow surrounded by the piece of furniture rather than sitting in front of it. After reading the official memo requesting that he clean out his office in the finance ministry, Jan slowly rose and was in the process of calling for his secretary when he suddenly stopped dead in his tracks—or rather, *something* stopped him. His mammoth form no longer fit through the door, and it was there, wedged in the doorframe for a good hour as he contemplated this turn of events, that Jan received his first epiphany. It came in one simple word: *mass.*

This monosyllabic uttering would be expanded upon in later writings detailing the inevitability of human desire and need, the ways in which the accretion of mass supplanted these needs, and the means through which the conquest of space—and by this Jan meant one's actual physical presence—had now become the single human telos. Jan's writings were abstract and philosophical, but he employed various acolytes adept at translating his teachings into layman's terms. Their slogans were simple and direct: *Does the world make you feel small? Get Big!* and *Our power is in our size!* The religious-minded were urged to *Celebrate the Holy Mass!* These catchphrases summarized a new and complex human philosophy, a "paradigm," as Jan liked to call it, measurable in sheer size and girth. They said it was a revolt against modelesque fashion, classical beauty, and contemporary advertising culture—a mantra for the plus-size woman, the all-you-can-eat-buffet aficionados, and the morbidly obese doggedly patronized by public health officials and medical experts. Within four years, it was evident that a sea of change was in the making as eating competitions were deemed *en vogue*, as "tipping the scale" became a euphemism for cool and as porcine physiques increasingly replaced slim, toned bodies in Hollywood blockbusters.

I was a small child the night Jan Huitzja appeared on international television and gave his famous Big Idea interview. I remember sitting on the living room floor running a toy fire truck back and forth over the carpet and receiving static shocks from the friction. My father was slumped on the couch, sipping a beer and watching *60 Minutes*. Huitzja—now an imposing 357 pounds—sat across from Charlie Rose, a lopsided grin on his face as he repeatedly peeled the wrappers from Snickers bars and gnawed off big chunks of nougat and peanut.

"Do you see yourself as leading a movement?" Rose was asking him.

"No," Huitzja said in between lip-smacking bites, "it's a quiet revolution. Martin Luther King had a dream, and I have the big idea that I want to share."

"And what is this big idea?" Rose plied.

"No," Huitzja replied, "you misunderstand. It's not *a* big idea. It's *the* big idea."

I recall looking up at my father, his face washed in the pale glow of the television. The Mass Electorate Party, the waif identification cards, and the coup were still three years away at this point, but I believe that on that night, I saw an expression of unease creep across his face, a portent of dread perhaps, or simply revulsion for the likes of a three-hundred-plus-pound prima donna like Jan Huitzja.

***

The doors slide open with a pneumatic hiss, and we enter. As expected, Crowley is the only one on the floor going through the ritual of taking inventory. He lays down his pad and pencil and puts his hands on his hips, affecting a managerial pose.

"Finally decided to show up for work? *Sooooo* thoughtful... You think inventory gets done by itself?"

I could remind him that nobody is interested in buying electrical goods anymore and that the trickle of customers we did have has dried up. However, there is little point. I let him play manager and walk with my head lowered as I gather my work shirt from my locker in the employee lounge. Nobody really comes to work anymore because they have to. They do it because it feels normal. I am as guilty of this as anyone else.

In the back, I find Brubaker shoveling empty boxes into his locker. His lips are smeared with chocolate glaze. Brubaker attempts to accrete mass by ingesting large quantities of baked goods every chance he gets. Unfortunately, it will only lead to the early onset of diabetes. Like me, Brubaker has been cursed with a killer metabolism. We simply can't accrete and so suffer the brand of irreformable.

I wish I had inherited my father's genes. When the Mass Electorate Party assumed power, my father was deemed reformable. He was ordered to report to one of the farms set up in the west where mass is accreted, and new citizens made. I haven't seen him since. I constantly keep my hopes up, though, and wonder if I will one day encounter him swooping down from the sky with extended arms. I know that if all went well out west, he would come back to find me. Of this, I have little doubt.

I am not certain of my mother's genetic makeup. I can only assume my metabolic imperfections come from her side. She left my father when she fell in love with a radio DJ from Detroit. It was something about his voice, apparently. Before leaving the two of us, she sat me down and tried to explain everything as best she could. When I asked why she had to go, she gave me an honest reply, which I can appreciate now. "Sweetie, your father is a milquetoast, and I was not raised to be married to a milquetoast," I remember this explanation because, at the time, I didn't know what a milquetoast was. Later, I looked it up in the dictionary and agreed it seemed a fair assessment of my father.

The real reason I want to accrete mass, though, is because Darcy can. Last summer, we were pedaling bikes along the downtown thoroughfares when I had to stop and remove my parka. She continued pedaling furiously down the street, never pausing or looking back. I loosened my coat as quickly as I could, hopped on my bike, and doubled my pace. My calves ached by the time I finally caught up and found her leaning against her bike, beaming a triumphant look.

"What gives?" I yelled, panting.

"I was wondering how long it would take you," she said coolly, deliberately checking her wristwatch.

"Didn't know we were racing."

"Didn't know *you* were that slow," she said with a roguish smile.

Things continued like this for a few weeks. Our bike rides together became competitions of speed and endurance. She dusted me every time, darting down streets and avenues like it was the Tour de France. I would always find her two or three miles ahead, shirt drenched and hair matted with sweat. One day, I was lingering around the train depot when I spotted a stash of old comic books in a box on the curb. I got excited when I saw a few of them were dog-eared issues of *Nancy Drew, Girl Detective*, Darcy's absolute favorite. When I arrived at her house to tell her the news, she was in the middle of an aerobic workout.

"Look at this!" I boasted, fanning out the glossy covers on the floor.

"Not now!" she huffed. "I'm busy."

"I thought..."

"Just go read them over there," she nodded, continuing with her oblique twists. "I'm almost finished."

The next night we were sitting on her roof watching Joanie play in the yard below. I was feeling hurt, although I didn't say as much. Without a word, Darcy began to cry. I started to ask what was wrong but checked myself. Instead, I slid my arm around her shoulder to comfort her. I had seen this in a movie once and thought it was the kind of thing a grownup might do in this situation.

"She's planning on building a feeding tray," she said with a weak laugh. "She thinks she can attract them, like pets."

"Who?"

She just shook her head, and I understood that this was not the reason for her tears.

"I'm up," she finally said.

"What?"

"Three pounds."

Those words rang like a death knell in my ears. I suddenly understood but tried to hide my distress. We didn't say anything after that for a long time. Dusk was descending. A thin layer of purple clouds hugged the horizon. I watched Joanie playing in the dirt below as the last glints of daylight faded and streaked the yard with crimson. *Why not her?* I remember thinking.

***

The second phase of the revolution began in Poughkeepsie, New York. It was there that a young engineer named Corey Sand invented poly-alloy knit fabric, a synthetic material composed of small metallic fibers capable of withstanding high-speed gradient winds. Sand was fond of sailing on Martha's Vineyard and designed the fabric to sail through category three hurricanes. That summer, he braved Hurricane Hector in a trial run and lived to tell of his feat. There is a now-famous picture of him standing in front of his storm-battered boat, *The Majestic*, defiantly holding up his metallic sail. The dock behind him is bathed in the golden light of late afternoon, evocative of the magnificent Indian summers that once drew tourists to the Martha's Vineyard area.

At first, the big ones posed little threat. They were sluggish and lethargic, often more amusing than menacing. The first attempt to conquer the mobility problem was a comic failure. High-powered Segways were manufactured with triple-reinforced wheels to sustain the driver's extreme weight. They looked like miniature tanks as they trundled along the streets and had a nasty habit of tipping over when exceeding speeds of more than five miles per hour. You would be walking along and find one turned on its side, the driver laying supine on the pavement or rolling about in a futile effort to get upright. Pedestrians gathered around, laughing and poking them with sticks. It's hard to admit now, but the Big Idea felt more like an elaborate joke in the early days.

Yet Huitzja and his inner circle were relentless. They purchased Sand's patent for the poly-alloy knit fabric and were mass-producing reams of it within months. The transition occurred so quickly. Everyone was caught off guard as the conquest of space was followed by the conquest of the air. It did not take a genius to realize a material capable of withstanding category three winds could get the big ones airborne. Almost overnight, they acquired speed and maneuverability; they could suddenly mobilize swiftly and with precision.

I remember the feeling that crept over me when I saw two of them pinning down a waif in the street. They were perched like bizarre predatory birds with bulging guts and hulking limbs.

"Whopper him!" one said to the other with an evil grin.

The waif shrieked.

From my hiding place, I watched as one of the big ones spread his arms wide and tipped his massive body forward, collapsing onto his screaming victim. The cry was cut short, followed by a nauseating squelching sound and demonic chortling. I had watched a man be compressed into nothing but a smear on the cement.

Later, when I recounted this story to Crowley, he gnawed at his lower lip and shook his head.

"Careful," he told me. "You don't always recover all the way from something like *that*."

At the time, I didn't comprehend what he meant, figuring he was referring to the victim who had been turned into human purée. Of course, you don't recover from that, I thought. You're dead! However, on mornings when I wake up washed in a cold sweat, I understood what Crowley was telling me. You don't recover fully. Not from that.

***

From the roof, we watch them swarm into the yard. They flash by in a rapacious blur of motion, whizzing from the sky to the ground and back. Joanie points at the gyre swirling in the cloudless afternoon sky. She is ecstatic.

"They're coming! They're coming!" she whispers with delight.

Joanie has constructed a large trough from plywood board running the expanse of the yard. For her age, she is quite ingenious. The stench of the slop draws them from the sky. On the first day, the trough attracted a mere two visitors. By the end of the week, there were at least twenty. Now it is a feeding frenzy. They formicate and crawl over one another like feasting larvae, their sickening grunts and smacking of lips filling the air.

Each afternoon, we come to watch. Joanie takes particular pleasure in the daily gorging, relishing in the fact that she can summon them. Darcy's concern is evident. She can't understand her little sister's fascination with these creatures. We pass furtive looks between ourselves in silence, keeping low to avoid being sighted. I don't know why it is at these times—when it is impossible to speak—I want to tell her of my concerns and fears.

My eyes drift across the seething mass below. I wonder if one of them might be my father returned from the west. He would surely come back to our old neighborhood in search of me. Each day, I find myself scanning the crowds of rotund bodies and clattering metallic wings that fill the yard looking for a familiar face, something recognizable and human.

Darcy places a hand on my shoulder. "Let's go," she says.

"But they're not done!" Joanie pules.

"But I am," she replies sternly, nudging me and leaving Joanie on the roof.

***

On the West Side, the Great Waif Rebellion remnants can still be spotted by a discerning eye: charred buildings, an overturned car rusting in the August sun, a ransacked Piggly Wiggly with a vandalized picture of the store mascot hanging in the grime-streaked display window. Darcy stares at the cartoon image of the smiling pig and traces a finger over the streaks of old spray paint.

"History," she mumbles.

"What?"

"Pieces of history. Or what passes for it now anyway."

"What? A cartoon pig?"

She nods silently.

The afternoon is still. There are more people about than usual. The weather report that morning on the radio warned of approaching high winds from the north later in the evening. Everyone walks along the streets furtively, like birds afraid of their own shadows.

I am suddenly uncertain why Darcy wanted to come here. We had heard rumors that the minimart on the corner of Ash and Grove was unloading cheap bottled water, but I can see that this has nothing to do with water or supplies. She is trying to connect with this place somehow but is finding it extremely difficult. Crowley has given me various accounts of the events that took place during the GWR, some of which seem contradictory, I might add. Yet here, I find it hard to connect these stories with the actual streets and rundown buildings I see, the alleys dotted with old plastic bags and crumpled wrappers. They just look like ordinary streets.

"History," Darcy is still mumbling under her breath.

On the ground, I watch as an old, balled-up hamburger wrapper begins to stir slightly in an oncoming breeze. Despite the afternoon humidity and sun, I pull my parka hood lower over my eyes.

"Maybe we should head back," I say.

Darcy remains silent, her eyes fixed on the cartoon pig.

I contemplate the balled-up wrapper dancing along the pavement like an omen prophesizing impending doom, and I shudder.

***

We inhabit a world of diminishing returns.

I once saw this phrase written on a wall. I was never sure what it meant, but it always felt like there was some poetic truth to it that I couldn't quite grasp. Mainly, I liked the sound of it. Sometimes if people ask my opinion on a certain topic like politics or store policies, I will shrug and repeat it. It has a sophisticated and wise ring to it.

On the day Darcy left, Crowley asked how I was holding up, and I simply repeated the phrase.

"What is *that* supposed to mean?" he asked, eyeing me oddly.

I told him I didn't know, and we left it at that.

Since then, he has tended to lay off me whenever we work the floor. He is less officious and reluctant to remind me of the tasks that need to get done. Sometimes, he catches me in the rec room, reading Darcy's letters to me. The old Crowley would have thrown a fit and pointed out that I am still on the clock, but he passes without a word these days. Mr. Popadokalus says he feels sorry for me, although I find it difficult to believe that Crowley could possess such a broad emotional range.

On the days I receive Darcy's letters, I read them three or four times. Life out west does not seem horrible from her accounts. She tells me about the school she attends, the new friends she is meeting, and her enrollment in preliminary aviation courses. The handwriting on the letters has gradually changed over the months. Her swirling Os and loopy Ls have flattened out and become more oblate. Her girly penmanship now looks clunky and less defined. Sometimes when I think about this, I get sad. It instantiates the time and distance that has been put between us, as though with each letter I receive, the Darcy I knew is progressively diminished.

Mr. Popadokalus can tell whenever I receive one of her letters, and he will usually put a hand on my shoulder or pat me on the back. "It gets better, kid," he tells me with a calm smile.

"I know," I tell him.

We walk over to Darcy's old house when our shift lets out. Nobody lives there now, but you can access the roof by the fire escape that runs along the side of the building. We climb up and sit there with our legs dangling over the ledge, looking down at the yard. The big ones soar around us, diving from the sky to Joanie's trough below, where a sea of bodies and gliders collide and tussle. Neither of us says much because there is nothing to say. We just sit there and watch the dusk quietly descend on the city. I no longer look among the horde for familiar faces. In a world of diminishing returns, nothing comes back.

I glance over and see Mr. Popadokalus staring into the welling evening shadows below, his face expressionless like it always is at these moments. He just sits and gazes, oblivious to the groveling that emanates from the yard. I sometimes wonder if he is lost in an old memory, or concentrating intently on the multitude beneath us. *Either way, they call him the veteran*, I think to myself. And in that instant, I can see it.

Here Feel We *the* Childing Autumn

Whenever I travel to Europe, my itinerary always includes a brief stop in Cologne to visit Kurt and Yvonne Hoffmann. The couple embodies the old-world charm and sophistication that I have always loved about Europe, and yet I would hardly consider them old-fashioned. They are savvy and oddly Americanized in their tastes and outlooks. I met Kurt and Yvonne when I was still a graduate student completing a year-long program of study at a German university. They are roughly the same age as my parents and, having no children of their own, they have come to consider me as something akin to a surrogate son. They have always taken an interest in my studies and work, are fond of ensuring I am well-fed during my stays in Cologne, and will never forget to send me a postcard when they go on vacation. Over the years, I have come to think of them as my European parents.

Last winter, I paid my customary visit to the Hoffmanns following a research trip in Denmark. I had been working incessantly for a month in a private archive located on the Danish coast. The town I stayed in was unremarkable and gloomy; the archive itself was rundown and hopelessly disorganized. Under the circumstances, work proceeded at an excruciatingly slow pace. The hospitality I received upon arriving in Cologne was welcome. On the last night of my stay, Kurt and Yvonne threw a dinner party in my honor. After the meal, a few couples remained sitting around the table conversing about politics or literature and sipping sweet dessert liquors. At one point, Yvonne mentioned I was finishing up a research trip. This naturally provoked questions from the other guests regarding the subject of my current study.

"I'm researching a scream," I told them.

The room fell silent, and a strange half-smile appeared on Kurt's lips. He was uncertain whether or not I was making a joke.

"You're researching *a scream?*" one of the guests asked, thinking that she had misunderstood my English.

I nodded.

It is not easy describing what I have come to think of as "my work." I have learned to anticipate the puzzled looks and blank stares I receive when I tell people that for the past five years, I have been attempting to track down a scream.

***

I discovered Helmut Leike when a colleague accidentally left a book in my office one afternoon. Pure curiosity prompted me to begin flipping through the leather-bound tome containing Leike's unedited letters. Although a contemporary of Nietzsche and Schopenhauer, Leike has been completely forgotten by current scholars. There exists no biography on the obscure nineteenth-century German philosopher, and the books he published during his lifetime are out of print today. The exact date of his death is a matter of speculation, although it is certain that he died in Skøvgaard, the small town on the craggy Danish coast where I would spend a month examining private papers and old folios in virtual solitude. It is difficult to see Leike's life as anything but tragic. Leike himself frequently remarked on the "chronic melancholy" that plagued him throughout his years in Skøvgaard where he taught at a small Lutheran university. In 1878, his wife, Eliza, took her own life, leaving him to raise two daughters on his own. The eldest, Augusta, died of consumption in 1893, and her sister was eventually confined to a mental hospital sometime around the turn of the century. Leike's letters from this period possess an almost Shakespearian quality at times in their ability to convey the interplay of human emotion and cosmic misfortune.

As I thumbed through the book, I came upon the passage of 19

August 1892:

When I entered the house, it was dark. I could hear Augusta having a coughing fit in the room upstairs. After administering my laudanum, I retired to the parlor and sat in the unlit room watching the shadows grow heavy and pregnant. My body felt heavy, my thoughts neither here nor there. The darkness of the room was like an endless abyss. I knew now what true absence and emptiness were. The sounds of the leaves outside in the wind, the ticking of a clock in my study, the spastic coughs coming from upstairs, the sound of a heart beating in a void. I sat motionless for a while drifting in and out of sleep. My dreams became written on the darkness. I saw horrid and perverse things emerge out of nothing and return to nothing. I hope that I never see such things again, for they were things that I could not comprehend. And then I heard a scream coming across the darkness, at first muffled and sounding like the drone of a fly but eventually amplified and piercing. Something told me that this scream was coming from a very great distance, echoing across space but also time, and I knew that somebody somewhere was having the very same dream that I was and that their world was as ripe with agony and pain as mine. It was this agony that was momentarily bringing us together, uniting us in some common fear and understanding. My body shuddered and the scream slowly dissipated, returning to the depths from whence it came. I was sitting in the parlor again. Upstairs I heard the convulsive coughing and gagging of a woman dying in a room by herself, of a child crying out in anguish.

At the time, I remember noting Leike's bizarre poetic diction and hallucinogenic imagery, but little else. The next day, I politely returned the book to my colleague and focused my attention once again on my own work relating to Renaissance verse and fifteenth-century Flemish patronage networks.

It is not untypical to encounter a word for the first time only to come across it repeatedly in multiple contexts shortly after learning its meaning. Whenever this occurs—and it occurs quite frequently—I am left with the knowledge that the particular word in question was there all along, waiting for me to make proper note of it and familiarize myself with its many uses and connotations. Only once we truly choose to recognize something can we understand just how common and omnipresent it really is. To some extent, this is how I have come to understand the scream.

Two months after reading Leike's letters, I was collating notes on Geoffrey Clyve's *Carmina et Recordatus*, a little-known book of verse commissioned by an influential Elizabethan courtier in the late sixteenth century. In the sonnet "Here Feel We the Childing Autumn," Clyve writes:

> *I hath ne'er forgotten that daemonic dream*
> *Which dost fore're plague my mind*
> *Whenst hark, there comes a mournful scream*
> *That art not fix'd i' place nor tyme*

In a similar fashion, the twentieth-century German essayist W. G. Sebald recorded waking from a strange dream while spending the night in a Northumbrian village during a trip taken in the winter of 1968. "An implacable echo rebounded across my waking thoughts," he scribbled in his notebook. "It was like the wail of some banshee, nightmarish and old, as though emanating from the primeval soil of this ancient land." The French romantic poet and novelist Gérard de Nerval is reputed to have disclosed to friends that his dreams had become haunted by the "ghostly shrieks of the past" a month before committing suicide in 1855.

Although spanning a half-millennium, these references to screams exhibit evident parallels in their relation to a state of dreaming, references to time, and the mention of a noise traveling *across* as opposed to *through* or *on* the air. These citations are only a small sample of an expansive body of testimonials, descriptions, and personal narratives recounting analogous experiences: patients in mental wards who have complained of nightmares in which they are paralyzed by the sound of screaming; an eighteenth-century Prussian official in Silesia who documented numerous reports of an "unearthly scream" that resonated through towns in the region one night in the spring of 1782 before mysteriously ceasing without rhyme or reason; the repetitive and nearly-obsessive imagery of a screaming mouth found in the post-war paintings of the artist Francis Bacon. "It would be no exaggeration," claims Bacon's biographer, Michael Peppiatt, "to say that if one could really explain the origins and implications of this scream, one would be far closer to understanding the whole art of Francis Bacon." Also noteworthy is Thomas Pynchon's cult novel *Gravity's Rainbow*, which, as one graduate student keenly informed me while I was carrying out my research, opens with the memorable lines: "A screaming comes across the sky. It has happened before, but there is nothing to compare it to now."

Scholars trained in the intricacies of exegesis and comparative textual analysis will tell you that there are rarely coincidences when it comes to syntactical replication across documents. One school of thought argues that textual repetitions stem from a shared cultural vocabulary central to the Western literary tradition. When we express ideas or convey personal experiences, we are forced to translate them into language. This process of converting raw experience into words is conditioned by a finite range of signs, symbols, and tropes particular to a specific culture, entailing that the ways in which we communicate any experience are predetermined in large part by the linguistic conventions that structure our thoughts. In other words, similarities found across multiple texts are not communicating identical experiences; they are describing different experiences filtered through a common mode of speech. Contrary to the cultural vocabulary thesis, a second line of thinking emphasizes the important role mimesis plays in the production of texts. According to this hypothesis, no text can be considered original or authentic. An author, whether consciously or not, is perpetually engaged in a referential game in which they mimic other works and passages, thereby accounting for unexplained similarities through a long and itinerant chain of imitative acts.

Neither of these explanations, however, satisfactorily explains the uncanny parallels linking Clyve with Leike and Sebald across five centuries. The references were too identical, too specific in their shared details. Moreover, upon further investigation, I discovered that the date of Leike's letter was not insignificant. In the fall, I was invited to speak at an academic symposium in Philadelphia. Afterward, I met an old friend of mine for dinner. Over the course of our meal, I casually mentioned the puzzle I had begun working on and even showed her a photocopy of Leike's letter which I happened to be carrying with me at the time. She pointed to the date at the top of the page. "I'm not certain," she remarked, tapping the slip of paper with her index finger, "but I think that was the same year that Munch began working on his series *Der Schrei der Natur.*" In actuality, Edvard Munch produced his first painting in the series a year later, in 1893. However, the first mention of *Der Schrei der Natur* dates from a diary entry made in January 1892, seven months before Leike recorded hearing the scream. As Munch recalled:

One evening I was walking along a path, the city was on one side and the fjord below. I felt tired and sick. I stopped and looked out over the fjord— the sun was setting, and the clouds were stained a blood red. I sensed a scream passing through nature; it seemed to me that I heard the scream. I painted this picture, painted the clouds as actual blood. The color shrieked. This became The Scream.

Successive generations of art historians have attempted to authenticate or refute Munch's account. Some have suggested that the story is a fabrication and the inspiration for the painting came after the artist glimpsed a Peruvian mummy displayed in one of the exhibition halls of the 1889 World's Fair staged in Paris. Yet if Leike's letter is brought into the equation, the details would seem to favor Munch's account.

Even more intriguing is the fact that Munch's series remains the best-known body of work in a broader phenomenon occurring among Danish and Scandinavian artists during the last decade of the nineteenth century. Berit Suiffjan, former curatorial assistant at the Nasjonalgalleriet and a fellow of the University of Oslo, is an expert on Munch and the modernist movement in Scandinavia.

At first glance, it would be difficult to peg him as an art historian of merit. Youthful, well-groomed, and always stylishly dressed, Suiffjan looks more like a high-end market consultant or trendy magazine editor than an academic. Yet his expansive knowledge of modern art and history comes out in conversation as he effortlessly moves from one subject to the next, discussing Munch, Manet, and the aesthetics of symbolism while commanding the rapt attention of his listener. Meeting over coffee in Oslo, I could immediately tell that he is without a doubt an excellent lecturer, a factor that perhaps explains the high enrollment levels in the courses he teaches every semester at the university.

For the past three years, Suiffjan has been examining stylistic forms in Scandinavian modernism and has spent a great deal of time devoting his analysis to the image of the scream popularized by Munch. While working at the Nasjonalgalleriet, he discovered a series of works by lesser-known Danish and Norwegian artists that bore a striking resemblance to Munch. "At first," he told me as he sipped at a steaming latté, "I thought they were imitations by painters and illustrators who had never quite managed to make a name for themselves. Ezra Pound once remarked that good artists copy and great artists steal. It seemed to me a case of the former rather than the latter." After studying the pieces for some time, however, and comparing them with the artists' personal correspondences and fragmentary notes, Suiffjan found that some of the works predated Munch's initial diary entry of 1892, sometimes by years. "At first, I thought I must be incorrect or looking at the problem wrong," he said with a weak smile. "The only other explanation was that Munch has actually been the imitator, a conjecture that would have really caused a stir in the art world." As it turned out, neither of these hypotheses proved accurate, and the entire question of who copied who has remained a constant enigma that Suiffjan has never been able to explain.

During my stay in Oslo, he showed me the pieces in the Nasjonalgalleriet's collection. As promised, the artists were obscure men barely recognized in their own day and to whom posterity has hardly been any kinder. Names like Albin Jaspaar, Konrad

Sjørner, and Carl Reider will not be found in scholarly monographs, let alone in the more standard art history texts books published by academic presses.

Occasionally, a reference to one of these artists will appear in an unpublished dissertation, and only then in the footnotes. As I looked over the numerous canvases and prints, I had the impression of receiving a privileged view into a forgotten world known only to Suiffjan and a select handful of specialists. Although stylistically different, a significant number of the works were redolent of Munch's masterpiece in their depictions of a single person in the act of screaming. The earliest of the works, a lithograph by a book illustrator named Fritjof Blegen, dated from 1885 and showed a man covering his ears, his eyes shut tight and mouth forming a rictus of agony. The stylistic renderings of the motif evolved over the years through the body of work, shifting from romanticism to the more abstract forms of expressionism fashionable by the early twentieth century. Some of the later pieces were clearly inspired by Munch while others only possessed a thematic similarity at best, but it was hard to ignore that there did appear to be a general theme and aesthetic at play spanning a period of over forty years.

Konrad Sjørner, "Impression of a Dream" (1898). Nasjonalgalleriett, Oslo.

Albin Jaspaar, detail from "The Screaming Man" (1887). Nasjonalgalleriett, Oslo.

One of the later pieces in the collection by the Danish artist Constantin Ingermann entitled *Efter Hyl (After the Howl)* particularly caught my attention. In the corner of the canvas was the date 1923 and under this, Skøvgaard. Further research conducted after I departed Oslo revealed that Ingermann had been a faculty member in the art department at the local university in Skøvgaard, the very same university where Helmut Leike had taught three decades earlier. During the early 1920s, the artist had resided at the Keyeraad House located on the edge of the town. The house is a picturesque home constructed in high Edwardian style that sits on a rocky precipice overlooking the North Sea. Over the years, the residence has amassed a long list of notable occupants, including the dramatist Holger Drachmann, the German novelist Alfred Döblin, and various members of the British royal family. Today it is an historic landmark of Skøvgaard with guided tours offered on weekday afternoons and twice on the weekends. Getting caught up in the details of the illustrious and historically significant residents who, for one reason or another, were attracted to the Keyeraad House over the past two centuries, it is easy to neglect the more unremarkable inhabitants who also passed their time and lived out their daily lives within its walls. One of these lives would be Helmut Leike's; Leike occupied the house from the mid-1870s until 1896 when he retired from academic life. It was in the famed Keyeraad House that his wife had taken her own life, that his daughter had become ill with consumption, and that he had recorded hearing the scream.

More unexplained repetitions, but repetitions rooted in geography and the particularities of place just as much as across space and time.

***

What is a scream? This is a question I have come back to again and again as I've carried out my work on the subject. It is certainly an emotional response, one intended to call attention to whoever is doing the screaming. Yet screaming is associated with a wide range of emotions. We scream when we are happy or excited, and commonly a scream can convey an expression of the utmost joy. Conversely, it also expresses danger, pain and fright—the anxiety of modern life that Munch was attempting to portray in his iconic image. From a more banal perspective, the so-called "Wilhelm scream" coined in the 1950s became the universally recognizable sound bit used in movies and television to communicate peril and imminent threat to audiences worldwide. Screaming also possesses a musical connotation, from wails that accompany tribal rhythms to the gritty vocals of heavy metal and hardcore rock bands. As an action in itself, it lacks a specific context or conceptual framework despite its many uses and depictions across cultures.

At a basic level, a scream is simply a noise, or more specifically, a sound. Like any other sound, it is generated by waves moving through a medium which cause variations in air pressure, a phenomenon typically represented in the form of a sine wave:

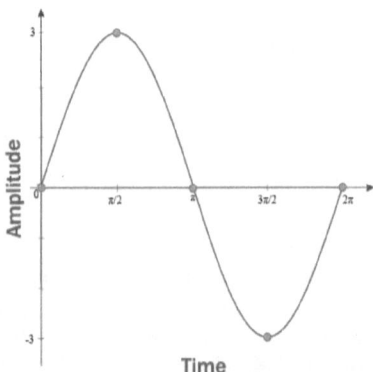

Sound is always moving and convulsing, and therefore it is conditioned by time as well as movement. Pitch—or the tone of a sound— is dependent on the frequency of the wave across time, with greater frequency usually producing a higher pitch. The basic formula for obtaining a sine wave is derived from the equation

$$f = \frac{1}{T}$$

in which f represents the wave frequency and T signifies time. Without belaboring the point, the important thing to recognize is the interdependency of sound and time. Without time we cannot conceptualize sound.

Dorian Tucker, a pioneer in hyper-physics at the University of California in Berkeley, has been studying sound synthesis and temporality for over a decade. His experiments have attempted to broaden our knowledge of ultrasonic wave forms and their movements through space-time. NASA briefly took an interest in his work when they were probing the possibilities of long-range radio communication across astronomical distances. The project was sidelined as advancements in laser technologies came to replace interest in radio wave transmission. Since then, Tucker has expanded the scope of his theories to assess the potential of sound to cross temporalities. "It's like time travel, but without the sci-fi stigma," he tells me as we step into his modest lab in Berkeley. "The idea behind time travel is that physical matter can somehow be broken down into photons and cross the temporal dimension. That's appealing to people. It entices their imagination. But if I told you that I was going to send a bit of sound back in time, you would probably just shrug. It just doesn't have the same appeal." Regardless, Tucker's work is attempting to construct a theory of sound-time that posits just such a conclusion: that sine waves can, indeed, cut across time as we know it. His studies have consisted of simulating sonic booms in a controlled environment that create large amounts of "sound energy." His hope is that the sonic brisance of these blasts might disrupt the relationship between sound and time as it is conventionally understood by increasing air pressure and generating sine waves that will actually travel faster than the speed of sound.

As Tucker explained the technicalities of his experiments and artfully broke them down into laymen's terms, I asked him whether he thought a human scream could be transmitted across time in the same way he hoped his sonic booms would. "Human vociferation just doesn't have that capacity," he replied, adding with a grin, "It would have to be one hell of a scream you're talking about."

Efforts to map human iteration onto time are by no means new. In 1863, the Spanish composer and amateur scientist Bartolomé Zubiri published an article speculating on the possibility of recording sound and speech by "writing on the air." In Zubiri's opinion, air was a medium not only through which sound traveled but upon which sound could actually be mapped and notated. Although his theory of etherography never held up under investigation, it did inspire a French piano maker named Émile Moreaux to begin experimenting with the effects of echoes in the late 1870s. Moreaux constructed a device with tapering metal bells used to catch and channel sound. The bases of these bells were outfitted with small rotating discs powered by a pneumatic pump that regulated air pressure and sustained sound waves as they were transported in a circular loop between bells. It was a primitive echo chamber of sorts that could, according to the patent Moreaux filed in 1879, theoretically prolong sounds ad infinitum. This claim was grossly overexaggerated, however, and Moreaux's *Répéteur* soon failed.

At the turn of the century, Barney Gyles Lewis, a London orchestral arranger and stage performer, advertised the use of Moreaux's device in one of his musical performances. For two weeks, his Symphonic Echotorium drew large crowds who came to witness an entire symphony performed without the participation of a single musician. According to the program drafted by Lewis, the music was initially played by an orchestra and captured by the *Répéteur*, resulting in a faithful reproduction of the performance note-for-note that repeated on a continuous loop of sustained echoes. Audiences packed the house night after night to experience the Symphonic Echotorium until the spectacle was revealed as a fraud. Lewis actually had an orchestra secreted away under the stage playing the music.

A poster advertising the Symphonic Echotorium in 1901.
British Library Collections.

Reoccurring sonic phenomena across time have equally been a subject dealt with extensively in theories on the paranormal. "Happenings" or "occurrences" (as they are known in the parlance of paranormalists) are frequently accompanied by otherworldly voices and sounds in most documented cases. In the opinion of Ramsey Keiffer, an expert on spiritualism and the occult, recurrence lies at the heart of what the general public commonly considers a "haunting." In his book *The Specter and Historical Time*, Keiffer dedicates an entire chapter to the predominant role that sound plays in such experiences, indicating that disembodied voices, creaking furniture, and ghostly footsteps constitute the primary means through which the traumas of the past momentarily press themselves onto the present. As Keiffer sees it, we perpetually exist in two types of time. There is the time that actively engages us on a daily basis—what he deems "the realm of individual temporalities"—and then there is historical time, "the realm of shared temporalities." The crux of his argument is that at certain moments and in certain locations, this shared historical time possesses a psychic energy that is capable of manifesting itself over and over again like a repetitive loop in sound and, less frequently, image. We do not exist in a world of ghosts who menace the living, in Keiffer's estimation; rather, we inhabit a world of palimpsestic times that sometimes cross and interfere with one another like two television signals colliding.

It is easy to write off Keiffer's theories as notional and unoriginal, but Leike's account of hearing the scream does exhibit many of the patent characteristics associated with paranormal activity noted in Keiffer's study. Leike himself interprets the dream as a reoccurrence, or more specifically as a multi-occurrent phenomenon—"I knew that somebody somewhere was having the very same dream that I was." His "somewhere" is not rooted in time, for as Lieke notes the scream he hears appears to echo across space *and* time, allowing for the possibility of a "somebody" existing in a past or future time other than his own. It is the experience of "agony" (the precise word used by Leike is *Seelenangst*) that is momentarily uniting those who hear the scream and, according to Keiffer, it is exactly this type of emotional resonance across time that enables paranormal occurrences. Given Leike's outlook and academic background, it is not a stretch of the imagination to believe that he may have interpreted this scream as the expression of a universal *Weltschmertz* that humanity has endured across the ages. Under this reading, Leike's dream is experienced as an inverted Ode to Joy, an *Ode an der Kummer*, or "Ode to Sorrow." Whereas Schiller's song of *Freude* (joy) possesses the "magic power to reunite" what is divided, Leike's scream of *Seelenangst* likewise unites man, only this unity is established through the recognition of a shared pain and suffering rather than the joy of human fraternity.

Various cultural anthropologists have also shown a keen interest in the paranormal and the persistence of ghost stories across societies. Dunya Jansen, a professor of anthropology at the University of Amsterdam, has studied America's fascination with hauntings and folklore, arguing that ghost stories and accounts of paranormal activity oftentimes serve as a means of addressing unresolved social grievances and past injustices. "Many ghost stories in the United States are connected with haunted plantations or Native American burial grounds," she explains. "Ghost stories are a way of expressing cultural remorse for the violent atrocities that have marred America's historical experience and which are commonly omitted from the master narrative of America's national origins." The familiar sounds associated with paranormal activity are, in this context, linked to the tensions inherent within a given culture or society and are, therefore, symbolic rather than real. Less concerned with documented cases of paranormal activity than with the tradition of the ghost story, Jansen does nevertheless address the issue of reoccurring paranormal phenomenon briefly in her monograph by relating it to Hegel's theory of historical repetition. She claims that the idea of historical recurrence has been central to Western historiography, informing the works of Polybius, Petrarch, and Machiavelli to name a few. Yet Jansen is practical enough to resist a paranormal explanation in her study and aptly concludes with a quotation from Karl Marx. While events of world-historical significance may occur twice, "the first time they occur as tragedy and the second time as farce." In Jansen's final assessment, paranormal recurrence is the burlesque parody of tragedy, an act that seeks to transform historical trauma into folkloric Kitsch and tourist attractions.

In the late 1970s, an international research team composed primarily of British and American scientists conducted a series of atmospheric experiments using high-powered radio telescopes. Over the course of their studies, they detected a faint crackling noise reminiscent of the dead static you might hear over the airwaves at night. When they broke down and isolated the sounds they recorded, the team hypothesized that the crackling was the remnants of the initial Big Bang, "relic" light and radio waves originating from the moment of creation some 13 billion years ago. These and other findings have suggested that we need not turn to the realm of the paranormal when it comes to explaining sonic and visual recurrence in the abstract. We are constantly surrounded by sound and light waves accumulating through—or perhaps in spite of—history, linking the present with the oldest and most primordial of traumas. What *is* required is the proper medium or instrument to snag these errant transmissions reconnecting us with that distant past.

***

On a balmy afternoon in late April, I am standing by an open window and enjoying the spring breeze. I stare out at the flood of traffic creeping along Amsterdam Avenue, my eyes absentmindedly passing over the taxi cabs, loading trucks, and bustling pedestrians below, but my attention is elsewhere. From a vintage reel-to-reel tape player set up in the corner of the room comes the clacking of drums and the tinny sound of an unidentified string instrument. Then the resonant voice cuts back in over the music, warbling and stretching syllables as it floats just above the scratchy hiss of the tape. It is like nothing I have ever heard before. "Not something you can exactly tap your foot to," Seth Vickers says, flashing a grin.

Vickers is an associate professor and self-appointed archivist for the Department of Anthropology at Columbia University. He has the trademark stooped posture and appallingly mismatched wardrobe of a seasoned academic; his graying beard, thick-rimmed glasses, and suspenders give him an appearance that can only be described as avuncular. Earlier that afternoon, Vickers had led me into the basement of the Schermerhorn Extension which serves as the department's B archive facility, although "facility" is not quite the right word to describe it. The B archive is a dimly lit room overflowing with all varieties of antiquated machinery, for-gotten belongings, and curios. Stacked boxes line the walls, as-cending haphazardly to the ceiling; a pile of carousel slide projec-tors molders in a corner, accumulating dust; mason jars filled with yellowing formaldehyde sit forgotten on shelves, the specimens suspended in the fluid no longer recognizable. Vickers likes to re-fer to the B archive as anthropology's dead letter office, although it seems more like a neglected museum. After a half-hour of fish-ing through boxes and packing crates, we located the materials that brought me to New York: two dozen reels of tape recorded by the late James Sanford Payne. When I first contacted Vickers to inquire whether or not the department still had the recordings, he chuckled. "Sure, they're here," he informed me politely. "It's finding a machine to play the damn things on that'll be the prob-lem." As it turned out, Vickers happened to have a friend still in possession of an old Sonora reel-to-reel player, and so I took the train up to New York, acting on a hunch that archive B contained something I wanted or, perhaps by that point, even needed.

James Sanford Payne is one of those curious historical figures for anyone interested in the modern discipline of anthropology. He made a name for himself traveling through French Equatorial Africa in the 1930s. The field trip had been self-funded, and when-ever asked whether he was conducting research or taking up Afri-can exploration as a leisure activity, he would respond with an ex-pressionless face and reply mirthlessly: "I'm following André Gide's trail, naturally." He was fond of telling his colleagues that after having read *Travels in the Congo* he planned to take up a life as a travel writer. There has been some disagreement over whether or not the Princeton-educated scholar hailing from a prominent New England family ever seriously intended to imitate the scandalous French novelist, but in the end, it is clear that Payne decided not to pursue a literary career. Purchasing a German-manufactured Magnetophon, he left for Africa and spent the next twenty-two months recording the dialects and music of the indigenous populations in Chad and the Congo. His fieldwork among the Laari, Teke, and Toubous peoples was already well documented by the conclusion of his trip, thanks in part to the efforts of a certain well-placed French anthropologist willing to publicize his findings. Payne returned to the States a celebrity, the American Africanist of his generation.

In the following years, Payne attracted public notoriety as a spokesman for the anti-imperialist platform then gaining momentum in the country. At conferences he explained that his desire to record the local languages and traditional music of indigenous peoples was motivated by the demoralizing realization that "native Africa" was imperiled by colonialism. "We have a duty, a solemn obligation as humanists," Payne implored in one of his speeches, "to record these cultures and languages before they vanish completely, to leave a record for posterity and to preserve a society which European colonization will fatally condemn to historical oblivion in a short time." The scholarly community has long been divided on the sincerity of Payne's anti-colonial politics, and even at the time many of his colleagues accused him of exploiting the movement to promote his own work and garner funding.

Payne's status as a prominent scholar earned him a comfortable position at Columbia and a steady flow of institutional financing over the next decade. Yet this was not the James Sanford Payne that had piqued my interest. The Payne I sought to explore was older, less idealistic, and respectively more embittered compared to the trailblazing Africanist of the 1930s. By the late 1940s, the limelight surrounding Payne had dwindled considerably. His articles no longer elicited the adulation of cohorts; his active research agendas had been supplanted by perfunctory lectures given to unenthusiastic students; it had been nearly a decade since the publication of his last book. In 1943, he began organizing a new research project modeled on his African adventures. Yet, rather than preserving "aboriginal Africa," as he had liked to say, he now chose a subject closer to home, easier to access and less exotic.

Armed with his portable recorder, Payne set out for the southern United States with the intention of recording the folk songs, spirituals, and local voices of the Mississippi Delta and Louisiana lowlands. Payne clearly recognized the commonalities linking particular styles of African music with African American folk music and spirituals originating in the Deep South. Yet from the notebooks Payne kept at this time it is evident that he did not plan to capture the sounds and culture of a dying world, as he had done previously in Africa. Payne went down south looking for something in particular—a specific song that, according to his notes, had been transported from Africa centuries before and which was still performed in certain remote communities in the countryside.

Payne's account of how he came to learn of this song is convoluted at best. In one entry, he claims that he encountered a group of traveling black musicians outside of Chicago who performed a song reminiscent of ones he had heard in Africa. "The rhythms were too unique and the singing too particular to mistake it," he wrote. "Just as with certain tribes I lived among in the Congo, words were chanted in a low, guttural drone before the singer let out an ear-piercing shriek mimicking a wild animal in pain. In Swahili, this screech is known as *miungu kilio*, the howl of the gods." In another entry, Payne records stories of rural populations located outside Baton Rouge using traditional African instruments. The singers were called "wailers" by the locals because they would punctuate the music with loud, prolonged fits of screaming. In 1942, Payne claims to have witnessed one of these performances near Hammond, Louisiana. "The blacks of the region will perform their spirituals and delta music during the day while in the company of whites. At night, they slink away into the woods to perform the *ancestral songs*, as they say. They use instruments nearly identical to the *ahoko* and *adungu*, mixing them with banjos and fiddles. The singing is a mix of chanting which then breaks into sustained, atonal screams that can go on for intervals of ten to fifteen minutes until the vocalist is exhausted." In other entries, Payne describes scenes of men accompanying wailers with pounding Batá drums, ceremonies in which individuals are possessed by spirits and shriek incessantly, and whole choruses consisting of nothing but bestial yelps and screeches.

Payne's accounts are the only records documenting this brand of tribal African music in Louisiana, although Payne himself notes that the whites in the surrounding towns dismissed the music outright as "devil songs" and voodoo unworthy of serious consideration. It was only in 1943 he became convinced that the music he was hearing was, in fact, a distinct variant of African music and not a creolized composition derived from distant African origins. That spring, Payne left New York intent on recording these performances in various localities throughout Louisiana and the Delta region. He sent field recordings and letters documenting his findings to a friend back in New York on a more or less consistent basis over the next year. These correspondences furnish a vivid picture of both his travels and state of mind at this time. He reported hearing compositions that consisted exclusively of screams. Through alleged interviews conducted with the performers, he eventually learned the significance behind these odd vocal iterations. "The wailers believe that they are perpetuating the screams of their distant ancestors," he stated. "These songs are conceptualized in genealogical terms because they attribute a power to the screaming, a means of connecting with their aboriginal essence. It is a primordial poetry without words; a scream that is sustained across time and multiple generations, uniting those in the present with those in the remote past. One quickly grasps the fact that our understandings of history, our very chronologies have no place among these people."

Photograph of James Sanford Payne while on exploration.
British Library.

Whether or not Payne did discover an authentically residual African music and culture preserved on American soil has gone unverified. The communities he allegedly visited have never been identified in subsequent anthropological or demographic studies of the region. Nor has anyone documented cases of folk music consisting purely of screaming. Payne's last letter to New York was postmarked on 23 August 1944. Three months of silence followed, after which friends began to believe something was amiss. They were correct. In December, Payne was officially classified as a missing person when local authorities failed to locate him. An FBI investigation was launched shortly afterward with similar results. Payne had vanished, leaving a cold trail behind him. In 1957, unidentified skeletal remains were unearthed in Adams County, Mississippi by a privately contracted surveyor working on the riverbank. The skull exhibited signs of severe cranial trauma suggesting foul play, and rumors circulated that the body was, in fact, Payne's until a medical examination discredited this assumption. Investigators attempting to solve the mystery of Payne's disappearance were hard-pressed to corroborate many of the details in his correspondences, and to this day his reports are considered fabrications, embellishments, or outright delusions. Yet Payne, always a trailblazer in many respects, did foreshadow the growing interest in Southern musical culture that would resonate in the years to come. In 1951, the anthropologist Harold Courlander directed a study on the music of the African diaspora, releasing *Negro Folk Music of Africa and America* as part of the Smithsonian Folkway musical heritage series. The jazz scholar Charles Edward Smith similarly documented the historical progression of African American folk music with *Music Down Home* in 1965. Neither of these records contained the bizarre type of music described by Payne, nor do they bother to acknowledge Payne's contributions to the field in the album liner notes.

As I listen to the tapes and watch the sky outside the window fill with crepuscular light, I realize I have come to sympathize with Payne. Like him, I want clarification, an answer to a nagging question that will not let me be. Above all though, I want *it*; I want to be in *its* presence. This singular desire had sent Payne down south and has brought me here to the obscure B archive facility in New York. And so I sit and listen, waiting to hear the scream that I have only read about, waiting for its mythic presence to emerge from the crackling hiss of the tape and fill the room.

***

In 1881, Helmut Leike described the Danish coast as "threatening and desolate; a landscape haunted by the type of ghosts populating the most banal of nightmares." Upon first glimpse from the train window, anyone would concur. A flat, pebble-strewn shore extends outward veiled in thick fog. Craggy projections rise into the air, their outlines soft and ill-defined against the sickly colored late afternoon light. Lying two kilometers inland, central Skøvgaard appears just as inhospitable. The streets are grimy and cheerless. People seem to wander about in a daze, reluctant to engage in conversation or even make eye contact. The church bells that ring on the hour sound awry, their tolls dampened by the fog that rolls in off the sea and descends on the city's narrow streets.

The municipal archives are located on Hamletgade directly opposite the local tourist bureau in a building which has clearly seen better days. The only archivist on staff—one Ula Fremde—doubles as the official tourist minister and, as a result, spends most of her time idling away the afternoon across the street making small talk with tourists who, for one reason or another, happen to find themselves in Skøvgaard. Once Ms. Fremde granted me access to the archival reading room and showed me where the dossiers were located, I was usually on my own for the remainder of the day.

After his death, Leike's papers and letters were left unclaimed. Following a series of transfers between distant family members in the Brandenburg area, the uncollected documents and notebooks were eventually returned to Skøvgaard and donated to the municipality. As I began sifting through the array of papers, it became obvious that they had never been formally cataloged or organized in any systematic manner. From nine in the morning when the archives opened until five in the evening when the building closed, I spent my time in the stifling reading room pouring over pieces of fragmented correspondences, notes written on yellowed paper, rough drafts of manuscripts, and receipt books. Although I formed a more introspective view of Leike's life as I rummaged through the detritus of his most personal impressions and thoughts, my efforts did not bring me any closer to the object I sought. Aside from the 1892 letter, there was no mention of the scream. A single book left in my office by an absentminded colleague four years ago had brought me here to the source, and now the trace had run cold.

On the day I exited the archives for the last time, I crossed the street to thank Ms. Fremde for her time and attention. The visit was purely customary, to say the least. When she asked if my time in Skøvgaard had been fruitful, I was honest. Then she asked me if I had taken the tour of the Keyeraad House located on the coast where Leike and his daughters had lived. "No," I said, and left it at that. It was only as I was packing my bags in the hotel room later that night that I thought again about her question. Why hadn't I paid a visit to the house, if only out of pure curiosity? Lying in bed, I let my mind wander. I closed my eyes and attempted to picture the rooms, to construct their interior contours and imagine the moment when an aged Leike, dozing in his parlor, heard that primal screech resonate across his waking consciousness. I could feel my body tense with the thought and knew it would be a restive night filled with hours of agitated pacing, self-analysis, and second-guessing. I buried my face in the pillow and tried to think of other things: my morning departure, the train ride to Cologne, Kurt and Yvonne.

Photograph of the Keyeraad House,
Skøvgaard Municipal Archives, c. 1918

***

The wind through the trees and the sounds of the coast are expansive in the night. The house comes into view. I do not pause as I navigate down the gravel drive and hear the sound of the pebbles under my feet. Reflections of light flicker across the rolled panes of glass in the windows. A wind chime rustles on the porch. There is a dream-like sensation as I reach out and touch the cold door-knob. It turns effortlessly, as I somehow knew it would. The scent of dust greets me, a smell of something moldering and long shut up as I step in and quietly shut the door behind me. I am alone, absorbed in the emptiness of the house. I take a seat on the floor in the parlor, squinting through the thick shadows to see if anything is there. There is nothing.

The fireplace is dark and cold, its hearth like a gaping eye socket that stares back lifelessly through the obscurity. I feel the floorboards with my hands and lean back into the corner across from the fireplace. My eyelids flutter. The house possesses a somnolent affect, its silence a lullaby sending me off to sleep. I watch as my breath materializes in the air and give myself over completely to the quiet. The thought of falling asleep in this place, of dreaming, of giving myself over to the empty darkness, the muffled sound of the wind cutting through the trees outside and the waiting for what will come.

What Hath God Wrought?

2 December 1846

Arrived in Houston last Monday, from where I was able to arrange transport to Austin and on to San Antonio. The territory, only recently annexed to our great union, looks nothing as one would be led to believe. The cities—should one be so inclined to consider them such—bear little resemblance to the bustling streets and gabled houses of New England. Here everything is flat, dusty, vulgar. The people have a peculiar character. They speak in long drawls and manifest a fiery republican spirit at odds with the decorum of respectable New England life. In the mornings, you can see boys escorting herds of longhorns across the plains and covered wagons bound west dotting the horizon. The region is not without its rustic charms and should provide an abundance of local color for the reports I am to send back to Boston by courier.

In Austin, the streets are unpaved and stony. Mud and dirt abound, and it is not uncommon to see horses parked in the middle of the road drinking from stagnant puddles. The low-lying houses have an ominous character, tilting and slanting at such angles as though they were constructed from nothing more than mud and twigs. The phrase made popular by Mr. Morse—*What hath God wrought?*—persistently enters my thoughts as I meander about the grubby main thoroughfare where the old governor's house sits, grey and dreary, on its perch along the hills. I have to wonder whether Morse had Texas in mind when considering his communiqué. What hath God wrought, indeed?

The proprietor of the boarding house in which I am to spend the night—a certain Widow Saunders—is a voluble woman. Upon entering her establishment, she cordially invited me to a glass of sherry and a hot meal consisting of meat steeped in red lentils. While I ate, she provided me with a concise history of the area, enlightening me on the Spanish missions and the recent war of independence that remains fresh in everyone's mind. Her husband gave his life for the cause, she told me with pride. When I informed her I was heading to Coahuila y Tejas to cover the current struggle, her expression darkened. She preferred not to speak of the events occurring along the Rio Grande and remained silent while I hastily finished my meal. I had the impression I offended her in some manner, although it is difficult to read the people here. A constant air of melancholy appears to linger over them, inscrutable yet present all the same.

7 December 1846

In the morning, I met my contact, Mr. Wicker, who arranged my travel to Ciudad de los Santos. When my driver learned I was a reporter working for an Eastern journal, his face lit up. During the three-day trek, he talked incessantly, informing me about the war and the bandit brigades running arms through the area. He mentioned the bodies strung from trees with a macabre grin and related how during his previous return from Ciudad de los Santos he had come across one such unfortunate individual hanging from a huisache tree. The body had been distended and encrusted with flies. Checking the corpse for any valuables, he discovered the man had been eviscerated, a common tactic used by the local gangs. These are the grisly details of the secret war ravaging the region, a war outside the battles waged by Taylor and Santa Anna on the front, a war that will, no doubt, be lost to history.

I abided my companion, laughing at his crude jokes and collo-quialisms. When the conversation lulled, I sat atop the wagon recording my impressions of the desolate towns and farmsteads we passed along the route.

Ciudad de los Santos is a dreary garrison town. Pulling in, one first sees the hovels on the settlement outskirts occupied by Tejanos. Military men in dirty uniforms mill about the streets, heckling prostitutes and arguing with local business vendors. On our approach, a crowd of reserves called out to us in broken Spanish and made gestures in the air with their hands. The horses kicked up clouds of dust, drawing angry looks from pedestrians.

Parking his cart before a small, clapboard building on the far end of the settlement, the driver flashed a smile. This is where I am to reside. Despite its squalid appearance, the structure is newly built and in much better condition than the other buildings we passed on our way in. To the east, an expanse of flat, parched terrain extends as far as the eye can see, emitting shimmering waves of heat. Descending, I noticed little puddles of mud dotting the earth, the remnants of last week's rain I was later told. A hundred yards out, a rotting animal carcass lay face-down in the fetid water, attracting vultures.

The station chief is a burly Ohioan named McAllen. He greeted me politely, showed me to my quarters, and introduced me to the main garrison commanders. Next, he gave me a tour of the barracks where half-dressed soldiers sat about playing cards and cleaning rifles. They cast furtive glances in our direction as we toured the grounds and McAllen gave me the lay of the land.

"They can be a bit suspicious when it comes to civilians," McAllen explained after we returned to his quarters. "Don't take it personally."

He authorized me to conduct interviews with the men if needed but urged me to avoid political topics in my discourse. He did not want Whig politics eroding morale, he stated candidly. I assured him he had nothing to worry about. Journalistic integrity and objective reporting were my stock-and-trade. This remark seemed to please him.

8 December 1846

Ciudad de los Santos is situated over one hundred miles from the front. It occupies a key position in the supply lines, serving as a transport hub for men and weapons destined for Buena Vista and San Gabriel. When I was told I was being dispatched to Coahuila y Tejas, I never expected to see combat. However, it is evident that even these garrison towns are not immune to the violence and destruction raging further west.

On my first morning, I awoke in good spirits. Taking my morning coffee by the window, I noticed a small Spanish mission on the horizon toward the north-east. The building is plain, earth-colored, and adorned with a bell tower that juts up into the sky. I have been told that it is derelict, which explains the building's egregious state of disrepair. The Spanish missionaries have long abandoned these parts. The building remains shrouded in silence, sitting on the horizon like an abscess growing out of the earth.

When the war first began, the garrison commanders used the mission as a stable to keep the horses. According to some of the men, the horses never grew accustomed to the confinement. They would whinny and run about during the night, creating a ruckus that kept the men awake. The horses are now sheltered in the barn with the food provisions, leaving the mission to molder in the dust.

I was studying this structure from my window when I heard the first gunshots. I immediately ran to the courtyard to seize a rifle, fearing we were under attack. Entering the courtyard, I saw a body sprawled on the ground. A pool of crimson streaked the dirt, spreading out like an oil stain.

Men in uniform stood about the courtyard in a semicircle. Butch Crommer, the garrison sous-lieutenant, was looking over his work with a grin. To his left stood a line of slovenly-dressed men, their wrists bound in twine. The fear on their faces was legible, having just watched Crommer execute one of their companions.

I asked the recruit immediately adjacent to me what was occurring.

"Brigands," he whispered, his eyes fixed on the prisoners. "Found them in the hills a quarter-mile from here."

"Were they surveying the garrison?" I whispered back.

"Most likely."

"And so he'll execute them?"

"Most likely." His expression was unflinching and expectant, giving the impression this was a regular occurrence.

Crommer began circling the line of prisoners like a vulture cutting a gyre, a Colt Walker clutched in his fist. He smiled and spat in the dirt. Some of the prisoners were visibly upset. A few retained their composure, head held high, resigned to their fate.

"Tejanos aren't exactly welcome here," Crommer was saying, training the barrel of the gun on the men. "'Specially those intent on stealin' from us."

Some of the troops grumbled their agreement, and Crommer's mean grin widened.

Settling on a man at random, he pressed the barrel to his forehead. A shot rang out and the man collapsed into the dust like a ragdoll. The troops cheered, and one of the prisoners began to wail.

Crommer went down the line, executing all five. I was powerless to intervene, although I wondered whether McAllen had authorized these killings or whether I was witnessing an injustice. When Crommer was finished, he looked down admiringly at his work and spit.

"Don't bother burying 'em," Crommer said as his men began clearing the bodies and dragging them through the dirt.

I later learned that there is a defunct well on the premises that is being used as an informal mortuary. A column extending into the bowels of the earth filled with corpses; the idea is ghastly.

"Welcome to the City of Saints," one of the men said to me as the crowd dispersed. He did not bother to hide the irony in his voice.

I have been here less than twenty-four hours and I have already borne witness to the sickening atrocities of war. I dare not speculate on what is yet to come.

Now, as I sit in the yard observing the night constellations and recording my impression, the image of those men continues to haunt my thoughts. I see them quivering and collapsing in the dirt, their bodies spasming like insects. A dark pool marks the killing grounds, the earth saturated with the blood of the fallen.

11 December 1846

The mornings here are still. I rise close to dawn and watch the sun cresting over the flat horizon. Its light is warm and radiant, bathing the landscape in fiery hues. Out here, the colors are extraordinary and vibrant, unlike anything I have ever seen.

The men take their breakfast in the yard, mumbling in low voices. I can feel their eyes directed at me as I pass. They have little trust for Yankees, especially one assigned by a newspaper. I am skeptical whether I will be able to assuage their suspicions and establish confidence among them.

Yesterday, McAllen requested to see me in his office. Upon entering, he lit a pipe and gestured for me to take a seat. He looked out the window with a plaintive gaze, blowing coils of smoke into the air. His eyes were fixed on the site of the previous day's atrocities. He lectured me on the grim realities of war and the need to keep up morale among the men, adding that such details may be difficult for a civilian like myself to comprehend. War was "existential," in his opinion. He asked me if I understood what he meant. I replied that I did, and he nodded.

"Do you think of the future?" McAllen then asked, drawing his pipe from his lips.

I did not know how to respond, but it appeared he expected no answer.

"I do," he continued. "It is filled with farms and towns spreading out across this savage land, of God-fearing men fulfilling a noble mission which does not belong to them alone, but to providence."

He fixed me with a cold stare.

I was under no illusions he intended me to quote this in one of the reports I will send back to Boston. Summary executions and wells packed with corpses have no place in this august narrative of manifest destiny. They are simply the grisly means to a more righteous end, the minutiae eclipsed by a far vaster plan.

I spent the afternoon conducting interviews with those troops willing to confide in me. They are amiable for the most part and excited to speak with a reporter. They constantly make certain that I have spelled their names correctly in my notes: Bosworthe with an *E*. Jesppson with a *double* P. All recounted stories of hardship and privation, of courage and sacrifice. Yet they are not reticent when it comes to speaking of the melancholy and horrors that afflict the average soldier, either. The brutality, the nightmares that plague their sleep. The toll of war runs deeper than the blood-drenched slaughter that wreaks havoc across this land. It is manifest in the weary faces and gritted teeth, the agonizing screams that pierce the stillness of the night as men cry out in their sleep, fists clenched, begging for absolution. I recorded these impressions in my notebook with an equanimous face.

In the later afternoon, I was walking along the outskirts of the garrison when I heard calls of "Newsman! Newsman!"

Looking about, I discerned no one in sight until my eye drift upward to a tall observation tower positioned against the fort wall. A sentry was waving his arms frantically in an effort to get my attention.

"I got a story for ya, too," he called down, beckoning me to join him in his roost.

Climbing the rickety ladder to the top, I was greeted by a view of the vistas and bluffs extending out into infinity. Flat, open space dotted by the occasional homestead as far as the eye could see.

The guard let out a soft whistle. "Think of all that empty space out there," he said, noting my gaze.

From our position, I could clearly make out the old Spanish mission. It looked small and diminished in the distance, like a warped dollhouse. Crimson light bled across the plains, and as my eyes scanned the landscape, I perceived a small procession making its way along the rocks and dirt to the east. The line was composed of five women. They walked in slow, measured steps, their colorful shawls flowing behind them in the evening wind. Each carried a basket in her arms.

I pointed to the line and asked who they were.

"The widows," the guard explained, his voice sober and inflectionless. "They are bringing flowers for the dead, most likely."

"The mission is still in operation?" I asked.

The guard shook his head. "Old habits die hard."

I wondered if they knew that their husbands' bodies were interred only two hundred yards to the west, left to rot in the shaft of a neglected well. Would they have dared to leave the flowers there at the final resting place of their beloveds? I watched as they ambled through the dust and entered the crumbling building, the procession mournful and with unspoken purpose.

Eventually the guard broke the silence. "That gonna make it into one of your stories?" he asked with a malicious chuckle.

I feel as though I am on a very tight leash here.

That night, I sat up in bed thinking of the women trekking along the mission trail. Before extinguishing my lamp, I turned my eyes out the window. A soft glow emanated from within the mission. I imagined the women placing candles around the courtyard and strewing the paving stones with dried flowers. Each widow stood in silhouette, solemn in the flickering light. In turn, each drew a rosary from their calico shawl and lay it on the earth. "*Tierra de los Santos*," they whispered. "*Nunca olvidamos.*"

Suddenly, a loud shriek cut through the night. I heard the shuffle of feet and murmurous voices coming from the barracks. "'S all right. We're here," the voices uttered. "They can't git ya here."

I listened to them soothe their restless companion, and eventually quiet consumed the barracks. For all their talk of courage, these are broken men, worn down by the hostilities and evil cultivated within this war-ravaged land. The City of Saints is populated with ruins and debris. There are no spoils to be had.

12 December 1846

Curiosity got the best of me. In the morning, I set out across the plain for the mission. The building is more dilapidated than I first assumed. At a distance, it appears somber and dignified, juxtaposed against the expansive landscape. Up close, it is a pathetic shell of crumbling stone and spotted plaster. Parts of the tiled roof have collapsed. The main entrance is a gaping black hole where a door once stood. Inside, the floor is littered with debris and stagnant pools of water. Ribbons of light cut through the holes in the ceiling, casting skeletal shadows along the walls. As I entered, I could hear animals scurrying in the darkness.

In the chapel beyond the foyer, I found a large, conical pit where the floor has caved in completely. Remnants of tallow candles were scattered throughout the room. A single woven palm basket sat on the floor, emptied of its contents. The fibers were moist. Further down the crevice of the pit sat a mutilated cattle skull, decomposing in the heat and gathering flies. I shivered. *Old habits die hard*, I recalled the guard remarking.

I refrained from mentioning my discovery to McAllen or the other men. I know not what I would say aside from giving a descriptive account of my wanderings. Even this seems obscure to me. I work with words, and yet words now fail me.

14 December 1846

On Wednesday, a convoy passed through Ciudad de los Santos carrying a platoon of troops. They were returning from Santa Fe where they endured heavy losses against the Mexican *permanentes*. All I could think was how tired their faces looked. They stood about in their dirty uniforms, smoking tobacco and discussing reports of the strange malady that has recently afflicted many of the officers and recruits on the front. From their accounts, it appears chronic somnambulation and melancholy are routine occurrences. One man noted an entire subdivision at Valverde seized by what one can only describe as madness. He described men walking about at night in a daze, muttering incomprehensible words.

"I seen it," he told me, pipe clenched between his teeth. "At Santa Rita, an entire regiment decimated in an unnatural way."

I informed him of recent medical studies documenting the phenomenon of mass mania and hallucinations. Under extreme forms of trauma, it is believed that the mind can be stricken with severe apoplexy, resulting in hysteria. The man nodded and smoked in meditative silence as I spoke. "Perhaps," was all he offered when I finished.

As the wagon receded into the distance, I thought about his remark: *in an unnatural way*. I am under no illusions that the natural world conceals the most arcane and beguiling secrets. Its study daily reveals such mysteries that man is yet to comprehend. *Unnatural* is merely a synonym for our profound ignorance. We cannot fathom what God designs. Nature is only what God allows us to see and scrutinize.

15 December 1846

I have taken to making daily excursions to the abandoned mission. I detect signs of visitation, although I have yet to see anyone enter the desolate construction. Small figurines carved from obsidian and melted candles are strewn across the floor like strange votive offerings. The cattle skull has vanished, and the aperture at the center of the pit appears to have widened. The diameter is now approximately three feet across, a hole big enough for a man. The soil is dry and friable, explaining the cause of such rapid erosion. Here, everything eventually turns to brittle dust.

Peering into the cavity, I could only discern an inky blackness without end. I tossed a pebble into the hollow, waiting for the sound as it hit the bottom. None came. I assume the earth below is covered in moss or some variety of undergrowth. All the same, it felt like tossing a stone into a cavernous void, the echo consumed by obscure nothingness.

I cannot say precisely what draws my fascination to this forlorn place. From my window, I keep close watch over the slumbering construction, anticipating the approach of the women to replenish the candles or leave additional tokens of mourning at the edge of the crater. Yet they have not returned. The mission slumbers in the thick evening shadows.

17 December 1846

Dinner in the officer mess this evening. McAllen appeared laconic, sitting at the table with a troubled expression on his face. He continually tapped the tines of his fork on the tablecloth, a peculiar tic that drew looks from the other officers.

After a few glasses of wine, Butch Crommer began to converse on the behavior of certain men housed in the barracks.

"They're calling it *Mexican fever*," he said with a sardonic laugh. "They say it's a psychological disorder incurred by intense heat on the brain."

"But it's not an *actual* fever," one of the officers interjected, leaning back in his chair. "The reports from Santa Fe detail somnambulism and incoherence. Nothing that would derive from miasmic properties."

"A swelling of the brain, according to Dr. Percival," another offered. "The product of this abnormal environment."

McAllen grimaced. "Which is exactly why this land should be cleared and made habitable."

"Godliness *and* cleanliness," Crommer reminded with a smirk.

"Not that again," replied a young officer with a scowl. "These people aren't heathens. We're not in Africa!"

"You follow what the French have done in Algeria?" Crommer asked, leaning forward across the table. "They're building roads, schools, doing what the savages can't. In a decade, Algiers will resemble Paris!"

"We're not fighting Muhammadans here!"

"We're fighting something worse," Crommer bellowed. "We're fighting wild dogs and jackals that refuse to be domesticated."

"I don't see what this has to do with this so-called *fever*," said one of the officers at the end of the table, clearly weary of the conversation. "I have twenty men in my company who can't sleep and wake up at night hollering to the high heavens, and you want to prattle on about the French killing Muhammadans in Africa!"

McAllen bit his lip and looked at me for the first time.

"Funny how none of this Mexican fever business has been

reported in the newspapers," he said. "One might assume it's nothing more than gossip."

The table fell silent and the rest of the meal passed in polite, labored conversation.

The meal concluded; I returned to my quarters. On the way, I decided to pass by the infirmary to satisfy my own curiosities. At the entrance, a cluster of medical orderlies stood about talking in sibilant voices. A dejected wail came from an open window, punctuating the stillness of the night. It was difficult to discern their visages in the moonlight, but I could feel the cold stares of the orderlies as I continued in the direction of my quarters without a word.

18 December 1846

As I set out along the trail in the early afternoon, the sentry posted in the observation tower began whistling.

"I'm beginning to think you might have a cache of whiskey hidden out there," he called down.

"A what?"

"I won't tell no'ne," he promised, adding: "though, *if* it is whiskey you got, a man can get mighty thirsty up here. Keep it in mind."

I assured him I would as I continued along the path winding through the ocotillo and mesquite. Walking, I had the impression of following a trail of footsteps accumulated across ages, a line scored in the dirt by ancient human traffic of men and women in search of God's salvation.

Inside the chapel, I found signs of recent activity: fresh candles, tracks in the dust, an abundance of stone figurines scattered across the broken tiles. The pit in the center of the floor was wider, extending over three-fourths of the chamber like a gaping maw ready to swallow the sky. Squatting by the edge of the carter, I thought I could discern faint voices emanating from the depths. My mind conjured up images of rotting corpses piled atop one another, forming a column of tangled and malformed bodies. Their jaws clacked together, trying to speak, trying to tell their story.

Slurred words conflated in the darkness, echoing across an immeasurable void filled with grief and suffering. Closing my eyes, I saw lines etched in light stretching out across a plain of darkness. They shimmered like constellations fallen to the earth, and I instinctively felt that these clusters of light were pulsating with human life and energy. Moiling like some strange species of luminescent insect, they combined to trace the outlines of towering buildings, centers of commerce, and thoroughfares limned in white radiance.

I cringed as the distant cry of a bird drew me from these macabre reveries. I blinked into the ribbons of pale sunlight, wondering whether I had been dreaming or seeing into some nameless future that had yet to be written in the annals of this cursed land.

19 December 1846

Morning light has now begun to bleed across the land, and yet even in the clarity of the coming day, I am still uncertain of the phenomenon which I have witnessed. I cannot remember when I first became cognizant of the low, puling sound coming across the night. It emerged slowly, a faint apian buzz gradually thickening into a plangent cry. Even as I became conscious of the noise, I had the curious impression that it had always been there, present, waiting for me to discover it. By the time I rose from bed to ascertain the source of the commotion, the wailing had saturated the air, subsuming the crickets and restless wind through the acacia trees.

Gazing out upon the starlit landscape, I saw stretching before me a column of half-dressed men trickling out of the barrack gates into the sprawling night. Their movements were spasmodic and juddering, like puppets being dragged along invisible threads. As my eyes drifted to the head of the formation, I immediately understood. The mission was bathed in a flickering glow and the men were marching toward it like insects attracted to a lamp.

Rushing into the night, I merged with the crowd, following its trajectory. With each step, the howling grew louder. I imagined a wounded animal crying out in pain. As my eyes drifted over the throng, I spotted Butch Crommer, his eyes wide and glassy. I waved and called to him, but his gaze remained fixed straight ahead as the column snaked toward the mission in silence. Sprinting ahead, I jostled against the men filing through the doorway and there beheld a sight that will forever remain imprinted on my memory.

The howling became deafening as I lurched into the chapel and filled my lungs with the foul, miasmic air. The screaming was coming from the cavity in the center of the floor, its perimeter now lined with concentric rows of teeth. The walls of the pit throbbed with each shriek, emitting an abominable stench. To my horror, I watched as the column of men entered the chamber one by one and without hesitation marched to the edge of the precipice and hurled themselves into its abysmal depths.

I wanted to shout, to raise my voice above the thunderous scream, but I remained paralyzed, watching as each, in turn, approached the gaping mouth and strode obliviously over the edge. As this gruesome procession continued, I saw McAllen advancing toward the lip of the chasm. I cried out, begging him to stop, but my words were inaudible. Yet as he teetered on the brink, I am convinced our eyes locked for a moment. His mouth appeared to open, and his lips formed a rictus on the verge of speech. And then, without a word, he lilted forward, his body spiraling into the cavernous abyss.

Along *the* Path, We Will Find One Another

Of course it was Arkady meandering along the path. Who else would it be? Jan slowed his steps, shifting the weight of his rucksack on his shoulder. Arkady was walking at an even pace, a silhouette etched against the pale evening light. Jan looked over his shoulder in the direction he had come. Violet and crimson streaked the sloping hills. A small cluster of gnats whirled in a frantic dance.

He would wait, he decided, kicking at the dust and keeping an eye on the lone figure making his way along the path ahead.

When Arkady finally arrived, Jan fixed him with an incredulous looked.

"So, it *was* you," he said.

Arkady's lips twisted into a grin.

Jan had been sitting at a brasserie in Trier musing over a regional guidebook. It was a generic guide at best, listing all the typical attractions one might expect in the Mosel region. He spread the map listing all the chateaux and vineyards of the lower Rhine across the table. Each location was marked by cartoonish bushels of dark grapes. A touch touristy, Jan thought, as he traced his finger over the glossy surface.

Drawing his eyes from the map, Jan rested his forehead against the windowpane and watched the pedestrians glide by the square in silence: an old woman carrying overflowing bags, men finicking with umbrellas, teenagers walking with their heads down, earbuds screwed into their ears. Trier had a deserted and dreary feel in the autumn. He wondered what it might be like in the summer when the *Brot und Spiel* festival attracted flocks of tourists. A different city entirely, he suspected, starting out at the greyish buildings and damp cobblestones.

He must have been lulled to sleep watching the pedestrians because when his eyes fluttered open, the light had changed. Squinting through the glass, he was certain he caught a glimpse of a familiar face in the crowd. He had only seen it for a moment before the individual turned and merged with the rest of the traffic, but the recognition had been instantaneous. Jan got up from his table and hurried to the door. He could just make out the person at the far end of the street, their sienna coat setting them apart from the crowd.

"Arkady!" Jan called, realizing that he probably couldn't hear him from this distance.

"Arkady!" he repeated, before remembering that Arkady had been dead for two years.

But now, here he was, traveling along the same desolate road in the middle of nowhere, a bit unkempt perhaps, but certainly alive.

"I thought you were dead," Jan said, feeling this was the only appropriate thing to say.

Arkady lifted his arms and performed a clumsy pirouette to indicate this was clearly not the case. "Obviously, you heard wrong."

Jan placed a hand on his shoulder. One last act of validation. He ran the textured fabric of his coat between his fingers, the threads course and slightly moist.

"What are you doing here?" he finally managed.

"Same as you, I imagine."

"You can't be here for the vineyards..."

"And why not?"

"The tourist season is over."

"And yet here we are."

Jan looked back over his shoulder to the hills of trellises and pergolas outlined in skeletal precision against the diminishing light. From this perspective, they appeared dark and menacing, like the spines of large, slumbering beasts. The wind had picked up some, creating a faint susurrous noise as it rustled the leaves.

Arkady cleared his throat. "Don't act so surprised," he said. "You know as well as I do that this is the best time to come. The vine-yards are practically deserted, and you don't have to bother with the tourists. You said so yourself."

"Yes..." Jan murmured, vaguely recalling saying something to this effect once.

"Well, found any gems?"

"A few. Weingut Grusel had some good selections. That was in Eitelsbach. There was one in Konz with an excellent Silvaner."

Arkady nodded.

It struck Jan how easily he had settled into this normal conver-sation, as though there was nothing else to speak of. Sure, they had discussed making a wine-tasting trip to the Rhine at one point, but that had been over three years ago. Before everything had oc-curred and before Arkady had died. It felt as though there were other things to be said, more important things than vintages and grape quality.

"Where's your bag?" Jan asked, noticing Arkady was carrying nothing with him. He couldn't have been walking along a country road with no supplies. They were miles from any town or village. "And a car? How did you *get* here?"

Arkady stared at him, as though to pose the same question.

"I've just come from a place down the road," Jan explained.

"A vineyard?"

"Yes, that's right. A place right down the road there." He turned and pointed into the distance. From this vantage point there were only rolling hills and the river. Not a farmstead in sight. He must have been walking longer than he thought.

"Well, it's somewhere back there," he continued. "Right past the bend of the hills."

"What was it called?" Arkady asked, picking at a hangnail.

"Well..." Jan wracked his brain for the name. Weingut Dieder, or Winegut Caspar. Honestly, he had visited so many in the past week that they had begun to blur together. There had been a young woman at one who smiled at him, he remembered, her sad expression so provincial, like a Millet painting. But that had been near Serrig, three days earlier. Where had he been that afternoon?

Jan drew the guidebook from his sack and began rifling through the pages until he reached the map. He scanned the brownish-green cartography, moving across the typographical grape clusters demarcating wineries. He settled on Serrig and traced the route to Sommerau.

"I was in Serrig three days ago," he explained, "and Trier after that..."

"Which was...?" Arkady asked. He seemed genuinely amused.

"Well, two days ago obviously."

"Yes, but which day?"

Jan paused and knit his brow. "That was Tuesday... I think."

"And what day is it now?"

"Well, Thursday naturally."

"And we are now...?"

Jan stared up at Arkady, annoyed. "Don't you know where you are?"

Arkady's expression remained blank. "Don't you?"

Jan narrowed his eyes and returned to the map. "Of course. I was just at the vineyard down the road there..."

"The name of which you can't remember."

"I can remember it. Just give me a minute. Weingut Müller, or Weingut..."

His voice trailed off and now he heard only the wind murmuring in the leaves. He returned to the map, searching for a name that would jog his memory. Yet the more he looked at the map, the more it resembled an alien landscape with odd names and expansive valleys. Surely, you could just follow the river and find yourself somewhere, he thought. But even the river seemed to bend and snake in awkward directions. More like the Amazon than the Mosel.

Arkady cleared his throat again.

"Had any reds on this trip?" he asked, changing the subject.

"Figures you'd ask," Jan said, letting his hands drop to his side. "This was my idea, *my* trip, you know." He tried not to grit his teeth when he said this.

The famed search for the perfect Rhenish red: Arkady had

always sniggered when Jan brought up the subject. For him, it was a joke, an object of mockery. "It's not a Rhenish red," he would always jeer whenever presenting a bottle to him in the company of acquaintances. "But hopefully it suffices for people with less re- fined palates." This was always followed by the same laughs and chuckles, the same unspoken scorn that would cause Jan to bite his tongue and narrow his eyes just slightly.

"You mentioned it a few years back, yes, but it's hardly *yours* to claim," Arkady said.

Jan glared at him.

"Look, this is getting off all wrong. I'm not trying to take away from your enjoyment. I'm really not."

Arkady began tracing circles in the dirt with the tip of his shoe. Jan noticed they looked dust-streaked and threadbare, as though Arkady had been walking for a long time.

"I asked about the red wine because I know a place not far from here that's known for producing it. In fact, I was headed there now. I wasn't following you if that's what you thought."

Jan returned his attention to the map, ignoring the remark.

"What's it called?"

"Not on that map," Arkady said confidently.

"It might be," Jan snapped, too quick for his liking. He began scrutinizing the map, more for show than anything else, waiting for Arkady to reveal the location. When he didn't, Jan folded up the map and curled the guidebook in his hand.

Of course, Arkady would know some *recherché* vineyard out here in the middle of nowhere. The more Jan thought about their chance meeting, the more he was convinced that Arkady had in fact followed him. The whole thing suddenly felt cruel and duplic- itous.

"I'm headed there now," Arkady said. "C'mon."

"With *you*?"

"Is there anyone else here?"

Jan looked around, realizing how foolish he sounded.

"Or we could go back to the place you just came from if the wine's good there."

He said this with such smugness, Jan cringed.

What had the place been called? Jan couldn't remember, nor could he remember what it looked like or the steward who had served him. A black veil draped across his memory. He had been walking along the road, as though emerging from a fog, on his way to somewhere. Where, however, he couldn't say, and Arkady knew it.

"No, I've already been there. We should try someplace new."

"As you wish," Arkady said, gesturing forward with his hands.

"And you haven't a car? A driver?"

"And you?" He cast a long look around the panorama of darkening hills and fields, indicating it was just the two of them. "I think I can get us there," he said. "Besides, we probably have a lot to talk about anyway."

"I seriously doubt it," said Jan as he yielded and fell into step with Arkady.

"Really? You haven't brought up Yvonne or Frankfurt."

"I knew it," Jan mumbled.

"Water under the bridge," Arkady assured. "I'm not as unforgiving as you might think."

Somehow, Jan doubted it.

***

In his Frankfurt days, anything seemed possible. There was an air of novelty that Jan relished. He had never known anything like it in his life. Having grown up in a sleepy town like Giessen where nothing ever changed and people preferred it that way, coming to Frankfurt was nothing short of a revelation. Social circles fluctuated with dizzying speed while each day brought something new and untold. Gatherings at artists' lofts. Trips to museums. Invites to plays and informal gatherings where people crammed into tiny apartments to drink cheap alcohol and discuss politics. Although his job in the financial sector had brought him to Frankfurt, Jan owed his newfound sociability to one source in particular: Yvonne and Arkady.

The couple took to Jan immediately. They had met at a charity event organized by Jan's firm. Jan could stomach the PR message of "strength in community" touted by the execs, but he was not blind to the fact that donations were a convenient means of outsourcing some of the surplus capital accumulating in the corporate coffers. "You don't seem like a company man," Yvonne had said to him, before introducing herself and her partner as "conscientious representatives" of the local arts council. He shrugged and made some remark about appearances being deceiving. A few glasses of wine, some polite chatter, and by the end of the night Jan found himself whisked away to the studio of an up-and-coming photographer that the couple knew. He was asked what he thought about the current state of the German arts, or whether he felt Gerhardt Richter was passé. He had no opinions on either topic, he told them. Yvonne and Arkady merely smiled and steered the conversation toward more neutral topics. In the coming months, however, Jan found he could articulate his thoughts on such matters, often with insight.

Yvonne had a habit of calling him by his given name. "Johann, would you mind...?" or "Johann, what do you think about...?" At first, it was irritating, although after a few weeks, he grew accustomed to it. It had a maternal ring. What he did not become accustomed to was Arkady addressing him in this way. The name had a belittling and slightly patronizing feel when he said it. "Johann, what are you thinking today?" or "Johann, what do you make of that?" Try as he might, he never sensed the same endearing quality that characterized Yvonne's delivery.

Jan had come to Frankfurt alone, and knowing nobody in the city, Yvonne and Arkady quickly became his social outlet. They knew anyone worth knowing in the city. While various threads of interest drew them together, it was Jan's interest in wine that seemed to cement a bond between the three of them. During his time at university, Jan had taken an interest in viticulture. Never possessing the agricultural resources or expertise to become a bona fide vintner, he had settled on acquiring a refined knowledge of wines instead. Beginning with the standard French and Spanish varieties, he moved on to New World varietals and later German blends. Yvonne adored it when he lectured on specific vintages or instructed them on how to properly tell a good finish. "So bo-bo," she would say with a giggle, imitating the way Jan would uncork and prepare a bottle. For her, it possessed a certain bourgeois-bohemian chic lacking in her life. Arkady was less enthralled. When it came to Jan's interest in Rhenish and Austrian wines, Arkady liked to joke it was a peculiar way of being a German nationalist. "Why bother with the Rhine and Danube when there are France and Spain?" he asked with a malicious laugh.

Arkady fashioned himself a poet, although he rarely published anything. He had a romantic streak for sure and could recite Régnier and Rilke by heart. Yet as to actual artistic merit, Jan was inclined to believe Arkady had little. It didn't stop Arkady from spouting his ideas on modern literature and the crisis of the poetic soul to anyone who would listen. And seeing as the couple was always surrounded by what Jan came to think of as "their entourage," there was always someone to listen. Jan was not afraid to admit he preferred Yvonne, who was a modest yet very skilled sculptor. He would sit for hours with her in her studio near Hanauer Landstrasse conversing and watching her work. There was something soothing in the way her moist hands molded the clay, the way her earth-stained fingers tore through the material like soft flesh. "A soft but firm touch," she always liked to say, running her hands along the contours of a vase or some figurine yet to be fully formed. In the coming months, it was that very same soft-but-firm touch that Jan came to love and anticipate. To think of that small room on Hanauer Landstrasse would evoke an exhilarating expectation that knew no words. And as his visits became routine, first weekly and then daily, Jan came to appreciate his Frankfurt life on a new and more intimate level.

Jan always wondered whether Arkady was suspicious. "He's not the jealous type," Yvonne told him one afternoon. He remembered it had been raining because he could hear the patter of the downpour against the corrugated iron in the courtyard below. "He's not the kind to get upset over some bo-bo indiscretion like this."

Some bo-bo indiscretion like this. The phrase stuck with him and would echo in his thoughts as he watched Yvonne mold and work her clay, giving definitive form to clumpy raw matter. Sometimes he would imagine her plying and sculpting his own body in such a way, transforming him into something new and unrecognizable, yet beautiful in accuracy and detail.

Yvonne was, of course, wrong. Bo-bo indiscretion or not, Arkady was the type to get upset, even enraged. In his typical dramatic flair, one night Arkady rampaged through their apartment like a bull in a China shop. After smashing everything that could be smashed, he booked a flight to Africa mentioning something about a Hemmingway complex. Within a week, Jan was living with Yvonne, filling the place Arkady had vacated. The entire affair left a bad taste in his mouth, but he tried not to think about it much. Truthfully, he even came to enjoy it. Within a month, he was attending the same social gatherings and events, only this time with Yvonne on his arm. Nobody among the entourage seemed to comment on Arkady's sudden disappearance or make sly remarks suggesting any ill will. Things carried on as usual: the same gossip, the same discussions, the same cheap wine filling plastic cups. The only difference was Jan was sharing a bed with Yvonne. There was a slightly surreal quality in thinking one man could seamlessly be replaced by another, but the scenario appeared to work, and in Jan's favor. Perhaps it said something about Yvonne more than Jan, but he didn't reflect on it much. Life was good, and he could play up Yvonne's bo-bo fantasies for as long as it lasted.

The problem was it didn't last long.

Six months later, he found Yvonne sitting in the kitchenette, a steaming cup of tea on the counter before her. Jan knew something was amiss since Yvonne usually drank tea after her evening yoga sessions. Without a word, she handed him a slip of paper folded into fours. It reported that Arkady had been killed in a rafting accident on the Zambezi.

"Just like that," Yvonne murmured, unclenching her fist and spreading her fingers to imitate an explosion. "Gone."

It wasn't too long after that Yvonne packed her own bags.

"You're just not that interesting," she told him as she jammed clothes into a duffle bag. It had the ring of a parting shot. Why Yvonne felt the need for a final jab was beyond him. Looking back, though, he realized many things had been beyond him from the start.

**

Had he felt sorry for what he did?

No, not really. Arkady had been a self-absorbed showman, always more talk than substance. He craved attention, even going as far as to stage his own romantic demise it now seemed. On principle, Jan had little sympathy for people who constantly demanded the spotlight.

Had he felt bad about not feeling sorry?

Perhaps. He had been deceitful, but seeing Arkady now caused any sense of lingering remorse to evaporate.

The sun was arcing toward the horizon. Jan watched their shadows stretch out on the path mimicking the movements of their legs and the syncopated sway of their arms. It felt like they had been walking for a while, but the sun had yet to disappear over the hills.

"And where is she now?"

"No idea."

"Just like that," Arkady scoffed, unclenching his fist and spreading his fingers wide. "Vanished."

"Pretty much."

The gnats were becoming agitated. A faint but persistent drone impregnated the air. It seemed to be coming from somewhere very far away over the hills.

"Almost there now," Arkady said without taking his eyes from the road.

Jan listed to the crunch of their footsteps on the gravel and the distant hum of the insects. He had questions, but there would be time for them later, maybe.

When they arrived at a path straying off the main road, Arkady paused and looked around at the fields dotted with vine-clad trellises. In the accumulating dusk, they resembled bones jutting from the earth. A cottage was visible in the distance, the windows filled with sallow light.

"This it?" Jan asked, skeptical.

Arkady nodded and turned onto the footpath. He began whistling. The melody was vaguely familiar, although slightly out of key. Just dissonant enough to make it unrecognizable.

As they approached the cottage, the darkness thickened. Looking over his shoulder, Jan watched the sun dropping behind the hills, a fiery half-disk hanging on the horizon. It hovered there just above the shadowy mountains like a glaring eye, scrutinizing and judging.

Would the vineyard even be open at this hour? The daylight was rapidly expiring and soon it would be pitch black. How had he let this occur, he wondered as Arkady pulled the long coil of string, producing a muffled chime inside the building. Not for the first time, Jan tried to recall where he had been earlier that day. The name of a vineyard or town. Anything. But his mind groped at nothingness.

The door eased back to reveal the sliver of a middle-aged woman. Her expression passed from surprise to suspicion as Arkady went into a long explanation of how they had gotten lost on the road.

"You can see we're in a slight bind," Arkady said, wrapping up. "It's dark and we're lost."

"That's true," replied the woman, without pity. "You are in a bind."

When Arkady asked whether the woman could possibly put them up for the night, her face hardened. If it was a question of money, Arkady assured her it was not a problem. He hadn't even bothered to consult Jan on this point, and when the woman quoted an exorbitant price for a single night of room and board, Jan balked. He was about to protest but caught himself. What was the alternative? Wandering around in the night hoping to find a hotel in the middle of the countryside?

They were ushered into a damp-smelling foyer. Wan light spilled into the hall, tracing the outline of a doorframe ahead. The woman shepherded them into a bare dining room and escorted them to an empty table. Jan took stock of the furniture. It appeared old, but not antique. The type of objects handed down generation after generation simply because nobody else wanted them. Looking about the room, he was drawn to the pale green wallpaper. The floral pattern was mottled with water stains.

"Charming," Jan said, taking a seat.

"Do you know anywhere better?" Arkady asked, sitting opposite him.

Just as Jan was about to speak, the woman reentered the room with a young girl in tow. She had a plain face with corn blonde hair pulled back in a bun. Jan had a vague sensation he had seen this girl somewhere before. In a painting maybe. It was that wistful provincial look popular in Biedermeier pieces. Even her clothing— a heavy-stitched skirt and white blouse—matched the period. They must do it for the tourists, Jan assumed. Nobody dressed like that anymore.

The girl proceeded to lay out glasses and silverware on the table, performing her task with care. There appeared to be a method to her work as she circled the table, arranging the utensils and folding the napkins. The cutlery was oddly shaped, as though each was intended for a very specific purpose: a carving knife with a convex blade, a fork with uneven prongs, miniature tongs with pointed edges. Picking up the knife and studying it, Jan was reminded of a surgical instrument.

While Jan inspected the cutlery, Arkady turned his attention to the woman, asking what would be served for dinner.

"Boar," the woman replied bluntly, keeping an eye on the girl as she performed her work.

"In that case, may we request a *pichet* of red wine to accompany the meal?" he asked, turning to Jan. A slight smile flickered across his lips. Arkady made it seem like he was doing him a favor.

Jan turned the carving knife over in his hands and chuckled. "And I'm sure they have it, don't they?" he said, more to himself.

"Of course," the woman said, furrowing her brow.

"Then it's settled," Arkady remarked, clapping his hands. "Boar and wine it is."

Once the woman and girl had left the room, Jan leaned back in his chair and cast a long look across the table.

"How long did it take you to arrange this?" he asked, picking at a loose thread in the napkin.

"Meaning?"

"*Meaning?* This is obviously some kind of joke."

"Is it?"

"Yes."

"A joke? Then what's the punchline."

"Arkady, I can't..." He rested his elbows on the table and inclined forward. "Arkady, what happened in the past—"

"Water under the bridge, like I said."

"No, it obviously isn't. Otherwise, why this?" waving a hand around the room. "This makes me feel less sorry for you, you know."

"I never wanted your pity."

"What are you after? A confession? A show of contrition? Fine, you can have it..."

"You seem to misunderstand."

"Do I?"

"Yes. I was walking along that road when suddenly there you were..."

"Exactly," Jan exclaimed, bringing his hands down on the table and making the cutlery rattle. He hated to let Arkady see he was getting under his skin. "You think that's a coincidence?"

"I've never believed in them, but look..."

His voice trailed off as the door opened and the woman appeared, bearing a carafe in hand. There was a slightly ritualistic quality to the way she tipped the carafe to fill their glasses, wiped the lip, and placed the pitcher in the center of the table.

Arkady held the glass up to the light, evaluating the wine's clarity. The way he intently gazed at the liquid felt slightly taunting.

Jan wasn't going to take the bait. Instead, he picked up his glass and took a sip. The wine had an unusually thick consistency, but the taste was immaculate. It was clean and floral, lingering on the palate.

"You approve?" Arkady asked.

"It's fine," Jan said, not wishing to add more.

"You won't admit it, will you?"

"Admit what?"

"That I brought you here, rather than the other way around."

"Knock it off, Arkady! Why is it always about *you*?"

Jan took another sip. The wine felt viscid and heavy in his mouth.

The door swung open, and the girl entered with plates balanced on each arm. Jan sat in silence as she once again circled the table arranging the platters of meat and steamed vegetables. As she did so, Arkady plied her with questions, asking about vinting techniques and the pH levels of the soil in the region. It was Arkady at his most transparent, showing off as usual. To Jan's satisfaction, the girl showed little interest.

"You do make this here, right?" he asked, holding up his glass.

The girl nodded without looking up. "Yes," she whispered.

"Does it have a name?"

The girl shrugged.

Jan watched her hands as she laid the plates on the table. He had not noticed it before, but her right hand was deformed. The fingers were thin and clenched together like a desiccated paw. She balanced the plates on her right forearm, transferring them to her more dexterous appendage. The girl must have noticed him staring because she began cradling the malformed hand closer to her body. He was being rude, he assumed, as he took another gulp.

The alcohol was taking hold of him. He could feel its warm, mellowing effect as he poured himself a second glass from the carafe.

Once they were alone again, Jan picked up the oddly shaped carving knife and poked at his food. He didn't have much of an appetite, but eating was a welcomed diversion. Arkady was shamelessly funneling food into his mouth and washing it down with large slurps of wine. In his carelessness, drops of wine splashed onto his collar, flecking it with heavy maroon blotches.

"You're not eating," Arkady remarked, pointing at his plate with a fork.

"I..." Jan began.

In the pale light, Arkady's face appeared ashen and swollen, his eyes clouded. They sank into his face like two alabaster stones encased by tumid lids, features more reptilian than human.

"Are you all right?" he asked, continuing to chew.

He must have drunk too much because looking at Arkady's collar he saw the wine stains expanding like an oil slick. Arkady continued to speak, but his lips did not move. The voice was coming from a large gash in his throat. Looking at his hand, Jan realized he was clutching the carving knife tightly, its serrated blade speckled with the same wine-colored red.

"I..." Jan tried again.

"Yes...? You *what*?" Arkady pressed.

"I think I should lay down," he finally spit out.

"But you haven't touched the boar," the slit in the throat said, sending a rivulet of red down the front of Arkady's shirt.

Jan sprang to his feet still holding the carving knife. Fleeing the room, he stepped into the hall and proceeded to feel his way through the dark, running his fingers over the plaster and wallpaper in a desperate attempt to retrace his steps. The darkness had an earthy smell and he felt as though he were not alone in it. Something was there with him, quiet and still just beyond the cover of darkness. When his fingers grazed the door, he threw it open and filled his lungs with deep breaths of night air.

Staggering into the starlight, he couldn't make out the road that had led them to the cottage. In every direction, fields covered in trellises and grape vines stretched as far as he could see. He began to run, tramping through the tangle of vines and soft earth.

He caught sight of the large trailing plant too late and stumbled forward. The vine was thick, coiling around itself like a serpent. From the position on his knees, he saw the clusters of grapes drooping from the stalk, their skin black and shiny. Jan had never seen a plant like it before, and as the grapes began to jostle, he understood the vine was wriggling through the dirt, alive. He groped for the carving knife, but it was nowhere. In the field ahead, he could make out the young girl, her figure limned in moonlight. She was approaching, moving through the undergrowth like a slinking cat.

Jan's hands fumbled in the soil, hoping to close over the blade. His fingers scraped against the soft tissue of the vine. It seemed to be erupting directly beneath him. Something was there. A large mass of organic matter. He began clawing at the soil, trying to unearth the root of the plant. Red wine pooled in the shallow hole. His fingertips touched the fleshy tip of the nose first. Wiping away the loamy residue, he saw Arkady's lifeless face peering up at him, the eye sockets and mouth caked with mud. Vines heavy with grapes sprouted from his chest and throat, sending leafy tendrils twisting out across the field in every direction. Jan let out a wail as the cavity brimmed over with the thick, red juice of the vine.

Behind him, he could now hear footsteps. Someone was whistling. The melody was vaguely familiar, although slightly out of key. Just dissonant enough to make it unrecognizable.

Lloyd Hammersmith, Importer-Exporter

I was not the first person to live in the attic. That's what the landlady told me the day I moved in. I was never certain whether the remark was intended to set my mind at ease or was just a simple statement of fact. In either event, I decided to call the derelict little room home.

I tossed my small valise containing everything I owned onto the bed. A cloud of dust rose from the sheets, filling the air with an acrid smell. The windows lining the east wall were coated in a fine layer of filth. If you squinted through the grimy panes, you could see the old docks on the street below and beyond that, the Penarth marina on the opposite shore with its weather-beaten stalls and forlorn seaside kiosks.

Given my situation, it was hard to complain. I was new to the city, earned a modest income as a freelance copyeditor, and had very few ambitions in life. Getting by was enough. It always had been. The secluded room felt just the place for me, and after a while, I did come to think of it as home.

The neighbors were a mixed lot. The couple on the fourth floor argued incessantly, often carrying on well into the night. The raised voices and pounding furniture began the day I arrived and never let up. Listening to them, you would have thought the apartment was inhabited by two prize fighters. After a few weeks, I grew accustomed to the racket and learned to work around the noise. The floor below the argumentative couple was occupied by a Moroccan named Ben, whom I came to know quite well during my period of residence there.

About a month after moving in, the couple kicked up a

commotion unlike anything I had ever heard: shattering dishes, violent screams, objects hurled with brute force against the walls. After some hesitation, I crept down the stairs and found Ben standing in the hall with an expression of disbelief on his face. From outside, the row sounded awful. Neither of us wanted to intervene. In the end, I was the one who knocked, rapping my knuckles forcefully against the door to hide any inhibitions I had.

The door flew open. I expected to be greeted by a burly man with massive arms. Instead, I found myself face to face with a petite, middle-aged woman clutching a pan in her right hand.

"What do you want?" she asked, visibly annoyed.

Behind her, a man in a white undershirt was slumped over a kitchen table staring dismally into a cup of tea set before him. He didn't look up or make eye contact as I peered inside. The room was in shambles. The sight of this intimidated man huddled there amid the chaos had a surreal quality.

"You're making a great deal of noise," I told the woman, trying to sound assertive.

She laughed and jabbed a finger into my chest. "You really should mind your own business," she said before slamming the door.

I looked at Ben and without a word we broke into fits of uncontrollable laughter.

After that, I thought a great deal about the cowed man I had seen sitting among the broken dishes and overturned furniture. There was something about the way he just sat there silently drinking his tea without protest I found brutally honest and suggestive about the world.

This was our little community. All except for the business that occupied the bottom two floors.

I noticed the sign the day I moved in, a tarnished metal plaque affixed to the redbrick advertising Lloyd Hammersmith, Importer-Exporter. As to what Mr. Hammersmith traded in, I had little clue. Nothing suggested a flourishing business or even that the firm was still operational: no men hurrying about with invoice slips clenched in their fists, no packing crates or lorry drivers, no employees entering or exiting the premises. The bottom two floors were as silent as a tomb. I assumed Mr. Hammersmith and his associates had closed up shop long ago, a vestige of the days when Cardiff was a bustling port city in Britain's global empire. Such wistfulness hardly seemed out of place among the dilapidated and peeling buildings of the bay area. Cardiff practically oozed imperial nostalgia. Each crumbling edifice was a reminder of prosperous days long since passed.

Of course, I was wrong.

One afternoon I returned home to find a thin, even-faced man standing in the hall. He looked like an office clerk with his starched white shirt and thick-framed glasses. The man gave no indication he was engaged in any particular activity. He simply stood outside the door on the first floor landing impatiently tapping his shoe on the tile.

"Hello," I said, eliciting a dismissive nod.

Ascending to the attic, I could hear the staccato rap of his shoe against the title echoing through the hall. In the afternoon quiet, it sounded like the measured ticking of a clock.

I had finally met the mysterious Mr. Hammersmith, and I was underwhelmed. For months I had imagined a dapper Victorian gentleman or an eccentric traveler scouring the world for curios. What I got instead was a nearsighted bookkeeper in shirtsleeves.

***

After the night of the commotion on the fourth floor, Ben and I became proper neighbors. We exchanged small talk whenever we passed in the hall. He told me about his construction work, and I filled him in on the bland details of copyediting medical texts. Nothing remarkable. The kind of pleasantries you would expect between strangers getting acquainted with one another.

On a balmy September evening, Ben knocked on my door and invited me down for tea. The text on hepatitis prevention I was reading scarcely commanded my attention and so I saw no reason to decline.

"Sure," I told him. "Better than hepatitis."

Ben's apartment was a railroad-style flat extending the entire length of the building. The rooms were sparsely furnished, although it was clear he had attempted to create a sense of domesticity from the meager possessions he did own. We sat at the kitchen table drinking tea and talking about nothing in particular. In the course of the conversation, I learned Ben had come to the United Kingdom three years ago on a work visa, leaving his wife and child behind in Rabat. Half his pay went back each month to support them. His plan had been to relocate his family at a later date. After years of writing to the Home Office, however, Ben admitted he was at a loss. Manual labor did not pay a great deal, I wagered. Certainly not enough to fulfill the high-income requirements and fees set by the Home Office.

He opened his wallet and removed a dog-eared photograph of a young woman and child. The boy in the picture appeared happy, the woman less so.

"My son is five," he told me. "The last time I saw him he was a baby."

I could sympathize with his dilemma, although it was probably no different from many other migrant workers who found their way into the country. Long days, endless bureaucratic formalities, socializing with foreigners who spoke of distant homelands in thickly accented English: I certainly didn't envy his situation. It seemed a lonely life, a life of constant estrangement and frustrating disappointments.

I was about to remark on the photograph when a noise interrupted. At first, I thought the couple upstairs was about to kick up their usual racket, but I realized that this noise was different. It sounded like a large animal running back and forth beneath the floorboards. The galloping went from one end of the apartment to the other, rattling the teacups in their saucers.

"What was that?" I asked when the noise ceased.

"It happens sometimes," Ben replied, almost apologetically.

"*That* happens often? Does he have an ape running across the ceiling down there?"

Ben shrugged and dabbed at the small drops of tea on the table with a napkin. He seemed fine with the fact that he lived in a building with rowdy neighbors.

"Have you met him?" I asked. "The man downstairs, I mean? He seems an odd fellow."

Ben admitted he had met the proprietor once or twice, adding that Hammersmith had come to his apartment and introduced himself personally.

"I suppose having to walk up to the attic would be too exhausting," I chuckled.

"He is interested in a book I have," Ben explained, mistaking my comment for irritation. "I don't believe he is a rude man."

"Book?"

He nodded and walked over to a thinly populated bookshelf containing a few volumes and paperbacks. Without much searching, he retrieved a leatherbound tome and placed it on the table. I could tell from the coarse pages that the book was old. The leather cover was embossed with looping Arabic script.

"It's been in my family a long time," Ben said as I began flipping through the pages.

I could not read the script, but it didn't resemble the handwritten Arabic I was accustomed to seeing in store windows along the city road. Under normal circumstances I would have given the book a cursory examination to be polite. However, upon opening the volume I discovered it contained a series of plates with detailed illustrations of spider-like men and minaret-studded cities. I was no expert, but I could tell the book was probably worth a significant sum of money. Perhaps Hammersmith was an eccentric in search of exotic curios after all.

Over the coming week, editing took up a great deal of my time as I worked over texts concerned with disease and public health. I read about millions of people stricken by influenza and cholera epidemics capable of wiping out entire city districts. My mind conjured up images of sick and coughing people, apartment buildings under quarantine, and families clustered together in small, ill-lit rooms. In between these apocalyptic daydreams, I took walks around the bay. On most days, cold rain lashed the waterfront and clouds hung low on the horizon. Through the hazy drizzle, the old shipping houses looked forlorn, almost menacing. Roaming about the abandoned esplanades, I came to despise autumn with its blustery gales and sunless skies. Here, brightly colored foliage and crisp air were nonexistent.

As per my normal work schedule, I made a habit of returning home just as night accumulated in the sky. Basking in the warmth of electric heaters, I sat up in bed late into the night, circling odd bits of text and correcting spelling errors in red ink. Hardly an exhilarating lifestyle, but one I had grown accustomed to. Lack of expectation was a virtue, I told myself. It meant a life bereft of disappointment, regret, and countless other miseries that gnawed away at most people on a daily basis.

These thoughts were heavy in my mind on the Thursday I returned home from my latest meandering. I stepped into the foyer and proceeded to remove my wet jacket just as the door at the opposite end of the hall creaked open. In the dim light, I saw Ben exit and close the door behind him. Our eyes met and I noticed a guilty expression on his face.

"I was visiting with Mr. Hammersmith."

"That so?" I asked as I fumbled with my stuck zipper.

"He is going to purchase my book," he continued, perhaps feeling he had to explain his visit. In all honesty, it was nothing to me if he was cordial with the other neighbors.

"Right-o," was all I could think to say. "Maybe one of these days I'll properly introduce myself. Maybe see what kind of animal he has locked up in that apartment. I only met him in the hall that one time."

At this, Ben's expression changed. "So you've met Mr. Hammersmith before?"

"Yes. The man with the glasses and crew cut. I can't say he seemed all that engaging."

Ben puzzled over my comment for a moment.

"Oh, him," he finally replied. "Yes, I know him, but that's not Mr. Hammersmith."

***

The clatter and scraping noises began sometime after midnight. I can't remember if I awoke or if I had been lying in bed on the verge of sleep. Muted voices echoed in the hall followed by the sound of jostling, bumping, and hammering. A thin line of electric light seeped under the door.

After a half hour, I crawled out of bed, braving the early December chill. I found the combative couple standing on the landing in robes and slippers. Neither of them looked up as I joined. They were leaning over the banister, heads angled downward toward the commotion.

"What is it?" I whispered.

The woman flashed me an irritated expression suggesting she couldn't be bothered to explain.

I craned my neck and saw three men at the bottom of the stairwell maneuvering a large packing crate through the front door. Its edges knocked against the walls as they navigated the object into the narrow hall. "Lift, don't drag," a voice instructed. The sound of footsteps and hammering on wood followed.

"No consideration," the woman grunted, elbowing her husband and receiving an obsequious nod.

I honestly didn't see how they were in a position to complain.

"Maybe you should go down and speak with them," I offered, not bothering to hide my grin. "Maybe *they* don't realize they've woken up the whole building."

I expected a sharp retort, but instead, a panic-stricken expression spread across the woman's face.

"I've said all I need to him," she replied.

"Oh, so you've met him too?"

A stony silence followed, punctuated by the sound of hammering and splintering wood below.

When she came knocking at my door three days later, I imagined she was going to have it out with me for my offhand comments that night. Who did I think I was making such insinuations? Why didn't I mind my own damn business? I answered the door ready for a fight. I didn't get one.

She glared at me in her usual way and then gestured to a woman standing at her side. The stranger was dressed in a long floral gown. A scarf covered her head, exposing a young face with deep-set eyes.

"She's looking for your friend," my neighbor said as if this settled the issue.

"I don't know where he is," I told her. "He's not here."

She shrugged and walked off, leaving me alone with the woman.

Unsure of what to do, I invited the woman in and offered her a seat. My room was hardly suited for entertaining guests. Loose sheets of text and crumpled papers littered the floor. Laundry, most of it in need of washing, was draped across the furniture. I apologized for the mess, although it didn't seem to bother the woman in the least. She sat in the chair and gazed at the floor, her hands fidgeting nervously in her lap. In the pale afternoon light, I noticed that the skin on her cheeks was chapped and peeling, marring an otherwise flawless complexion.

"You're looking for Ben?" I asked.

She said nothing.

I was trying not to stare and busied myself with preparing the kettle. I had no desire for tea at the moment, but it filled the silence and gave me something to do. My eyes continued to fix on the restive hands cupped in front of her, the way they contorted and enclosed one another like two wrestling animals. Every so often she unlocked her fingers to scratch at the dried patch of skin on her cheek before returning them to her lap.

"You're his wife?" I said, realizing I was talking to myself.

The woman bore a certain resemblance to the one I had seen in the photograph. Her face appeared more drawn than I remembered, and the scarf concealed her hair. No errant locks protruded from under the fabric. It looked taut, as if stretched across a bald scalp.

As I took all this in, the woman began rocking back and forth in the chair, her eyes darting about the room like a frightened animal. I ignored it at first, but the swaying became more violent.

The front legs of the chair rose off the ground and landed with a dull thud. She was mumbling quietly to her herself, although the words eluded me.

"Are you...?" I asked, placing a hand on her fists to calm them and steady the chair.

Her hands were clammy to the touch and for a split second, I thought I felt movement. Not the agitated wrestling of hands and fingers, but a slithering just beneath the skin. I recalled a summer spent at an aunt's house long ago where earthworms crawled through the garden. On lazy afternoons, I would sit in the grass watching their writhing bodies twist in the dirt. This image jumped into my mind as my fingers grazed her moist, spasming flesh.

As if able to read my thoughts, the woman recoiled and for the first time looked at me. I withdrew my hand as her mouth contorted into a sneer and she released a low hissing noise like a cat.

It was an hour before I finally found Ben in his apartment and explained the situation. A smile crept across his lips.

"She's arrived," he trilled and bounded up the stairs.

The woman was exactly where I had left her, and I was happy to have Ben take her off my hands. I wasn't sure what to make of the whole thing. Then again, it wasn't my problem either, I told myself. I reheated the kettle with the intention of resuming my work, but concentrating on medical texts proved impossible. Instead, I drank tea and listened to the patter of the afternoon rain against the window, wondering what was taking place two floors below.

By the time I descended the two flights, I had already convinced myself I was just checking up rather than satisfying my own curiosity. Ben was sitting at the kitchen table, not doing much of anything. I noticed the head scarf and gown the woman had been wearing crumpled up in a ball on the carpet. She was in the other room sleeping, I was told.

"Your wife?" I asked.

He nodded without adding anything. He looked tired. I decided not to press the issue.

"And your son? I assume..." I nodded in the direction of the bedroom door.

Ben turned his eyes to the floor. "That is a different arrangement," he murmured.

I might have asked whether he was referring to the Home Office, but I didn't need to. I was already grasping the situation, remembering the book and Ben's expectant look the day he exited Hammersmith's apartment. Lloyd Hammersmith, importer-exporter: I repeated the phrase over in my mind realizing the sick joke.

***

The next day I walked down and banged on Hammersmith's door. The officious-looking man with the glasses answered. I was prepared to wedge my foot in the door and confront him, but there was no need. The man smiled and welcomed me into the office.

Shelves containing books and decorative boxes lined the walls. Some had taxidermy animals perched on them, birds mostly, although I spotted a small wildcat with a fading coat. In the middle of the room sat a large mahogany desk, and behind it a wall filled with a variety of ornamental clocks, all ticking away the measured seconds of the day at their own pace. At the far corner was a door leading into the back rooms of the apartment. From my position, I couldn't get a clear line of sight into the first room, but it looked to be packed with boxes.

What struck me as odd were the other objects scattered throughout the room. You might expect to find books and *objets d'art* in the office of a trading firm, but interspersed with these were ordinary, everyday objects: a coffee percolator, a chipped mug, a child's toy model rocket, a rock with a heart painted on it. Each of these objects was displayed in the same manner as the others, creating the impression of a collection with little logic or coherence.

"Sorry to say we haven't met yet," the man said, offering me a seat opposite the desk as I studied the objects on the shelves. I was slightly unnerved by the glass-eyed stare of the mounted wildcat and assumed it was positioned directly across from the seat to create this precise effect on visitors. "My name's Clayson. Martin Clayson."

"An associate of Mr. Hammersmith?" I asked.

The man chuckled and asked if I wanted any tea or coffee. He seemed put off when I declined and got down to business. "So, what brings you here?"

"A client of yours."

"That so?"

"Benjallun Majid, the man on the second floor."

Clayson's eyes lit up behind his thick lenses. "Ah, yes. The man with the book. He was not a client of mine. My client was the man who wanted to purchase the item. A minor detail, though. He was in possession of a very unique manuscript. Imagine, a fifteenth-century facsimile of *Ma Baed al-Nujūm* here in Cardiff. Amazing how you can discover such treasures where you least expect them." He smiled, although it was not a warm smile.

"Can I ask what you paid him for it?"

"I'm afraid that would violate confidentiality," Clayson replied.

"Look," I began, "I don't appreciate people taking advantage, especially when somebody's in a tight spot. Or would you like me to involve the authorities in this?"

I thought my threat would change the tone of the conversation, but Clayson only stared at me from behind the desk, his mouth half-opened in a smirk. Then he began to laugh. "Authorities? You make it sound like a crime has been committed."

"Hasn't one?" I said in an even voice.

This remark provoked even more laughter.

"You have quite an imagination," Clayson said once his laughter subsided. "You could go to the authorities if you want. I doubt they would pay you much attention."

He looked at me over the rim of his glasses. His eyes were as cold and dead as the stuffed cat.

"I assure you, my dealings with Mr. Majid were fair and

equitable. I delivered on my end."

As Clayson said this, a noise came from the back room: a rustling sound followed by a soft thud, like pulp slung against a wall. Clayson froze and cast an apprehensive glance at the open door.

"What was that?"

"Just some deliverymen," Clayson said in a thin voice. "They're unpacking a few recent acquisitions."

Something about his expression implied we both knew this was a lie. A long pause followed. He was challenging me to confront him, to call him out.

"And where is Mr. Hammersmith? Is he around? I suppose I ought to meet him too," I finally said, breaking the silence.

Clayson fixed me with an impenetrable look. He began to laugh again, but this time the laugh was mirthless. "You didn't *really* think there was a Lloyd Hammersmith, did you? It's a name, a corporate entity."

I was about to contest this, but Clayson interjected and began drumming his fingers on the desktop. "Your problem is you don't belong here," he told me. "You're not like them."

"*Them?*"

"Yes, *them.*"

He reached into a wastebasket beside the desk, drew out a crumpled ball of paper, and placed it leisurely on the desk. Staring at it, I suddenly knew that were I to unfold this balled-up piece of paper I would find a section of medical text marked up in my own careful hand.

"When I look at this scrap of paper," Clayson continued, "do you know what I see? Nothing. It's completely blank to me. It can't be read or deciphered. It can't be *figured out* because there's nothing *to* figure out. It wants nothing and it gives nothing."

I stared at the balled-up paper. It looked minuscule and insignificant sitting there on the large surface of the desk.

"It doesn't belong *here* among all these objects, all these things with decorative features and functions. Do you see what I'm getting at?"

I didn't, but I suddenly wanted to be far away from Clayson and whatever was in the back room. So I nodded and said I had to be going. I left with the vaguest impression that my abrupt exit had in some small way suggested I agreed with his odd statements. The feeling did not sit well with me as I stepped into the hall and the door shut behind me.

Walking back up the stairs, I heard the bellowing and crashing begin. The neighbors were at it again, their argumentative voices filling the corridor. As I passed the apartment, I noticed the door was slightly ajar. Through the crack, I saw the man sitting at the table, his shoulders hunched, a dejected expression on his face as he gazed into the bottom of his teacup. The woman was hollering at the top of her lungs, screaming to the world that her husband lacked initiative and that all successful men needed initiative and drive if they expected to make anything of themselves. What did he have? Did *he* have initiative? Did he have *drive*? The floor was littered with smashed dishes and random pieces of silverware, and by the sound of it, the debris was only going to keep accumulating. It would accumulate until it filled every room in the apartment. Until there was nothing left to break or smash or throw. Until the detritus reached the ceiling, burying them alive in their own destruction.

The Artist's Apartment

I t was August when I moved into the artist's apartment. That was how we referred to it—*the artist's apartment*—although no artist had lived in it for almost a century.

"Maybe an interior decorator somewhere in the interval? Someone who drew cartoons for literary magazines?" Joshka teased, eyes turned to the ceiling as he admired the crown molding and cornices. "One of the lesser-known creative types somewhere over the years?"

But no. There had only been one.

On the day of the viewing, the real estate agent provided me with a tour and what amounted to a brief history lecture. It had been spring then, and raining. I had sat across the street at a café watching water cascade off the storefront awnings, waiting for the agent to arrive.

"Apologies," was all she said as she took the keys out of her pocket and slid them into the lock, as though this simple word was the only one required to explain her lateness and, perhaps, the afternoon's bad weather.

"The building, as you can see, is quite old but well-preserved," she began as we filed up the narrow staircase. "There are not too many like it on the market in Copenhagen these days." And then, with a knowing look and half-smile, "Old money has the nostalgic urge to cling to old things."

I nodded, unsure of what she meant.

Empty rooms have always elicited a certain sadness in me. They evoke no sense of life or home. Footsteps sound hollow and unabsorbed in them. There is an oppressive, hygienic feel to the vacuity.

I can't help but think of a mortuary.

"...and in addition to the charm," the agent went on, her heels rhythmic on the wood floors, "it should be added that Constantin Ingermann once lived here."

The name was unfamiliar, although I knew by the way the agent pronounced it, I was expected to recognize it.

"Ah," was all I replied, turning my attention to a standing mirror in the corner of the bedroom. The hand-carved frame looked old. I ran my finger along its edge and listened to the rain beat against the window. "And do the articles in the place come with it?" I asked, changing the subject.

Constantin Ingermann has been called the Danish van Gogh, although the comparison should not be drawn too far. His works have never been featured in any of the major national galleries, nor are his paintings in high demand on the international art market. Even his style, while modernist, bears little resemblance to the master. In fact, the only similarity seems to be that he died poor and virtually unrecognized in his lifetime. In Denmark, his name will raise some eyebrows and a few of his larger canvases dot the walls of the Statens Museum, but in Paris or London he is a veritable *inconnu*. When the Nazis occupied Denmark, they didn't bother to send the Ingermanns back to Berlin with all the other valuables. This detail was the one I liked repeating best to friends and relatives: I was inhabiting the former apartment of an artist that even the Nazis found tasteless.

However, it did add a certain charm to the apartment, as the agent said. I had never lived in a place with a pedigree, no matter how minuscule. My previous apartments had been modern studio types, quickly built and architecturally bland at best. Nobody remotely famous had ever lived in them. The closest was a previous tenant who had appeared in a commercial for sporting goods. It gave me a nice anecdote with which to edify guests.

Joshka acted unimpressed, of course, but even in his snarky references to "the *artist's* apartment" I could detect a hint of envy. In fact, his secret jealousy became one of the most appealing qualities of the apartment.

***

It takes time before you feel completely comfortable in a new apartment. The first week you busily rearrange furniture, unpack belongings from boxes, and try to create an environment that accommodates your particular daily rhythms. The nights breed a feeling of unsettledness. The creaks, the hum of the electricity, the sounds that echo from the hall; everything is unfamiliar. On the first night I slept in the apartment, I lay in the dark catching glimpses of myself in the standing mirror. This object was what an anthropologist might call "a trace," an artifact, in this case one left by a previous tenant. Naturally, my thoughts then turned to the anonymous people who had lived within these same walls, who had carried out their lives, slept, dreamed, and loved within the confines of the very same space I now occupied. "Man does not have a single consistent life," Chateaubriand once wrote. "He has several laid end to end." I could not help but wonder if the same might be true of living spaces, whether they too possessed several lives laid end to end as old occupants moved on and new ones took their place.

By the third week, I began to feel settled and decided on a date for the customary housewarming party. I invited some colleagues and friends, with the proviso that they should not come bearing gifts. Some ignored my request, leaving me with a set of cheese knives that I never used and a potted Gardenia bonsai that died three weeks later due to neglect.

During dinner, I was in the middle of telling guests about my new neighborhood when Joshka, a bit drunk by this point, let out a snicker.

"Alain, I can't believe you haven't mentioned the artist yet."

People exchanged puzzled looks as I glared at Joshka across the table.

"That back room," he continued, "it surely must have been his studio, no?"

"Whose studio?" someone asked.

"Constantin Ingermann's of course," Joshka replied, smiling.

"The *artist?*" another asked, eliciting a murmur around the table.

I explained that the apartment had once been rented by him, passing off this information with an air of nonchalance. I had been waiting to inform my guests of this fact over after-dinner drinks. Joshka, in his usual brusque manner, had spoiled the moment.

"And *this* was his studio?" a woman asked.

"That room right back there," Joshka replied. "Right where Alain's desk and chair are now. You can tell by the coloring on the floor..." he said as he beckoned everyone to follow him. "See those slightly discolored boards in the wood? Linseed oil. It's used as a solvent for oil paint."

"Whose apartment is this?" I asked him with an annoyed smile. "You seem quite the expert on it."

"Weird," a colleague of mine replied, bending down and rubbing the tips of her fingers over the off-colored section of the floor. "You *know* his paintings are in the museum here?"

"Right. Weren't good enough for the Reich."

"Come again?"

"Never mind. Bad joke," as I attempted to herd everyone back into the dining room.

It was after that we began collectively referring to it as "the artist's apartment." At work, colleagues would ask, "How are you settling into the artist's apartment?" If I went out with Joshka, he would inquire what the going rate was for an artist's studio in my quarter or whether I knew that blueprints for an artist's apartment were customarily sketched in pastel. Naturally, this was his form of a playful running joke, but taken together it was adding up to an unspoken presumption: the apartment was not considered properly mine. Nobody said *Alain's* apartment or *your* apartment. I lived in *the artist's* apartment, as if I were a houseguest temporarily keeping up the residence until its proper owner returned.

About a week after the housewarming, I was sitting at my desk reading when I noticed one of the strips of wallpaper above the radiator had come loose at the edge. The rising heat had moistened the solvent, causing the paper to crease and curl back slightly. I snapped my book shut and was about to flatten the crease with my palm when I saw that the small patch of wall beneath was black. Mold, I suspected, as I peeled back the paper a little, already wondering if the estate agent might have omitted a few details regarding the state of the property in her sales pitch. However, all I found was more black followed by a patch of egg-shell white and a speck of crimson. The paper loosened with a sticky tearing sound to reveal what was unmistakably a human form.

By the time Joshka arrived the next evening, I had practically denuded the back wall of my study.

"Redecorating, I see?"

"Unbelievable, isn't it?"

He scratched his chin and looked over my discovery.

Beneath the wallpaper lay a series of painted images on sheets of linen. Each featured a human figure against a black, formless background. The figures were pale and thin looking, their limbs posed in various gestures suggesting actions. In some, the bodies appeared maimed and disfigured with flecks of dark red staining the flesh; others gleamed with a skeletal brilliance under the light. The faces were crude, but not undistinguished. Care had been given to convey emotion in the dark pitted eyes and expressive mouths.

"I remember reading about some Michelangelo frescos found on the walls of a church in Italy," Joshka said as he studied the images. "I think they ended up going for a few million. Think you'll get that?"

"Seriously?"

He laughed. "You'll be lucky if they don't stick you with the bill for the wallpaper. Michelangelos are works of beauty. These..." He shrugged.

"Ingermann?" I asked.

"I can't say I know what his stuff looks like. Maybe. Makes sense." Joshka ran his fingers over one of the paintings and grimaced. "Not a fan of the new look you're going for. A bit... violent... creepy... macabre. You know?"

I nodded.

My study was now decorated with murals reminiscent of Goya's

Disasters of War.

***

I remember the leaves most. They seemed to shrivel on the branches and hang there like desiccated insect skins. When the wind blew, they made a sinister respiratory sound as though the entire earth was trying to breathe. The dry husking noise haunted my dreams. I heard it upon waking: every grey, wet morning, that cadence echoed along the coast, beckoning in some inhuman language.

The first night I arrived at the cabin, I noticed a rusted chime hanging from the eaves of the porch. For days, the violent wind belted out a perpetual cacophony of notes. Thinking it must have been somebody's idea of a joke long ago, I tore it down in anticipation of a few good nights of sleep. That was when I became conscious of the rustling noises swimming through the silence and understood why the former lodger had tolerated the din day in and day out. Most nights, I refrained from lighting a fire in the hearth and slept huddled in my coat. It was difficult to light matches in the damp and the smoke from the chimney would be visible for miles. I contented myself with the sallow glow of oil light, watching my breath materialize before me in the frigid air, listening to the distant crash of the surf on the crags, and eating preserved fish from cans.

On the days the rain ceased, I wandered along the beetling cliffs of the coast. Seventy meters below, a pebble-strewn beach extended into the ocean. I sat in the wet grass for a while and watched the heaving foam dash upon the rocks. I naturally wondered if anyone had ever thrown themselves from the cliff, perhaps motivated by unrequited love or simply boredom. At great heights, this idea always fixes itself in the mind. A human obsession with our own mortality. Isn't that what he had said to me once as he took my hand in that familiar way he had? We are obsessed with our own demise. These were what passed for sweet words between us, and I loved him for it. I did.

One afternoon, I spotted a person walking along the beach. He wore a heavy slicker and had a fishing pole slung over his shoulder. From the window, I watched him meander along the water's edge, his head bent against the wind. He was the first person I had seen in weeks and all I *could think was, "God, I'm not alone."*

***

In the east wing of the Statens Museum there is a small room exhibiting the paintings of Constantin Ingermann. The canvases—eight in total—are a mix of portraiture, landscapes, and vignette. The largest of the canvases is a full-length portrait of Fru Ingermann, wife of the artist. She is dressed in a blue coat, standing in three-quarter pose. Despite being indoors, she wears a matching blue cloche hat from under which stream curls of blonde hair. Her face is plain, even homely, with a narrow nose and thin lips. The eyes are the most captivating feature. They give the impression of a fixed stare that meets the viewer's gaze from every angle.

"There is something indescribable about her, isn't there?" came a voice behind me.

I turned to find a petite, mousey woman with large glasses. She was exactly as I had pictured.

"No need to stare," she told me with a smile. "We have a post-card in the gift shop for purchase."

As we walked through the wings of the museum, Linette Jespen gave me a biographical sketch of the man she had spent two years of her life researching while completing a master's in art history. Constantin Ingermann led a reclusive life, most of which remained undocumented and, as Linette added, with good reason. He experienced a brief period of fame in the mid-1920s, working primarily in Copenhagen and Skøvgaard, before falling out with the established circles of Danish modernists and withdrawing into obscurity. Ingermann had never managed to attract wealthy patrons in Europe or the United States, a cardinal sin in the art world destined to condemn even the most promising talent to a life of inconsequence. After divorcing his wife, he left Denmark to continue his career in Paris.

"Truth be told," Linette concluded as we entered her private office in the curatorial department, "it was only in France that he managed to establish any kind of reputation for himself, and that only because he changed his style."

"I see," as I took a seat across from her desk.

Up until this moment, I had been relatively convinced that the paintings decorating my study wall were not Ingermann's at all. They were stylistically distinct from the canvases in the museum collection. Comparing the two required a broad stretch of the imagination. I removed three photographs from an envelope and placed them on her desk.

"Into a style like *this*?"

She examined the photos carefully. "No, not exactly. Definitely more abstract and darker, but not as defined as these works. And *these* are...?"

"From my private collection," I said, explaining the story.

When I finished, she furrowed her brow and remained silent.

"Have any other artists lived in that apartment?" I finally asked.

"I am sure I would not be able to tell you that," she said as she leaned back in her chair with a thoughtful expression.

Outside, a quiet rain beat against the windows.

After we finished talking, Linette led me into an adjoining room housing the special collections. She removed a large folio from a set of drawers and began flipping through a series of sketches done in Conté crayon and charcoal.

"Most of these were drawn in your apartment," she said, turning the pages slowly. They were sketches of everyday objects: half-finished hands and torsos, detailed nudes etched in black chalk and graphite. The paper rustled slightly as she turned the pages. "Strange to think, isn't it?" Her thoughts seemed to be suddenly far away.

"Who is this?" I asked, pointing to a boy sitting cross-legged on a bed. He was present in several of the drawings, his body posed casually, his eyes communicative and always fixed directly on the observer.

"I have wondered the same thing," as she traced the lineaments of the boy's face with her index finger, suggesting a familiarity. "Officially, he has never been identified, but I have some hunches."

She paused, wondering whether she was boring me with tedious details. When she saw I was interested, she continued. "Existing letters indicate that Ingermann hired a German boy named Arthur to model for him in the late twenties. He never appeared in any finished works, but this could be him."

"But you don't believe that?" I asked.

She shook her head and walked over to a second drawer to fetch a slip of cardstock. Laying it down on the table, I recognized it immediately as the postcard of the Fru Ingermann painting hanging in the east wing. "Look at the faces, the eyes... Quite similar, aren't they?"

"Slightly," I admitted, comparing them.

"I think this might have been a relation of Ingermann's wife. I have absolutely nothing to back this up, mind you. Just a likeness. Not that it matters," she said, closing the folio with care. "Old drawings hide their secrets well. They divulge only as much as we allow them to."

"What an odd thing to say," I laughed.

She was smiling as she put the folio back in the drawer and slid it closed, perfectly aware of her idiosyncrasies and, moreover, quite comfortable with them. It was an attractive quality, to say the least.

***

The Russian writer Ivan Turgenev once remarked that a drawing showed at a glance what ten pages of writing took to convey. In the early twentieth century, the newspaper editor Tess Flanders summed up this sentiment with his pithier and more memorable saying, "A picture is worth a thousand words." We are inclined to prize the image over the word, if only for its immediacy. Yet what if there exist no pictures? What if the word is all that we have with its subtleties and digressions?

Anyone searching for Constantin Ingermann will quickly realize that there are no significant pictures of the man. In fact, only two exist. One is a grainy photograph taken at a distance. He stands bundled in a bulky overcoat on a street corner, a low-brimmed hat drawn down over his face. His wife, equally undistinguished, stands beside him, her arm locked in his. It could be any couple out for a stroll on a winter afternoon. The second is of a stooped, elderly man hunched over an easel in a Parisian studio in the late 1950s. Ingermann's back is to the photographer, his face partially concealed as he looks over his shoulder. This timidity extended into his work, as he never painted the customary self-portrait. There is no serialized presentation of an aging artist over the span of a career as one finds with Rembrandt; no impression of changing moods and stylistic experimentation familiar to van Gogh. It would seem that Ingermann deliberately rejected the artist's most essential object: the self as subject.

Words are equally scarce. Birth and death certificates were issued for Constantin Ingermann, but these stand as bookends framing a great vacuity. There exists no official documentation verifying the existence of his wife, and I could find no marriage license for the couple on file at the hall of records. Her full name—Helen Madsen Ingermann—is known only through a single entry in the diary of the Danish modernist Stefen Knudsen. On 18 November 1928, he records having dinner with Ingermann and his new bride, giving her maiden name. According to the entry, the couple had just returned from Germany—presumably their honeymoon—allowing for a vague chronology of events. In the few surviving letters and papers written by Ingermann, his wife is strangely absent. There are few accounts of conjugal life, and those that do exist are troubling. Ingermann's notes are peppered with references to domestic disputes that arose while living in Copenhagen. "Tonight, we fought furiously," he writes in October 1929. "Why is it we will drink to excess and descend upon one another like wild animals with our petty jealousies and recriminations?" he asks in another note a year later. "And always with such violence, as to make me wonder what the neighbors must think." It can be inferred that these quarrels paved the way for the separation that occurred at some point before Ingermann left for France, yet there is no proof of a legal separation or division of commonwealth in the record office. Fru Ingermann appears, struts across the stage like a ghost, and quickly vanishes, leaving little trace of her presence.

The more I began looking at Constantin Ingermann, the opaquer he became. The most vivid pieces were those left by the artist himself: the landscapes of places he visited; the sketches of the objects that he surrounded himself with; the portraits of those with whom he socialized; the repeated drawings of an ephebic youth stretched out across a bed, sitting tranquilly by a fireplace or standing nude in contrapposto like a humbled David. It was this child—the suspected Arthur—that proved the most intriguing. The initial A. appears in Ingermann's papers on various occasions, although with very little substantive detail. His slender body and distinctive face fill the pages of Ingermann's drawing books, and yet he never appeared on a finished canvas. More puzzling is the fact that one of Ingermann's notes dating from 1930 alludes to a session in which A. sat for a painting in his studio.

"Yes, the suspected lost piece," Linette stated with a wry grin. We were standing in the center of my study examining the wall murals. As she listened to me recount my detective work, she twirled the stem of an empty wine glass between her fingers, rotating the bowl back and forth in a contemplative gesture.

"You know, solving this might be quite simple," she finally said after examining the paintings for some time. "Ingermann had a son. Francis, I think. He oversees his father's estate. I received a letter from him years ago when I was working on the museum catalog. I imagine the family could authenticate these."

"I don't remember anything mentioned about a child." In fact, I had specifically made a point to search family birth records.

"Yes, *here* in Copenhagen," Linette replied, looking at me over her glasses. "Ingermann remarried later in life. The family, as far as I know, still lives in France."

Then Linette crossed her arms and concentrated on the paintings again. "You know," as she pointed to the panel on the end of a figure curled into a fetal-like position, "I think this piece belongs *under* the one beside it. See the white strokes on the bottom there? They connect with the one's right in the corner here."

I examined the two canvases and saw that she was right. In this configuration, the image was not of two bodies situated side by side, but rather a curled-up body positioned underneath a standing figure with a series of foreshortened lines dividing the plane between them.

"Any significance in that?" I asked.

She bit solemnly at her lower lip. It was evident she did not like to have her expertise tested in such a manner. "In Christian iconography, saints are sometimes depicted standing above defeated heretics, but I think that's a stretch. It looks like someone standing on a roof with the other person sleeping below them."

I felt like we were grasping at straws and then recalled Linette's comment on the day of our first meeting about pictures only divulging as much as we allowed.

That night, I sat at my desk and began composing a letter to the Ingermann estate. As I worked, I was conscious of the faces gazing down at me from the wall. In the thick silence, their hollowed eyes felt judgmental, conspiratorial even. I remembered having seen some old blankets stored in a back crawlspace filled with small boxes, so I stopped writing and went to fetch them.

The crawl space was roughly three feet high and ten feet deep. It smelled musty and was filled with a variety of items left by the previous tenant: volumes of the *Nouveau Larousse* illustrated encyclopaedia; packages of obsolete electrical fuses; vintage tumblers delicately wrapped in old newspaper. I unwrapped one and noticed that the yellowed paper carried stories from 1951. I pulled these sundry boxes out into the hall and retrieved the blankets piled in the back. I told myself that out of curiosity I would examine the contents of the boxes at some later date and began unfolding the blankets and draping them across the wall paintings. Once the images were out of sight, I was able to continue my work for the evening without interruption.

***

A kilometer to the east I found a copse that opened onto a lake. The trees lining the shore were bare, their branches extending toward the grey clouds like skeletal fingers. The shallow water tended to freeze on most nights when the temperature dropped low enough. Some mornings I ar-rived to find a thin sheet of ice flecked with snow. Its flat, opaline surface had a mesmerizing effect; an unadorned winter jewel hidden among the stripped foliage.

I took to testing the ice with my weight, entertaining the idea of walk-ing clear across the frozen water to the opposite shore. I set the task as a challenge for myself, considering it a respite from my otherwise dull days. I built up my courage slowly, at first walking out only a few inches but gradually expanding my distance from the shore each time. After two weeks, I managed to cover ten meters. A week later, fifteen. I heard the ice creak under my steps as I edged myself out farther. Occasionally, I saw opaque shapes moving below and wondered what variety of aquatic life they might be. As I walked to the lake each morning, I pictured the surface splintering underneath my feet and the water swallowing me in body-numbing oblivion.

By the month's end, I had made it to the center of the lake. From this position, the world felt expansive and unencumbered. A nacreous sky opened around me and I watched as small birds cut vectors across the clouds. Below my feet, large fish churned, their movement just perceptible through the frost-streaked ice. I heard the ice creak and jostle. Cautiously, I got down flat on my stomach to distribute my weight more evenly and prevent the ice from cracking. As I lay there with the cold against my cheek, I stared through the rime and watched the writhing life below. It looked abstract and magnificent, almost incandescent. The forms ac-quired a greater consistency as they rose closer to the surface before plunging back into darkness. I watched in silence as the shapes became more recognizable. Suddenly, the flash of a foot; the glint of smooth ab-domen; a hand pressing itself against the ice. The outline of a human form materialized beneath me, and I gazed silently into the familiar eyes with-out judgment or question.

"You're not here," I whispered to my lover beneath the ice. "I know you're not here."

I pressed my lips to the ice, momentarily imagining the feel of his em-brace. I recalled evenings in the flat, the smell of mineral spirits and burnt kerosene mixing with the humid summer air. We would lay in bed, our naked bodies entwined, a breeze drifting in through the window making the curtains tremble. As he dozed, I would lay awake and stare at us together in the long mirror opposite the bed. In the dark, we looked beautifully inhuman wrapped in each other's arms.

"You're not here," I groaned, but I was only speaking to the fish and the mute darkness below. I lay there still for a long time, feeling the blistering cold seep deep into my body.

***

One evening, Joshka suggested meeting for some drinks along the Nyhaven. Seeing as how it was in my general vicinity, I had no objection. He was the one who had to travel across town and back, which never seemed to bother him. Joshka had an almost slavish inclination for mingling with the tourists and fashionable sorts. I sometimes wondered if he found them generally amusing or simply thought these types of people were constantly "at the center of things," as he would say. "What *things*?" I always asked, to which he would usually roll his eyes. I was clearly on the periphery, although I was perfectly fine with this verdict.

I arrived early and sat alone at a table. The sky was streaked with twilight. A steady stream of people walked along the canal, dodging cyclists and the evening dinner crowds occluding the sidewalk. I noticed a button on the floor under the table and was on my knees inspecting it when Joshka's shoes materialized in the corner of my vision.

"What are you doing?" he asked, unwinding his scarf.

"Being in the middle of things," I told him, reseating myself.

"That again? Okay, so here's the plan—"

"We have a plan?"

"We don't have a lot of time."

"Time for *what*?"

But I could already see as he turned and waved to two women who had just stepped through the door.

"Her name is Alana," he explained in a hushed voice. "I don't know her friend's name. You can inquire. I'll explain later. Just act naturally and you'll do fine."

"Am I auditioning?"

Joshka gave me a pained grin as the two women approached.

Over drinks, Joshka did most of the talking. He lied incessantly, informing Alana he was a magazine writer and had just returned from China. The details of his story shifted at times, but the women didn't seem to notice at first. I engaged her friend in banal chatter. When she inquired what I did, I decided to follow Joshka's lead and lie through my teeth.

"I'm an artist," I told her.

This seemed to satisfy her curiosity and I switched the subject.

Toward the end of the meal, Joshka's deceit started to become evident, and it was at this point that he suggested moving our little gathering to my apartment. I could not help but suspect he intended to verify my identity as an artist and, by doing so, add some credibility to his own web of lies. I was about to jettison the proposal when my appointed date cut in, stating it was a "splendid idea."

**

"This place is... unique," Alana remarked upon entering.

I just smiled politely, asking if red wine was okay.

"And is this *your* work?" my appointed date asked, alluding to the wall paintings.

"Yes," I told her. "They're all mine."

As I opened the wine, I realized I did not have enough wine glasses. "There should be some in that box by the hall," I told Joshka. "They're tumblers. They just need to be washed."

"Classy," Joshka replied, and then asked Alana's friend if she wouldn't mind fetching the glasses from the box while he enlightened Alana on the wall paintings. The friend deferred with a roll of her eyes and disappeared into the hall. A moment later, an ear-piercing scream rang out.

"What?" Joshka bellowed.

She returned visibly upset. "There's a rat in the box!"

We all migrated into the hall and approached the box cautiously. Nothing stirred or scuttled as you might expect a frightened animal to do. Finally, after kicking the box once, Joshka worked up the courage to reach inside. We gathered around, holding our breath. As he rummaged through the box, his face suddenly contorted. He let out a cry that melted into a peal of laughter.

"Gotcha!" he wailed, pulling his arm out with ease. In his hand was clutched a brunette wig made for a woman.

"What is this?" he asked, staring down at the object in his fist.

"A wig?" Alana said, bemused.

"Look, there's another one," said her friend, reaching in and pulling out a matching wig, this one red.

"Something you haven't been telling us, Alain?" Joshka asked with a smile, examining the wig in his hand. It was caked with dust which rose into the air as he turned the wig over in his palms.

"That's not mine," I protested.

"Sure, sure," Joshka teased dismissively, draping the wig over his head playfully. "I think I might be a better redhead, no?" he said, smiling and turning to Alana. "What do you think?"

"I think this is getting weird," she said frankly, looking at him in disbelief.

"Maybe we should go," her friend added.

"Don't be silly," Joshka said, removing the wig. "I was just messing around."

The mood had changed, though, and nobody showed much inclination for wine or conversation by this point. Twenty minutes later, the women called a cab and left. Joshka and I spent the rest of the night sitting on my couch passing the bottle of wine between ourselves until we were good and drunk. By the time I awoke in the morning, he was gone. The two wigs sat on the couch with a note attached to them in Joshka's neat hand: *Don't Forget. Thursday is Ladies' Night at Club Hive.*

***

I was roused by the sound of scraping snow. My eyes fluttered open to see a blur of trees and sky. I instinctively recoiled and felt my weight give as I landed on the cold ground in a sitting position. I scampered backward, checking that my hairpins were fixed and properly fastened.

The man in front of me let out a gasp as I kicked tufts of snow at him. He had been carrying me on a makeshift stretcher assembled from splints of wood and a blanket.

"So, you're alive?" the man asked in a thick country accent.

My eyes darted around, taking in fragments of trees and rocky hills. The sky had darkened, signaling the slow approach of evening.

"Found you out on the ice," the man said, looking at me curiously.

I got on my feet and recognized the man as the fisherman I had seen down by the shore a month earlier. He was middle-aged with a rough, wind-chiseled face. Flecks of snow stuck in his poorly groomed beard. He had the look of a lumberjack just slightly past his prime.

"What were you doing out there?" he asked, extending a hand to help me over a puddle of grey water.

I stared at it coldly and remained still.

"I won't bite none," he said, smiling.

"I thought I saw somebody out there," I told him, shaking snow from my coat.

We were just beyond the lake. I could make out the trail carved in the thin layer of snow by the stretcher.

"What's a thing like you doing out here? Aren't a lot of folks out here."

I looked about the landscape and oriented myself. He saw the direction of my gaze and frowned.

"That old cabin's abandoned," he said.

I turned to walk away, and as I did so he barred my path with one of his legs. I met his gaze with an expressionless stare. He flashed a wan smile and withdrew his leg.

"Don't you at least say thank you?" he asked.

I didn't respond. My steps made a crunching noise across the damp, stony soil.

"I saved your life," I heard him call to me. "We usually say thank you for that 'round here!"

I remained silent as he continued to call out to me. After a while, the *rustling sound of the breeze coming off the coast blotted out his voice completely.*

***

After Joshka discovered the wigs, I took a full inventory of the box. I found an old autograph album filled with names I had never heard of and a jar of ball bearings in addition to the other items already noted. None of the items seemed linked or related in any way. They were a random assortment of objects, the residue of past lives and former tenants accumulated over years. I left the wigs on the shelf in my bedroom, hardly giving them a second thought. As the days passed, I turned my attention to other matters.

One night I had a dream in which I was wandering through a cave. I thought I recognized it as Lascaux, but the primitive drawings of bison and horses on the rock walls were replaced with images of twisted bodies and bone-white faces. I awoke in my bedroom. The room was dark, and I was uncertain of the time. Still slightly dreaming, I thought I perceived another person sitting across from me in the dark. It took a moment to realize that I was staring at my own reflection in the antique standing mirror propped in the corner. I threw back the covers and turned on the light, taking in the sight of my naked body in the length of the glass. It dawned on me that we rarely see ourselves fully as others do. Our limited perspective reduces us to nothing more than a pair of animated hands, two feet, and an incomplete body—an assemblage of parts that somehow add up to a whole.

As I let this thought settle in, an inexplicable feeling of déjà vu crept over me. Many years ago, a person had stood almost exactly where I was now staring at their own body in this exact same mirror. I had no logical reason to suppose this. It simply occurred to me, as if the layers of time were momentarily being peeled back to reveal a dim and indefinite past. Was it a man or a woman? I wondered, as I stretched my limbs and examined the fullness of my body. A woman, I finally decided.

As if to confirm my assumption, I removed the red wig from

the shelf and placed it on my head. Adjusting it, I returned my gaze to the mirror. My body was by no means feminine, although my thin frame coupled with the curls of red gave a certain androgynous character to my appearance. I shifted my weight, trying to perfect what I imagined was a feminine posture. Fixing my attention on the face swathed in red hair, I marvelled at how unrecognizable I appeared to myself. Then, whatever spell had come over me suddenly broke. I removed the wig from my head and stared at my reflection, uncertain.

I went to sleep that night thinking I would never relate the incident to anyone. It was not that I couldn't explain my actions. Certain things are not meant to be shared. They are meant to remain sequestered, concealed within old boxes and confined to eternal secrecy.

***

One afternoon, a surfboat appeared offshore. From my vantage point on the cliffs, I could see the fisherman below on the rocky beachhead. He sat in a meditative silence smoking a pipe as he waited for the boat to touch ground. Once ashore, he greeted the three men and helped them unload a few boxes onto the beach. They talked for a while and then the men got into the boat and departed. As I angled my body to get a closer look, the fisherman turned to me and waved. I had assumed that the protruding rocks standing between the cliffs and the shore would conceal me, but I now understood that I had been in plain sight the whole time.

Thirty minutes later, the fisherman came walking up the cliffs. He was humming a tune and in his left hand he carried a bottle that swung at his side.

"Afternoon," he said as he approached uninvited. I was seated in the grass not doing much of anything. I nodded and continued looking out over the shore.

He took a seat beside me and put the bottle down between his feet. It was whiskey.

"Pleasant afternoon," he said, unscrewing the cap and taking a sip.

"Those your friends?" I asked.

"Acquaintances. They come every few months." He took another slug of whiskey and gestured to the bottle. "Supplies," he explained with a smirk. "They have a large shipping vessel that goes between Copenhagen and Porto."

He held out the bottle of whiskey to me. I accepted it without a word and took a sip. It had been months since I had last tasted alcohol. It stung my lips and settled into the back of my throat with a warm sensation. I gagged and the man laughed.

"A hard drink for a woman," he said, taking the bottle from my hand.

"And they bring you these goods without the captain of the ship being aware," I stated rather than asking.

"You're a perceptive one."

"Doesn't anybody notice it's missing?"

"Not if they do it correctly."

"And these people, do they transport other things as well?"

"Supposing..." He eyed me furtively and took another sip. "Depending on what your market is."

"Do they transport people?"

The fisherman nearly balled over laughing. "I thought you were going to ask about morphine or British powder, not a cruise line."

"I'm serious," I said.

"How many?"

"Just one."

He nodded his head slowly and we sat there in silence for a while. I curled my fingers around a rock in the grass waiting for him to respond.

"I'd ask, but I'd rather not know," he said after a long pause, and I relaxed my fist.

"Can it be arranged?"

"Yes," he said to me, "it can be arranged for a price."

***

It was early January when I received the letter from Francis Ingermann. It was printed on expensive cream-colored stationery adorned with a heraldic estate seal. In no uncertain terms, he requested an audience and the opportunity to view the paintings for himself, although he let it be known that their authenticity was highly doubtful. I was instructed to bring the works to a lawyer's office near the Phoenix Hotel where he would be staying. In the postscript, I was politely reminded that the estate board was the only body authorized to authenticate the work of Constantin Ingermann. It possessed the ring of a veiled legal threat.

I carefully removed the canvases from the wall and rolled them into cardboard postal tubes. Afterward, I contemplated the bare walls. They were hardly recognizable now, and it occurred to me that I had forgotten the pattern of the former wallpaper.

Francis Ingermann was a large, barrel-chested man with an aged face and set of piercing eyes that seemed to fix upon you and never let go. He smiled and was polite enough as I entered the office, asking if I wanted a coffee or cup of tea. I noticed a thin, silent man standing toward the back of the room, his gaze alternating between us and the window. I assumed this was the lawyer.

"So, you believe that these were produced by my father?" he said in English as I began unrolling the sheets of canvas on a mahogany table situated in the middle of the room. His voice was inflectionless and bore no trace of an accent. It was that type of English that is acquired at high-priced language schools, neither British nor American.

As he scrutinized the images, I took the opportunity to study his profile. His face had an unmistakable familiarity. It struck me the moment I had laid eyes on him. I hadn't had to speculate as to which of the men was Francis Ingermann. I simply knew. His eyes possessed the same cold fixity I had first glimpsed in the gallery of the Statens Museum months ago, and this troubled me.

After a minute he shook his head. "I am sorry to say I have wasted your time."

"So, they are not your father's work then?"

"Definitely not," as he rapped his knuckles on the tabletop with the finality of a seasoned businessman. "Stylistically, there may be a few small similarities..." He paused and a thoughtful expression crept over his face. "When you wrote to me, I had hoped these might be works connecting my father's Danish and French periods. Have you taken the time to read up on his career?"

"A little," I admitted.

"Then you may know there is a gap between the two periods, and it has always puzzled me. The stylistic change..."

Although I nodded, I had ceased listening. I was fascinated by his gaze, those eyes possessing a dark intelligence that I was able to place with such certainty. I began rolling up the canvases and inserting them back into the postal tubes.

We shook hands and Francis wished me well. Then, before I exited, I decided to ask the question that had been nagging me since my arrival.

"Your mother was Simone Fereaux, Constantine's *second* wife, correct?"

He stared at me blankly.

"Yes, I was born in France. I see you *have* done some research then," he replied with a smile, but he could tell something troubled me about his answer. "Why do you ask?"

"No reason in particular," I said, tucking the postal tubes under my arm and heading toward the door. "I was just making sure I had my chronology straight."

"Well, it would seem you do," he assured.

The next few nights passed without event. I stayed in, occupying myself with emails and some light reading. I did not bother to remove the canvases from the postal tubes. I preferred the smooth bare walls. My meeting with Francis Ingermann had left me unsettled, although it was difficult to say why. I constantly felt on the verge of some conclusion that had first dawned on me in that office, one that never quite congealed into words. This vague impression lingered for a few days before slowly dissipating. At best, I could only describe it as a feeling of something amiss, but not obviously so.

By the end of the week, I made the decision to stash the postal tubes in the crawl space. There, they would accumulate dust with the other sundry items, adding yet another layer to the accumulated history of the apartment. I proceeded to drag the box out into the hall and in the process the old cardboard tore, spilling its contents onto the floor. There was the sound of breaking glass and a metallic shower of ball bearings rolling across the hardwood. I watched as all the ball bearings migrated down the hall and pooled beside my desk in the study. They sat there, motionless atop the slightly discolored boards. I found their movement peculiar and scooped them up to re-enact the scenario. At first, the tiny balls shot out along different trajectories as they ricocheted off the hardwood, but within seconds all of them assumed the same path, converging in the exact same spot. There was an obvious declivity in the floor, a space approximately two feet by three feet demarcated by the off-colored planks.

I repeated the experiment again. The result was the same.

By the fourth time, the ball bearings tumbled from my hand, my fingers too unsteady to clutch them.

***

It was afternoon when he arrived. I had been sitting on the bed by the window with a pad in my lap sketching figures in charcoal. Some days I could sit for hours attempting to retrieve his face from my memory and render it on paper: the lineaments of his cheekbones, the expressiveness of his eyes, the way the corners of his mouth turned down ever so slightly. His face would emerge out of a nebulous blackness, appear momentarily, and then dissipate like a flash of ephemeral light as I furiously sketched. Day by day, the characteristics became less distinct, the features more general. Each drawing marked an act of forgetting as though to render some part of his likeness was to erase it from my recollection. He was fading, and soon I would draw the face of nobody in particular, at which point I would cease drawing anything real altogether.

I put the pad aside as he entered, mindful of his gaze. I could smell alcohol on his breath as he told me that in two days' time, I was bound for La Havre.

Since the afternoon of our first conversation, I had kept an eye on the fisherman's comings and goings, noting his daily schedule from my vantage point on the high cliffs. He lived in a cottage near the shore. His work consisted of labor-intensive trips between his home and a fishery located a few kilometers down the shoreline. From early morning until mid-afternoon, he routinely checked the nets and traps along the coast and transported his catch to the fishery.

On the day of my departure, I awoke at dawn and sat up on the cliffs eating a breakfast of sardines and canned peas. After the sun rose above the sea, the fisherman exited his cabin as usual and began his trek along the shore. Once out of sight, I began my descent. It took nearly forty minutes to walk down the steep cliffs, the path of hewn rock winding in a zigzag pattern.

I was struck by the simplicity of the cabin's interior. A dining table with a single chair filled the center of the front room. Two dishes and two cups were found in an otherwise empty cupboard. Various fishing poles and bands of netting were scattered throughout. I began rifling through drawers and compartments, seeking the obvious places where one might keep a cache of money. When I found nothing, I turned to the adjoining bedroom which was equally plain.

On the stand beside the bed was a dog-eared Bible. I opened it to a marked page where a verse from Isaiah was underlined in black:

And the fishermen will lament, And all those who cast a line into the Nile will mourn,

And those who spread nets on the waters will pine away.

I turned the page and discovered that the rest of the book had been hollowed out to form a compartment filled with rolled-up Kroner notes. I pocketed the notes and returned the Bible to the stand.

I looked over the house one last time to ensure that everything appeared as it had when I entered and then proceeded to exit the front door. It was then that I saw the fisherman leaning against the guardrail of the front porch, a serrated fishing blade clutched in his hand. I attempted to make a beeline from the door to the porch steps, but he easily blocked my path with his massive body and pushed me back into the cabin. As I tried to dart past him again, he grabbed me by the hair. My body did not twist, but I heard the cascade of hairpins on the wooden floor. We stood staring at one another in silence, his eyes wide and moving between me and the tuft of blond hair clenched in his fist. I am still uncertain whether he flinched as I planted the hairpin deep into the side of his neck, unleashing a rivulet of blood.

I sat in the corner for what felt like a long time after that. The blood pooled in the same way it had the very first time, quickly cooling to the consistency of wet paint.

After calming myself, I proceeded to drag the body across the shore. The air inside the fishery was thick with flies and the smell of decomposing haddock. I hauled the body onto the salting table and rolled it into the brine. It wavered in the buoyant substance, drifting lazily down to the bottom of the tub like a leaf suspended in air as it melted into the cloudy liquid. By four, I was back on the beach with my small valise in hand. It contained everything I now owned in the world.

The waves tossed us about as the boat maneuvered away from the land.

"Miss, you should sit down," one of the oarsmen said to me. "It might be a little rough until we reach the liner."

I had been standing and staring at the rocky cliffs in the distance, wondering what a person sitting on the heights might look like from this perspective. An insignificant dot on the horizon no bigger than an insect was all I could imagine.

***

Man does not have a single consistent life. He has several laid end to end. Yet what if the pieces do not constitute one life? Must we examine the discontinuities? Or do the myriad fragments, when laid end to end, comprise the totality, the life itself?

These thoughts ran through my mind as I stood in the hall. Neighbors milled about, drawn from their Saturday routines by the sight of uniformed officers and the sound of splintering wood. They craned their necks and cast judgmental glances at the ribbon of yellow police tape stretched across the doorway. I tried to avoid their eyes and stayed silent.

Now and then I threw glances through the open door. Debris hung thick in the air and swam through the pale sunlight. It looked like it was snowing. And I could smell it. A faint acrid scent of dust, funerary, and old.

"We're going to have to call in a hazmat team," an officer was saying, but the voice sounded far away. My eyes fixed on the cavity in the floor and the shriveled form nestled there amongst the broken planks. All I could think was that it looked to be smiling. Why did they always look like they were smiling?

***

Thirty-six hours of solitude. I passed the time confined to my room studying the Danish passport in my possession. During my nights in the cabin, I sometimes wished I had kept the small photo cut from the document as a memento mori. In moments of sheer anxiety, we are prone to forget the nostalgic urges of a susceptible human heart. We do not think of the future, for in the depths of horror, no future is conceivable. We are conscious only of the immediate and contingent.

Through the small portal, I watched as the dim light of the coast blossomed in the dawn. I packed what I needed and threw the rest into a canvas sack weighted with old bolts and washers. In the pre-light, I crept aboard and tossed the sack into the heaving waves. Re-entering the quarters, I saw a freshly risen crew hand walking the halls. We nearly brushed as we passed one another in the narrow corridor, and he muttered a weak apology. I thought nothing of it as I placed my hand on the knob of my cabin door.

"I doubt that's your room," I heard the crewman say.

"Oh?"

"No funny business," as he pushed my hand away from the knob. "There's a woman in there and I don't think she's keen on being disturbed at this hour."

I squinted at the door in feigned confusion. "My mistake," I said. "Wrong room."

He eyed me suspiciously, trying to determine my accent.

"Wrong room. That's all," I said with an obsequious smile and continued down the corridor. I could feel his eyes on me until I turned the corner.

I walked aimlessly through the bowels of the ship for a while rehearsing my French. Eventually, I found myself on deck again. A few crewmen ambled about in the translucent morning light fastening lines and preparing for debarkation. Overhead, I heard the cry of a gull and knew that we were nearing the coast.

"Ten minutes," somebody shouted.

When you have nowhere in particular to go, ten minutes is the same as an eternity.

Requiem *for a* Winter's Night

It had begun to snow again. From his position at the window, Emile watched the tiny flakes fall through the ribbons of pale light projected onto the neighboring courtyard wall. The scene was hypnotic in its own way and momentarily drew him from the din of conversation and clinking glass filling the room. High End was lively tonight, attracting its usual weekend crowd of Berlin hipsters and tourists. Notwithstanding the surrounding revelry, Emile was content to sit by the frost-glazed windows and stare out at the snow quietly accumulating on the streets and buildings below. It provided a nice distraction whenever conversation lulled, and now was just such a moment.

Colby was recounting the latest foreign exchange gathering held earlier that week. The event had been a dull affair consisting of polite conversation over tables packed with baked goods and coffee urns, the usual hospitality the university liked to show towards its foreign students. Admittedly, a banquet with no alcoholic beverages and no prospect of decent conversation was hardly Colby's idea of a good time. His vested interest in attending the event had been an American student named either Jill or Jen Hersching whom Colby had had his eye on for a while. A few minutes of bland chatter, however, dispelled him of any such luck.

Just about the time Colby had given up hope of an extracurricular rendezvous, a new group of exchange students came barreling through the door and attacked the remains of the baked goods on the banquet table. The leader of the troop, a big lumbering student named Foster Greeley, began stuffing his face with brownies and moving in on some of the girls in attendance. He was visibly drunk and lurched about the room, asking girls at random if they wanted to dance. The third girl he propositioned noted there was, in fact, no music playing.

"A minor setback," Greeley assured with a lop-sided grin as he extended a hand.

"Where's the damn tunes?" another hollered through a mouthful of petit fours.

Colby watched the gang run from group to group trying to pick up any girl they could with amusement. As the crowd progressively thinned, he found himself entrenched in Greeley's little entourage. Colby had to admit he preferred Greeley's bawdy antics to anything he had witnessed thus far, and so, with the event at an end, he followed the gang to a watering hole in Prenzlauerberg.

One of Greeley's mates, a stocky and barrel-chested student named Martin Pykes, took to Colby instantly. Not only was he a fellow Brit, but it seemed that they both shared the ambition of shagging one Jill or Jen Hersching. Crooning over some pints, they made a small wager over which of them would be the first to seduce the object of their mutual desire. Meanwhile, one of Greeley's boys had purchased an armload of condoms from a dispenser in the men's room and was in the process of distributing them among the group. Unwrapping the prophylactics, Greeley and his mates began inflating the vermiform latex, making crude balloons that they tossed into the air and kept aloft like beach balls at an open-air concert. It was around this point that Pykes, drunk on beer and gin tonics, scribbled down an address for Colby on a bar napkin.

"Not to pull back on our little wager," he said, sliding the napkin across the bar, "but if our kitten turns out to be inaccessible, you can find adequate compensation here."

Colby stared at the writing on the napkin blankly.

"*Viel Spaß*, I assure you."

Colby said nothing as he tucked the napkin into his pocket and looked down at the floor littered with deflated condoms and shiny foil wrappers.

Emile, slumped in his chair, listened to all the details in a half-attentive silence. He continually found his attention drawn to the window. A low drone of ambient music filled the interior. The nightly partying at High End was beginning to crest as the rooms filled with bodies.

Not that he was prudish, but Emile found stories of aggressive preening and coed sexual adventurism tasteless. If his college experience had been routine by most standards, it had nonetheless been bereft of the typical courting, late-night hookups, and emoji-laden text messaging that passed for romance on American campuses. Two years of undergrad and six months on foreign exchange, and Emile still had yet to explore that complicated phenomenon that analysts never tired of branding "the college dating scene."

"Sounds like I missed a party," Emile said impassively.

Colby shrugged and rattled the remaining ice cubes in his tumbler. "Bit o' fun's all. Good blokes. The kind that're a ball to get pissed with but would probably be insufferable when sober." Then, following Emile's gaze, "It's really coming down out there."

Emile nodded. "You know, back home in Louisiana I'd never seen snow before."

"That so?"

"Yeah. I mean, I had seen it in movies and pictures, sure. But to actually see it in person is different. You know?"

"I see what you're getting at."

"The day it started snowing, I went outside and walked around for a while. I felt like I wanted to *experience* snow, not just see it. And you know, the first thing I thought was that it's really cold, as if snow and cold had never actually been associated in my mind. Stupid, right?"

Colby raised one thin eyebrow. "Any ponce could have told you snow is cold." He was rattling the ice in his glass again. "Looks like I need a refill. I suggest that you follow my lead and get something a bit harder that'll put some fire in your gut. It'll keep you warm when we're out there."

"What's out there?"

In the diffuse light of the bar, Colby's grin looked more like an impish smirk.

Out in the snow, Colby's tracks veered from one corner of the sidewalk to the other like the footprints of some ungainly bird, no doubt the effects of the four Black Labels he had gulped down at High End.

Emile hunched into his overcoat, his shoulders peppered with white. "Where are we going?" he asked.

"*Viel Spaß!*" Colby warbled as they proceeded along the deserted street. He paused and threw his head back trying to catch the falling snowflakes in his open mouth. "Here's how you *experience* snow. See?"

Emile was not amused.

"Jesus, lighten up, chum!" as Colby collided with a bicycle chained to a lamp post and almost careened face down onto the pavement.

In the distance, a light flickered in the wind.

"You hear that?" Colby asked, stopping and leaning up against the wall for support.

Emile cocked his ear, feeling the cold tickle of the snow. He thought he heard the faint sound of music.

"What? That music?"

"Like chanting."

Emile listened closer and heard voices mixing with the howl of the wind.

Up ahead, a fire was burning in the middle of the street. Plumes of smoke rose into the night air. For a second Emile thought it might be an automobile accident, but as they got closer, he made out a cluster of bodies huddling around what looked to be a burning garbage receptacle.

"Listen," Colby instructed, placing a finger to his lips.

There was the sound of voices murmuring.

"Are they singing?"

On the corner up ahead, four vagrants sat in a semi-circle, faces etched in warm firelight. They cupped their hands to the flame and exhaled breaths that materialized in the frigid air. A few sang, the plangent melody resonating in the night like an elegy. Emile listened and tried to make out the words, although the German was unintelligible to him.

Colby shuffled through the detritus of wrappers, crumpled newspapers, and beer bottles littering the pavement. These articles had once been contained in the garbage can but were now being used by the vagrants as fuel. Emile watched as an old man slowly balled up some fast food packaging and fed it into the fire, the paper shriveling, blackening, and disappearing into the flames.

"What a dump!" Colby wailed, kicking at the trash. He said it loud enough for the four men to hear.

"*Amerikaner?*" one asked as they passed.

"Wrong side of the pond, mate," Colby leered, as though to confuse a Brit with an American was a cardinal sin.

"A euro?" the man asked, holding out his hand. The skin was chapped with deep ridges of dirt caked under each fingernail.

Colby looked down at the hand in disgust.

"Maybe if you sing a little more of that ditty, I'd think it worth it," he said, a mean grin spreading ear to ear. "This little barber-shop quartet you got *might* be worth a euro!"

The man stared at Colby, expressionless.

Emile tugged at Colby's arm. "C'mon. Let's go. Leave 'em alone," he whispered, aware that he sounded like a remonstrative parent.

Colby shrugged off his grip and fixed his eyes on the man. "Sing!" he commanded. "Make it worth my money."

Emile stood aside, mortified, watching the two through the falling snow.

"A euro?" the man repeated with an imploring hand gesture.

At this, Colby laughed and began kicking tufts of snow at him. "Think he knows snow is cold," he said, turning to Emile, smiling.

The man flinched and rejoined the group nestled around the fire without a word. *What a dick*, was all Emile could think as he watched Colby continue to taunt the man from a distance.

"What'd you do that for?" he asked once they had resumed cutting along the side streets. He was still bewildered by what had taken place. Something about Colby's lack of compassion or even decency left a sour taste in his mouth.

"Trash," Colby hissed. "Handouts for everyone."

"You could have just ignored them."

But Colby's thoughts were already elsewhere.

Emile could still hear the singing a block away as their feet crunched in the snow and they entered a narrow alley. It almost sounded tribal, a chant calling forth something numinous and terrifying across the night as it mixed with the distant noises of stray cats and gurgling storm drains.

"Colby, you know where we're going?"

"I know, I know," he slurred, his steps uneven and faltering.

"This isn't some shitty discotheque, is it?"

"You'll see."

Emile paused and watched his breath evaporate into the night. Up ahead, Colby let out a belch that echoed through the passage.

"Hey, wait up!" he called, breaking into a light trot and keeping an eye on Colby's meandering tracks.

He found him midway down the alley standing in front of a metal-plated door. Looking between the number on the door and the writing scrawled on the folded napkin, Colby shrugged and rang the bell.

"This is it," he said.

Emile glanced down the alley. It was empty with little indication of foot traffic. The passageway extended into oblivion, a flat carpet of uninterrupted white enclosed by two brick walls. Hardly the setting for a nightclub or *recherché* discotheque, he mused. As they waited in the cold shifting their weight from foot to foot, Emile had to wonder whether this whole thing had been a ruse. He was about to suggest as much when he heard a heavy bolt being unlatched. The door inched open, and a man's face appeared, middle-aged with black shoulder-length hair neatly combed back and falling just to the trim of the white collar around his neck. He looked like a storekeeper, Emile thought.

"We must have the wrong address," Colby stammered once it was evident the man was waiting for them to speak.

"That depends on what you were looking for," the man replied in English, flashing them a grin.

"A friend gave me this address, but..."

"Then you are probably in the correct place," he said, holding back the door and gesturing for them to enter.

They stepped into the foyer. Soft, multicolored light from a Moroccan lamp filled the room. The walls were patterned with looping floral designs, the kind of lining paper you'd expect to find at grandmother's house. Colby, eyes wandering around the room, tried not to gawk at the statues and ornamental kitsch placed throughout the room. They waddled in, soles dragging across the arabesque tile floor, appreciative of the warmth.

"This way, please," the man instructed, heading down the hall.

Emile gazed at the pictures lining the wall: old frames, a mix of paintings and photographs running from antique to modern—all portraits vacantly gazing back at the spectator. The motif was odd, if not unsettling. Emile paused to scrutinize the deadpan face of a woman in a daguerreotype, noting the still expression and blank eyes created by the silvering effect.

"*This* way, please," the man repeated, prompting Emile to continue down the hall.

The next room was better lit than the foyer, drifting more toward the red-orange range of the spectrum. A table and some chairs were arranged beside a standing lamp with a fringed shade. The man made a gesture, and they took a seat. Neither said a word as they sunk into the soft velvet cushions. Colby pointed to the small Turkish teacups set before them.

"What is this place?" Emile whispered.

Colby shrugged and ran his fingers through the lampshade fringe, eliciting a rattle of glass beads.

The man returned with a tray bearing a teapot and sugar bowl. Placing it down in the center of the table, he took a seat between them and proceeded to pour two steaming cups.

"Sugar?" he asked, gesturing toward the bowl.

Colby shook his head and accepted the cup.

They sat in silence with nobody making much of an attempt to generate conversation. Colby sipped his tea while Emile stole glances around the room, taking in the figurines, candelabras, and baroque crown molding. Thick shadows welled in the corners where the red lighting refused to penetrate.

It was finally Colby who broke the silence.

"Nice statue," he said casually, angling his head toward a half-sized marble sculpture of a Greek deity.

The man nodded. "A very exquisite piece of work," he agreed. Then, with a half-smile, "What would you pay for that statue?"

"Oh, I wasn't..." Colby replied, confused, fingers moving through his neatly cropped crewcut still wet with snow.

"Simply a question. Indulge me."

"I couldn't say. I wouldn't even know what it's worth."

"So you didn't come here to purchase something?" he asked.

"I don't..." a shrewd look began to dawn on his face.

"An offer is innocent."

He scanned the room as though appraising the items in it. The statues, the lamps, the rugs—everything looked expensive, looked *authentic*, Emile thought, following Colby's sweeping gaze. For a moment, in the red glow of the oriental lamps, he thought he saw Colby lock eyes with him before moving on to the other objects.

"Fifty euros," he finally said, biting his lip.

The man laughed. "That statute is worth at least four times that amount."

"That so?" as he withdrew his wallet from his coat pocket and began running his thumb through its contents.

The man reached out and placed a hand over his calculating fingers. Colby responded with a ridiculous grin, dropping all pretense of knowing how to play this game.

"You're good for it," the man said, rising from his chair.

"Yes, of course. Absolutely," as he watched the man once again disappear into the back room.

Emile had observed all this in silence, and now he saw a worried expression creep across Colby's face.

"Spot me fifty," he whispered, eyes darting to the back door. "I'm solid for it."

"I'm not..."

"C'mon. Don't be naff. I mean, you weren't...?"

A confounding silence. He was right of course. Just being in this place was making Emile edgy and evoking memories of those anxious nights at college parties when he would beat an early exit, dreading the moment when people would begin pairing off and disappearing into vacant bedrooms. He never wanted to be the single guy sitting around uncomfortably while the party transitioned into the inevitable make-out sessions and breathless encounters upstairs; never wanted to endure those awkward conversations filled with ambiguous body language and innuendos or face the humiliating question "That's *it*?" to which there was no redeeming answer. There were names for people like that. Names that wove their way into the general campus chatter and haunted you for years. And yet, here he was. Following Colby, he had walked right into it.

The man emerged from the back room with two women in tow. They appeared to glide through the soft light, their long dresses trailing along the tile floor. When they approached the table, the first woman extended a hand to Emile as though expecting him to kiss it. A quaint gesture, he thought, staring at the smooth skin, unsure whether to take the hand offered.

"Elena," she said, smiling at him.

The man cleared his throat and nudged his head in Colby's direction.

"Ah, yes," Elena said, retracting the hand and extending it toward Colby. "You are the man who likes the statue."

Colby, mouth agape, nodded. "Yes," he managed, taking her hand and allowing himself to be drawn to his feet like a puppet on a string.

"And would you like to see the other statues we have in the house?" as she led Colby away from the table, her feet whispering across the tile.

Their voices and footsteps retreated into the thick stillness of the room. Elena's hips had a rhythmic sway to them, Emile noticed, as Colby disappeared through the dark doorway arm in arm with Elena. It was a practiced and deliberate movement, hinting more at technique than natural grace.

"I'm sure you can attend to our other guest, Eva," the man said with a wink once they had left the room.

Emile turned his defenseless gaze toward the woman, feeling as though he had just been assigned a babysitter. Eva was slightly older than Elena. Her dress was not as elegant or as formfitting. She had a pretty face, although there was a plainness to it that maquillage and heavy eyeliner could not completely hide. The look of a provincial girl dolled up for a night on the town, Emile thought.

"I give them five minutes," he said, trying to lighten the mood as Eva slid into the seat beside him.

"Don't have a high estimation of your friend," she replied, abiding.

He drummed his fingers on the table wondering what they were going to do in the meantime. Five minutes was wishful thinking, he realized. An awkward silence ensued in which Emile drained the last of the tea from his cup. Eva had a bored expression that suggested she didn't much care what they did or talked about. Taking account of the weather and the fact that it was a Tuesday evening, Emile assumed this is what passed for a slow night.

"What do you do here?" he asked to break the uneasy silence.

Eva fixed him with a puzzled expression and then gave a mirthless laugh. "Adorable."

"Well, shouldn't we do *something*? Or do we just sit here?"

Leaning across the table, she placed a finger softly on his lips. "We can do whatever you want."

Emile stared down at the single painted nail just under his nose, trying to decide if she was being playful or mean. When she saw the wince, she removed her finger, sat back in the chair, and let out a frustrated sigh.

"Why don't we go to the variety room," she suggested, motioning for his hand. "It usually helps with first-timers."

Emile offered no protest, his mind still on the way her fingertip felt against his mouth and the lingering salty taste it had left on his lips. His hand was warm and sticky. He tried to wipe it on his pant leg first before she took it in hers.

Leading him through a maze of halls covered in red vinyl

wallpaper, Eva hummed a tune under her breath. Emile took note of the portraits on the wall again and tried to slow their pace. Walking along, he thought he recognized a few. A narrow-faced, elderly man resembling his current history professor, an athletic-looking youth that could pass for Foster Greeley. The faces glided by, one by one, each containing more than a hint of familiarity.

"Who are all these people?" he asked as she pulled him along.

"People who have been here, I imagine," she said with a shrug. "Maybe your friend's face will be up there soon. Maybe yours."

The thought sent a shiver through his body, although he could not say why. Something about the blank, lifeless stares on all the faces, the way the facial muscles seemed carefully set as though by a mortician.

It took a moment for Emile's eyes to adjust to the dark as they stepped into the variety room. Shapes and objects materialized slowly in the blackness. Emile saw they were standing in a semi-circular room. A stage with a curtain lay at the far end, opposite which was a satin-upholstered divan. It had the look of a small theater. Frames covered the black walls, although in the dark Emile could not make out the faces enclosed within them.

He was about to ask Eva why she had brought him here when he heard the click of a switch. A faint light illuminated the stage in blues and reds, followed by a mechanical grating noise. From each side of the stage entered an automaton, their bodies carried along a hidden tread in the stage floor as they met in the center. Their features were crude, and the clumsy, motorized movements gave the impression of life-sized puppets operated by invisible strings. However, it was clear from the papier-mâché faces and old-fashioned clothing that the automatons were gendered, one male the other female. In a sequence of contorting gestures and creaky motions, the automatons began to act out various compromising positions, imitating a penny arcade peepshow.

"Neat, huh?" Eva said as she took Emile by the hand and escorted him to the divan.

Emile watched, half-embarrassed and half-mesmerized, as the two armatures went through their repertoire, joints squeaking and motors whirring. The simplified human anatomy left some things to the imagination, Emile noted, as his eyes moved between Eva and the sexless torsos banging and knocking together. The thought that people might find this grotesque performance titillating disturbed him.

After about five minutes, the gears began to grind again and the automatons parted, vacating the stage. Emile jerked as Eva wrapped her finger around his clammy hand resting on the divan cushion and gave a squeeze.

"I won't bite," she whispered.

On the stage, a second automaton came into view. Unlike the first, this one resembled an old man dressed in rags. A large floppy hat sat atop the head, partially concealing the wax-like face. Two shining eyes glared out at the couple, burning in the dark like cinders. A gangly arm extended outward, palm upward, the ill-fitting joints emitting a weak squeaking sound as the arm drifted from side to side.

Eva's giggling transitioned into laughter and Emile felt her hand begin to caress his cheek and draw him closer. Her breath was warm on his face.

Trying to wriggle free of her busy hands, Emile fixed his gaze on the stage where the automaton stared at them in silence. Something about the gesture, the way the hand dangled in the air imploring recognition, filled him with dread. "A euro?" Emile imagined it saying, scrutinizing the features of the face and trying to recall. Through the half-light of memory, all he could muster was a silhouette stenciled against the falling snow, an outline devoid of content.

"That's..." he heard himself muttering as Eva turned his face toward hers and their eyes met.

In the indigo radiance, her face looked different, older. Thin shadows accumulated in the creases by her eyes and the recesses around her lips, blotting out the former youth and attractiveness. A squeamish sensation coursed through him as their lips grazed and Eva twisted her body, leaning into his. She seemed to be directing him, guiding his hands to the correct places with short fits of discouraging laughter.

"Oh, this is... You've never..." he heard her murmur.

He fought back the urge to pull away as his hands fumbled along her back. The body beneath the dress felt spongy and form-less. There was a distinct sensation of fingers sinking into doughy flesh, of submerging his face in wet clay. His mind fastened on the sound of rickety gears coming from the stage. Repositioning his head to see the next exhibit, Emile felt a tug and heard a sickening tearing noise like tape being peeled from a wall.

Standing on the stage was an upright human body, its limbs slack and lifeless. Every inch of skin had been removed to expose the creasing layers of sinuous muscle and ligaments. A smooth skull-like head lolled on the neck, eyes bulging and reflecting the stage light in their glassy surface. The muscle was shiny. The body had been freshly skinned.

On the verge of screaming, Emile touched his cheek, and his hand came away coated in viscid gore. He squinted into the dark at Eva seated on the divan. The face that peered back was smeared and disfigured on one side, a mass of torn flesh and muscle run-ning together. The arm that had moments ago been around his neck now lay on the divan cushion, severed at the shoulder, the fingers still squirming and groping. A choked sound came from her yawning mouth.

"That's it," Eva slurred through a mess of teeth and flesh.

As his shoes skidded on the tile, Emile realized it had not been a question. He backpedaled and sprinted out of the room.

Stumbling through the halls, his thoughts turned to Colby and the countless photographs on every wall. He cut corner after cor-ner, his eyes racing over the portraits in a feverish blur. Could he imagine wandering these halls forever, searching, like Theseus in the labyrinth? Passages led on to other passages until he had the impression of running in circles. When he eventually did spot a door at the end of a long corridor, Emile bounded toward the exit with a forceful charge. Arms reeling and feet lurching, his body hurtled forward through the air as he tumbled into the snow.

Face down on the pavement, he could still hear singing coming across the night, its resonant tone sounding more ominous and cautionary than earlier. He lay there, lulled by the music, feeling the cold paralyze his body. He wondered how long he could remain there. How long before the cold seeped in and turned his blood to ice? How long before the plangent music became a requiem and the accumulating snow claimed its dead? Rolling over onto his back and staring into the night sky, Emile found no answer.

About *the* Author

Alistair Rey is a writer of dark speculative fiction and the new weird. His work has appeared in numerous magazines and anthologies over the years, including *Juked*, *The Berkeley Fiction Review*, *The Lowestoft Chronicle*, and *Weirdbook*. He currently resides in Cardiff, Wales.

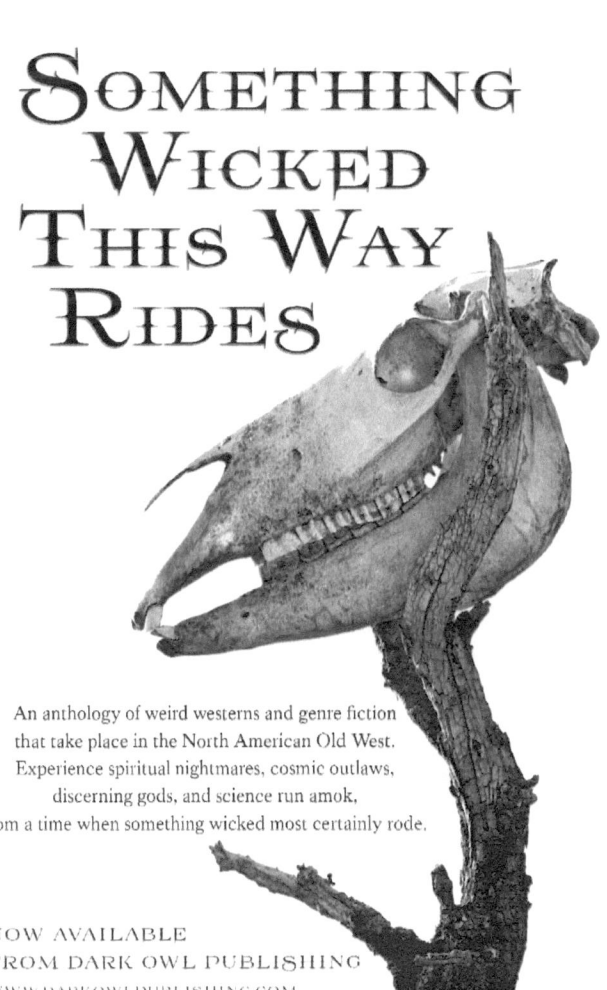

THE DARK

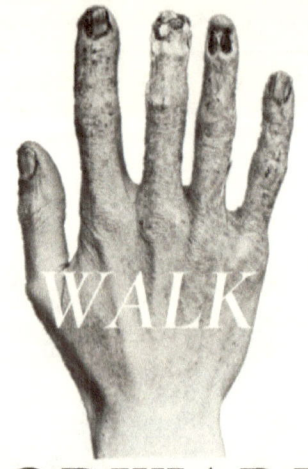

WALK

FORWARD

A HARROWING COLLECTION BY
JOHN S. MCFARLAND

Available in paperback and on Kindle from
DARK OWL PUBLISHING, LLC
www.darkowlpublishing.com